THE
BUFFALO
BUTCHER

JACK THE RIPPER IN THE ELECTRIC CITY

A NOVEL

Other Titles by
ROBERT BRIGHTON

Avenging Angel Detective Agency™ Mysteries

The Unsealing

A Murder in Ashwood

THE
BUFFALO
BUTCHER

JACK THE RIPPER IN THE ELECTRIC CITY

A NOVEL

ROBERT BRIGHTON

The Buffalo Butcher: Jack the Ripper in the Electric City
A Novel by Robert Brighton

Cover and Interior Design by The Book Cover Whisperer

979-8-9876964-7-7 Hardcover
979-8-9876964-8-4 Paperback
979-8-9876964-9-1 eBook
979-8-9891680-4-0 Audiobook

Library of Congress Control Number: 2023946077

Find out more at
RobertBrightonAuthor.com

For EBD

CONTENTS

A NOTE TO THE READER

Those of you who have read some, or all, of my Avenging Angel Detective Agency Mysteries will find this book both a departure and a return.

As a departure, the Avenging Angel Detective Agency doesn't figure in this book. But as a return, we travel back to 1901, and again (as we did all too briefly in *The Unsealing*) make a visit to Buffalo's historical high point—the Pan-American Exposition.

Eight million people—about one in nine Americans—came to Buffalo, New York, to see the "Pan." The cynics thought it was nothing more than yet another bloated world's fair. But most found the Electric City to be an expression of all that was good and hopeful: the unity of North and South American nations, the triumph of Man over Nature, and the advent of the modern scientific and engineering marvels that would herald a new century of peace and prosperity.

We can debate which camp won out, but one thing is certain. The assassination of President William McKinley in the Pan-American's Temple of Music drew a curtain forever over the promise of the Pan— and left Buffalo with a bitter legacy that is remembered even today.

The Buffalo Butcher also takes us into a darker side of bright, up-and-coming Buffalo, then the nation's fastest-growing city. We visit the back alleys of the Tenderloin District, a large red-light zone in the heart of downtown, where most anything was tolerated by city officials and police, so long as it stayed put. Hundreds of brothels and low-end dives huddled together in the Tenderloin and existed—for the most part—on the exploitation of young women who often had no other good option.

As I've mentioned in previous books, I've left prices in dollars as they were then. If you want an idea of what things would be worth (or cost) today, multiply the dollar values you read here by between thirty and fifty. Thus, the daily admission ticket to the Pan-American, at fifty cents in 1901, would be the equivalent of about twenty dollars in 2023.

The Buffalo Butcher, I hope, will give readers—in addition to a good story—a sense that the Gilded Age was exactly as Mark Twain meant the term when he coined it: shiny and glittering on the outside, but just beneath that gilded surface, made of dark and common stuff.

Robert Brighton
October 2023

The life of a wild animal always has a tragic end.

— ERNEST THOMPSON SETON,
WILD ANIMALS I HAVE KNOWN

PROLOGUE ::
VINE ALLEY

Buffalo, New York
The Tenderloin
Late June 1901

T he first body was found next to a rotting shed along Vine Alley, near the corner of Elm Street, and behind one of the worst dives in that part of the Tenderloin—Buffalo's sprawling red-light district. The corpse was discovered early Sunday morning by fifteen-year-old Louise Harris, who had been emptying chamber pots into an abandoned well in back of the place.

The wells had long ago been poisoned by a rising water table of blood, shit, and urine from the area's concentration of tanneries and slaughterhouses. By day, Vine Alley was alive with the bleating of sheep and the bellowing of cattle, sounds abruptly cut short by the stroke of a blade. By night, the low, desperate moos were replaced with the din of rattling pianos, drunken singing, and the angry scuffling of men—and sometimes women—who had come to Vine Alley for the cheapest fun that the vice district had to offer.

Emptying slops was every new girl's early-morning chore, usually performed while the prostitutes were still sleeping off the previous night's debauch. No one liked doing it, but it developed a strong stomach— a requirement on Vine Alley. After the pots were cleaned and replaced under each bed came collecting soiled laundry and, every once in a blue moon, scrubbing the floors.

That morning, Louise had dumped the dregs of Saturday night's bacchanal into the old well and was about to return to her other chores when she decided to tarry a bit and sneak a cigarette behind the shed. On Sunday morning things moved slowly on Vine Alley, and she wouldn't be risking the madam's wrath. And, with any luck, she might find one of the working girls there, too.

Louise liked talking with the older girls and looked up to them. They had the kind of scarred, sardonic humor that sprouts when all illusion has been plowed under, and they liked to shoot the shit, swear, and smoke. And talking was the best way for Louise to acquire the hard-won secrets of the hired girl: how to appear eager to fuck a client, no matter how foul his breath or his body; how to bring him off quickly; what douches and tonics could prevent pregnancy; and, if it came to it, where one could go to have things put right again. All this lore would make the first night of her *real* work—less than a year away, now—go much more smoothly.

The night before, Louise had bummed a couple of smokes while flirting with clients waiting their turn upstairs. As she rounded the corner of the shed, she removed one of the precious cigarettes from her skirt pocket and planted it between her lips. She could almost taste the smoke when she realized that she had left behind the parlor match she had pinched the night before. It wasn't well to carry them about: parlor matches, or snapping devils as the girls called them, needed only friction to cause them to ignite. This was convenient, but in a handbag or—God forbid—a skirt pocket, loose parlor matches could, and did, cause serious injury.

Louise held out her pocket and peered into it, hoping that she was mistaken, but there was no match. She removed the cigarette from her mouth, replaced it next to the other one, and with a sigh picked up her pail again to return to the dive. When she looked up, she spied what seemed like a roll of old carpet lying next to the far corner of the shed. That didn't make much sense, since the rag-pickers of the Tenderloin—who scoured the area for the tiniest scrap of old fabric—would never have overlooked such a treasure.

She walked over and saw that the object was part of an old horse blanket, draped over some other item. She kicked it gently with the toe of her shoe. It was soft and yielding. Louise bent down and pulled back the blanket, and immediately ran back into her brothel screaming.

THE DECEASED'S SURNAME WAS unknown. In the dive, she went only by Lizzie, and to her regulars—affectionately it was thought—she was Dirty Legs Lizzie. Why "dirty legs," no one knew. She was as clean as any of the others in her third-rate cathouse, and certainly more sanitary than a common streetwalker, but Lizzie wasn't a fancy girl, either. She was a workingman's throw, the kind a tired butcher from the slaughter-houses might avail himself of after a few drinks to wash the smell out of his nostrils. And while at thirty she was getting long in the tooth, madam and clients alike agreed that Lizzie still had a few good years left in her.

Her body was lying face up against the tottering back wall of the old shed. Her skirt and chemise had been pulled up over her hips and bunched up just above her pubis. Equal money was on two possibilities: either that she had been taking a squat behind the shed or had snuck away to service a "random" for a little unreported pocket money. A good prostitute was trained to bring a man to climax in two minutes or less, and even in a busy dive any girl could sneak off for five—plenty of time to make a few extra bucks. Madams didn't like it, but it was tolerated, provided the girls still made their nightly quota inside the house.

As the eye scanned upward from Lizzie's exposed genitals, it would detect nothing out of the ordinary until it reached her collarbone. That's where things got very interesting. Lizzie's collar was saturated with dried blood, which had gushed out from a somewhat ragged cut that meandered from just under her left ear, across her windpipe, and then stopped at the right clavicle. The cut was so deep that the inner struc-tures of the neck had been exposed. Lizzie had died staring at her killer, and her eyes still retained a kind of eerie intensity very unlike the glazed look of death.

The madam, Louise, and two horrified prostitutes were gathered around Lizzie's corpse when Patrolman Michael Scanlan sauntered up. He had heard Louise's screaming and thought he'd see what fresh horror was afoot at the corner of Vine and Elm.

"What's going?" he said as he came up behind the group.

"Someone murdered one of my gals," the madam said.

"You don't say." Scanlan bent over to take a look at the dead woman, hands on his knees. "What's her name?"

"Lizzie," all four ladies said in unison.

"Lizzie what?"

The women all shrugged or murmured something inaudible.

"I'll call Detective Cusack," Scanlan said. "But it's going to take a while. Someone vandalized the call box on Elm, so I'll have to hoof it to Eagle and call from there. Don't let anyone back here until I get back. I don't want to tangle with a bunch of rubberneckers on a Sunday morning."

He ambled off down Elm in the direction of Eagle, whistling and swinging his stick. A half an hour later, he returned with a second cop and the detective.

Detective Cusack was a somewhat rumpled, balding man, wearing a suit that seemed a size or two too large for the body inside. Perhaps, like the flowing robes of the Bedouin, the baggy outfit helped him keep cool in the humid Buffalo summer. Or, more likely, he'd got it at a remainder sale at Meldrum's, which was famous for selling cheap but functional goods, usually in off-sizes.

The cops, Cusack, Louise, the madam, and the two whores all stood and stared silently at Lizzie, who stared silently back.

"I called the coroner," Cusack said to no one. He knelt in the dirt, and with his thumb and forefinger, spread open the flaps of skin bordering the fatal neck wound. The four ladies leaned over Cusack for a better view.

"Don't you all have something else to do?" the detective said over his shoulder.

"Yeah," Scanlan said, prodding Louise with his stick. "You've done your bit. Now scram."

The ladies scurried away, whispering.

Cusack crouched over Lizzie's corpse, closely examining the cut. It resembled the kind of cut one might make in filleting a fish—neat and clean, very deep, but not quite straight. Still, straighter than one might think if a murderer was trying to cut the throat of a struggling woman. The wound had to have been inflicted quickly, Cusack thought, in a single stroke—and with the confidence of experience. This was not the work of someone unaccustomed to the blade. He could think of at least six butchers within a block, and any one of them could have managed the job. But then again, he knew them all pretty well, and for the most part they were broken-down, quiet types, and—if anything—weary of gore after spending twelve hours a day in it up to their boot-tops.

The killer had done his work, and then had slipped away unnoticed. Yet given the quantity of blood—even though quite a bit of it had soaked into the dirt—it would have been impossible to commit this sort of crime without coming away drenched. But Cusack knew even that wouldn't earn so much as a raised eyebrow on Vine and Elm. Half the men wandering home from work, or stumbling along drunk, were coated in the stuff. It was only part of the passing parade in this desperate part of the city, where death was the stock in trade and blood a badge of brotherhood.

"All right, I'm done," Cusack said, standing and dusting off the knees of his baggy trousers. "Cover her privates up, will you? When the coroner's wagon gets here, tell them I'll meet them at the morgue to make a report."

Scanlan nodded, and the second cop, Patrick Mahoney, knelt down to restore Lizzie's modesty. He pulled on the hem of her skirt, but the rear of the garment had stiffened in the clotted pool of blood under her body. Mahoney reached under the corpse and was trying to free the back of her skirt, when Scanlan stopped him.

"Detective," he said, looking at Cusack, "did you see that?"

"See what?" Cusack asked.

"*That*," Scanlan said, touching his stick to the smooth skin just above Lizzie's pubic mound.

Cusack bent over again. "Hmm, that is interesting."

Faintly incised into the dead woman's skin was a pentacle.

⌐

A KNIFE-WIELDING MURDERER WHO had killed a prostitute needed
a good name. "Jack the Ripper" had already long been taken, and for
good, by the mysterious whore-killer of Whitechapel some thirteen years
before. So the Buffalo newspapers—not unmindful of the enormous cir-
culation increase enjoyed by London's penny dreadfuls after Saucy Jacky
had made his debut—had to think fast to find a name that would sell.

Their first attempt, "The Tenderloin Ripper," seemed almost like
plagiarism, and was roundly rejected. Then they went after the "Vine
Alley Marauder," which was a mouthful. Finally, a young newspaper-
man hit upon one that combined the city's name with the predominant
trade around Vine and Elm: *The Buffalo Butcher.* That one was clear and
memorable, even if it did cast a bit of shade over the city's reputation. It
stuck immediately, earning the young reporter a ten-dollar bonus while
putting tens of thousands into the coffers of his employer.

The pimps and the madams of the Tenderloin did their best to reas-
sure their girls that the Butcher's choice of victim was nothing more
than happenstance, but the streetwise working girls were having none of
it. All they could talk about was where or when another murder might
occur, and which of their unofficial sorority would get the cut. And
every man who came to any of the brothels was viewed with such suspicion that many of the girls froze every time the door closed behind a
client. Some refused to go outside at all, even to run errands. A few even
considered moving to Cleveland.

Every girl had her own suspicions about who or what had swung
the deadly blade. Few believed it could be the work of a woman; too
much strength would be required to pin a struggling whore to the
ground and open her throat with a single stroke. A man, then. But what
kind of man?

The criminal's catchy name provided a clue. A butcher, slaughter-
man, or knacker were the most likely suspects. Vine Alley may have
earned local renown for its concentration of slaughterhouses, but in a
city where horses outnumbered people five to one, every neighborhood
had at least one knacker. The knacker was a fellow of strong constitution

who disposed of old, diseased, or otherwise unwanted horses. He killed and bled them, and then stripped off the hides to make leather, rendered the bones and hooves into glue, and minced, cooked, and sold the flesh as pet food. The knacker, it was said, left behind nothing but the whinny.

There was only one other possibility—a medical man. A doctor or a mortician would be handy with a knife and unfazed by blood. But doctors had taken an oath to do no harm, and morticians—well, whatever they got up to in the basements of their undertaking parlors was likely more than enough to satisfy the most ghoulish appetite.

One curious element gave the girls of the Tenderloin pause. London's famous Whitechapel murderer had gotten his jollies from the extravagant mutilation of his victims, without ever having left a trace of traditional sexual activity—the frenzied violence itself having served, presumably, as a surrogate for orgasm. That was not the case with the Buffalo Butcher's victim. Inside Lizzie's vagina, the medical examiner found evidence of a very recent seminal emission.

Apparently, Buffalo's killer liked to take his fun with a side dish of murder. It certainly would be easier to cut a woman's throat while in the process of humping her, and outdoor fun and games were almost always carried on in strict silence, too, for fear of discovery. That would jibe with the lack of reports of any unusual screams or cries for help. Of course, there remained the hideous possibility that the killer had taken his pleasure after Lizzie had given up the ghost.

THE CORONER'S CONCLUSION WAS brief. *Willful murder by person or persons unknown. Cause of death, exsanguination due to severed left carotid artery.* On autopsy, it was determined that Dirty Legs Lizzie hadn't been too far from the grave, the Butcher notwithstanding. Years of heavy smoking had damaged her lungs, ten or twelve whiskeys a night had rotted her liver, and her heart was almost twice the normal size. She likely would have been a dead woman in a few years, or a few weeks, depending. But that, of course, didn't change the fact that she had been hurried along to the next world by a very sharp instrument, which the medical examiner assessed to have been a straight razor.

This came as something of a surprise. Most everyone had expected the murder weapon to be, of course, a butcher's knife, but even the keenest of those would have left a bigger kerf—the width of the cut. The blow that killed Dirty Legs was a slice more than it was a cut, and the fine, stiff steel of a man's razor would have been both sharp and strong enough to make the fatal incision.

The incision itself had started deep on the left side of Lizzie's throat, deep enough to find the carotid artery buried an inch under the skin below the ear. That would have been enough to finish her in a matter of a few minutes—the blood loss from a severed carotid is catastrophic—but the killer had an apparent penchant for symmetry, and had drawn the blade in an ascending and ever shallower arc across the front of the throat and then to rest against the opposite clavicle.

Without the carotid's supply of blood to the hungry brain, unconsciousness—or at least shock—would have been almost instantaneous. Yet the swooning brain would still command the heart to keep working, harder and harder, compounding Lizzie's problem as her blood pressure dropped. In only a few minutes her heart would have so little fluid left to pump that it would have to accept defeat and stop entirely.

This was precisely how flocks of sheep and trainloads of cattle went to their deaths every day, not two blocks from Lizzie's murder, but no one—not really—had thought much about how it actually worked.

But now it was most of what occupied the minds of the prostitutes of the Tenderloin, as if they hadn't already more than enough to contend with. Their better sort clucked their tongues, the ministers railed about the wages of sin, and the newspapers secretly wished for another murder.

That wish would be granted, and soon.

Meanwhile, only a few trolley stops north of Vine Alley, the Pan-American Exposition—the Electric City—was finally getting going in earnest. May, and most of June, had been cool, but the weather had at last begun to cooperate. As July approached, the fair, the heat, and the killing were all about to reach a climax.

:: PART ONE ::

HOPE

CHAPTER 1 ::

HELEN

March 1901
Three Months Earlier

S he stood five feet five, a little on the tall side. At 130 pounds, some said she could put on a bit of flesh; but if anything, Helen would have liked to lose a little, even though her figure was svelte and sleek. Without a corset, she was shapely; with one, she could have modeled for any newspaper or fashion magazine.

Her oval face was framed by dark, wavy hair, swept up, mostly, which gave her the look of a woman perhaps even a year or two younger than twenty-one. Her lips, full and with a perfect Cupid's bow, were perhaps her best feature; after that were her large, dark eyes, moist and alluring.

By any standard, Helen Crosby would be any young man's prize, but for the fact that she had been orphaned at only nine years of age and had grown up under the thumb of a rather stern, old-fashioned grandmother in Hamilton, Ontario. Such an upbringing had left her with a deep sadness that many men found unappealing, or at least complicated.

Hamilton was a pleasant enough town, but Helen had never felt truly content in Canada, a small and somewhat provincial country. She wanted to go south to the States, especially to New York or Chicago, where great things were happening and where a beautiful young woman could find both good employment and an advantageous match. At least that's the impression she had gleaned from dreaming over countless ladies' magazines.

She'd considered the stage, for a while, but Grandmother had said that actresses were all sluts and whores, living off the largesse of rich men who waited hungrily at stage doors. Now, at twenty-one, without voice, dance, or acting lessons—not to mention a chronic lack of funds—that ship had safely sailed, much to Grandmother's relief.

Helen had a slightly older sister, Eva, who had left Hamilton for Buffalo several years before. There she had established herself as an independent milliner. Millinery—at a time when every block had two or three of them—wasn't much of a living, but it was independent, and it was independence that appealed to Helen.

If she could go to Buffalo in the great Pan-American Year, she could easily find some paying position and stay with her sister while she got her feet on the ground. And while Buffalo was not New York or Chicago, it certainly wasn't Hamilton. So Helen chose a practical dream, a half-step, and bought a one-way ticket for Buffalo, trusting to good luck and the insuperable confidence of youth.

When she stepped off the train at Exchange Street Station, two hours and a world away from Hamilton, she fully expected that she would immediately become anonymous in the passing crowd.

She was very wrong. A beautiful girl like Helen was bound to attract attention, and some of it of the very worst kind.

THE GRAND OPENING WAS less than sixty days away, or so the newspapers insisted. Day by precious day, the ever-more panicked organizers reassured an ever-more skeptical public that, no later than 8:30 a.m. on May 1, three hundred fifty acres of pastureland would indeed have metamorphosed into the greatest spectacle the world had yet beheld—the Pan-American Exposition.

But at this late date, an on-time emergence seemed unlikely. Rising from the foot-deep brown slush—a crusty confection of snow, mud, and manure—was little more than a ragged skeleton city of wooden scaffolding. There was still no Midway, no Electric Tower, no Venetian canals: only miles of roughly graded pathways, trenches filled with melting snow, and spools of wire connected to nothing.

There was, however—just inside what soon would be the fair's main gate—a hopeful little clapboard structure, tidy enough, and with a deep front porch over which hung a broad sign that read:

EXPOSITION EMPLOYMENT.
INQUIRE WITHIN.

Under the overhanging porch hung a series of boards tacked with hundreds of curling slips of paper, each describing an employment opportunity. Although intended to be temporary, like the Exposition itself, for new arrivals to Buffalo, "Pan-Am work" provided a toehold in the booming city—and, if that didn't work out, free daily admission to the spectacle.

A great many of the jobs weren't of tremendous appeal to a pretty, young woman with big-city dreams. Cleaning ladies, candymakers, and ticket-takers—why, positions like that had been available back home in Hamilton. And becoming a sideshow barker or "spieler," or joining a troupe of dancing girls, were hardly ladylike employments.

This was unexpected, and Helen tamped down a rising wave of disappointment. Her small savings had been invested in her train ticket, leaving her entirely dependent on Eva's tepid support. The very first evening after her arrival, while Helen was still unpacking her single, small trunk, Eva had started grousing about the cost of room and board. Of course she'd agreed, and so here she was, combing the weather-stained slips tacked onto the board.

Perhaps there will be something tomorrow, she thought. I'll tell Eva I'll come back then. She was about to turn away when one small, neatly printed slip caught her eye:

HELP WANTED—FEMALE. COMPETENT, PLEASANT
YOUNG WOMEN OF SOUND CHARACTER
AS BELL TELEPHONE OPERATORS.
NO EXPERIENCE NECESSARY.

Her heart skipped a beat. Now this sounds like a good one.

What could be more modern, clean, and precise than being a telephone operator?

She darted into the little frame building, where there were two old women sharing a long desk.

"Hello," she said, trying to appear competent, pleasant, and of sound character. "I should like to enquire about the Bell Telephone Operator position. Positions."

The two old ladies looked her up and down. "Are there any of those still open?" the one said to the other.

The second lady riffled through a large ledger, running her finger down the pages. "Yes," she said, after what seemed like an eternity. "One opening left. What's your name, young lady?"

"Helen Crosby," she said, almost wanting to jump with joy. "I've come to Buffalo to—"

"You're very pretty, and that's what they're looking for," the old lady said, handing over a large sheet of paper and a stubby pencil. "Fill this out. Where it says position, just put Bell Telephone Operator."

"Of course," Helen said, her hands shaking. "I'd be delighted."

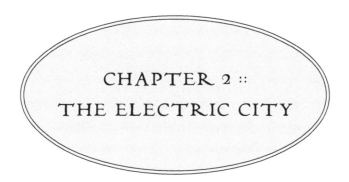

CHAPTER 2 ::
THE ELECTRIC CITY

It wasn't supposed to be in Buffalo at all.

Originally, the Pan-American Exposition—the Electric City—was to be built on tiny Cayuga Island, not far from Niagara Falls. And despite a great deal of puzzlement over the location, on a sweltering day in 1897, President William McKinley had dutifully appeared on the nondescript patch of riverbank to turn the symbolic first shovelful of soggy earth.

The "Pan" was billed as the greatest fair the world had ever seen, or ever would see; and it was certain to cast the last big one, Chicago's Columbian Exposition of 1893, in permanent shadow. Building a temporary city in a seasonal tourist resort like Niagara Falls was fitting in a way, yet the selection of the honeymoon mecca—which needed no additional publicity—was galling to the many cities that had been bypassed.

Nearby Buffalo—a *real* city, the nation's eighth-largest and fastest growing—took it hardest. The mayor, the aldermen, the big businessmen—all looked bad for having been overmatched by a mosquito-infested plot of boggy alluvium. On paper, Buffalo had every advantage: two hungry train stations, the Erie Canal, a favorable location on the Great Lakes, and all of it within a four-hour train ride of half the population of the United States.

So the shamefaced city fathers made pilgrimage to Albany and to Washington to supplicate the truly powerful that Cayuga Island was a quaint, well-meaning mistake. And yet the decision-makers had faces to save, too, and Cayuga Island stood the storm. For a while.

But then in February 1898—only six months after McKinley's ominous shovelful of earth—fate intervened in favor of Buffalo. The USS *Maine*, a warship anchored in Havana Harbor to keep a watchful eye on American interests in Cuba, detonated late one evening in a massive explosion heard as far away as the tiny wintering ground of Miami, Florida. In moments, nearly three hundred sailors went to the bottom with the shattered hulk, taking with them—unbeknownst—Niagara Falls's hopes for the Pan-American.

While it was highly likely that the vessel had been blown to smithereens by a fire smoldering in its own coal bunkers—an unfortunate but not particularly unusual occurrence—such small facts were not about to stand in the way of much larger interests.

For some time, Cuba had been trying to extricate itself from the Spanish Empire, and if the island and a few other imperial possessions could be jarred loose, they could easily be made fast to the nearby United States. Those who envied other nations' empires, notably Assistant Navy Secretary Theodore Roosevelt, who had presidential aspirations, predictably blamed Spain for the ship's destruction and clamored for retribution. War!

Many were opposed, but the newspapers—wars sold papers, after all—put their thumb on the scale, hard, and soon enough everyone was singing the same tune, even if reluctantly. When the rarest bird of all, a group called Humanitarians for War, began bleating in favor of rescuing the supposedly starving Cubans from their Spanish overlords, it became inevitable. War was declared, and other matters had to wait. Accordingly, the Pan was postponed until 1901, and Buffalo had bought some time.

War or no war, a phalanx of Buffalo boosters quickly mounted a full-scale assault against the flanks of a distracted governor and Congress. Wave after wave of blowhards pelted lawmakers with facts and figures: the city's hundreds of restaurants, thousands of hotel rooms, umpteen miles of train and trolley lines, and abundant available labor. But politicians had already become jaded by large numbers, so the well-intended rows and columns of statistics were greeted mainly with yawns.

With hopes fading, a delegation of Buffalo's who's who went to

Washington for one final push. But after another fruitless Capitol Hill meeting with both of New York's senators, it seemed that the cause was, at last, truly lost. With his fellow envoys in a funk, the least likely member of the delegation—one "Popcorn" Charley Willard, who owned a sketchy hotel, The Alzora, and several lesser dives in Buffalo—decided to mount a last-ditch action.

Willard had been invited to join the delegation as the lone representative of the kind of cheap lodging that most visitors to the Pan would likely seek out. How he had been chosen wasn't entirely clear. He was *connected*, that everyone knew, though how or why were mysteries. Popcorn Charley certainly didn't have what the blue bloods in the delegation could claim—good breeding, college education, or flawless personal hygiene. But what Charley possessed in abundance was something that the others did not: what was called sand, grit, moxie, or—in Charley's world—*balls*.

As the downcast coffle of bureaucrats filed slowly out of the Capitol to catch the train back home, Popcorn Charley buttonholed one of the bored senators himself, pulling him aside whether he liked it or not. He thanked him for a moment's indulgence and offered him a cigar, a good one—Cuban, of course—which the senator gladly accepted.

"Your Eminence," Charley said, without a trace of irony. "Allow me to apologize for my fellow delegates."

"Whatever for?" puffed the senator.

"Because I don't know about you, but if I hear one more speech about civic pride, I'll put a bullet in my brain."

The senator studied the glowing ash on his cigar. "Willard," he said, "you put it rather tartly, but you're not far off. Believe me, sir, nothing would give me more pleasure than to see Buffalo prevail. The mayor and council of Niagara Falls certainly haven't done *me* any favors over the years. But without *something* else, I just don't see how we could justify—"

"That's the problem with all those characters," Charley said. "Not one of them said a word about Buffalo's biggest advantage."

"I'm listening," said the senator.

"What other city in New York State, or anywhere, has not one, but *two* red-light districts?"

The senator squinted through his cloud of smoke, either indignantly or possibly suppressing a laugh. "A little decorum, if you please, Mr. Willard. We *are* in the United States Capitol, after all." Then he turned on his heel and strode back into the shelter of the great dome, leaving Charley grinning to himself.

In less than a week, it went out from on high that the distinguished delegation from Erie County had won the day, and that Buffalo had been selected for the new and improved 1901 version of the Pan-American "based on the city's manifest natural advantages." The decision was now final and irreversible: millions of visitors would be directed toward Buffalo, and lonely Cayuga Island would have to settle for its millions of mosquitoes.

It was well that it had been decided quickly. American expeditionary forces—with Teddy Roosevelt and a few of his favorite reporters conspicuously in the front, naturally—took fewer than three months to wrest Cuba, Puerto Rico, Guam, and the Philippines from centuries of Spain's grasp. As American flags rose over its new territories, the unfortunate Cubans, in whose harbor it had all begun, soon discovered that they had no more say in their new government than they had in the old one. And they were still starving.

But the land-grab had puffed up the United States rather nicely. Roosevelt and his fellow imperialists had acquired their empire, and almost for free: The whole adventure had been financed by a temporary excise tax levied on long-distance telephone calls. The war was decisively won in ten weeks, and the temporary tax was still being collected a century later.

But none of that, telephone taxes or starving Cubans, mattered to Buffalo. America may have won a bully little war, but Buffalo had won the battle for the Electric City. And Popcorn Charley Willard had led the charge up Capitol Hill, even if he'd never be given credit for it.

POPCORN CHARLEY WILLARD HAD his faults, but lying to elected officials was not among them. He had been scrupulously correct. Buffalo, with a tenth of the population of its cross-state rival New York City, boasted twice the number of whores.

The smaller and rougher of Buffalo's two red-light districts, The Hooks, was located hard by the waterfront—the wharves, the slips that handled the Lake Erie steamers and the Erie Canal itself. The ten-block area catered to the down at heel, the dangerous, and the diseased. The throngs of conventioneers, country bumpkins, and respectable gentlemen visiting the Exposition would be having nothing to do with The Hooks.

Instead, they would gravitate to the city's second, much larger, if only slightly more genteel pleasure zone—the Tenderloin. It had borrowed its name from the original, in New York City, but Buffalo's had been there for at least as long as Manhattan's. Bounded by Michigan, Washington, Seneca, and Exchange Streets, the Tenderloin was a half-square-mile chockablock with saloons, dance halls, cheap hotels, and brothels, a tolerated if technically illegal vice district in the very heart of downtown. And—best of all—the whole thing was only a ten-minute trolley ride away from the Pan-American Exposition.

What Popcorn Charley and the distinguished senator had grasped was a simple calculus that could not be discussed in polite society, however obvious and incontrovertible. From May to November, ten million people were expected to "do the Pan." Four million of those, conservatively, would be adult men. And of those four million, at least three-quarters did not intend to let abstinence spoil a good time. That meant that an army of males—one as large as the entire population of New York City—would be looking to get laid. And it was in the brothels, bawdy houses, bordellos, and dance halls of the Tenderloin that their desires would be fulfilled.

Popcorn Charley and his fellow dive-keepers stood to reap a once-in-a-century windfall.

CHAPTER 3 ::
WHORECRAFT

There was one other thing that put the Tenderloin in good stead for the Pan-American spree, and that was the well-meant but hopelessly stupid Raines Law, passed a few years before by the state legislature. For years, working men—who worked six days a week, with only Sundays off—had bitched that in New York State it was impossible to get a drink on their day off. By law, alcohol sales were forbidden on the Sabbath.

Working men didn't like it, and neither did saloonkeepers, restaurateurs, and hoteliers, who made most of their money serving up liquor and beer. Salvation came in the person of New York State Senator John Raines, who developed the bright idea to allow the sale of alcoholic beverages on Sundays—subject to certain prudent limitations. Under his plan, Sunday sales of alcohol would be permitted, but only in hotels, boarding houses of at least eight rooms, or if served with food to keep the firewater from going too quickly to a fellow's head.

Contrary to its intention, the Raines Law opened the floodgates for vice. A tidal wave of applications for hotel licenses swamped courthouses across the state. Saloonkeepers partitioned off the upstairs or back rooms of their dives into eight tiny compartments, some smaller than their equivalents on a half-decent overnight train; trays of stale bread, bits of moldy cheese, and—in the case of Charley Willard, stale and grimy popcorn—began appearing on bars to meet the food requirement.

And with eight or more vacant rooms suddenly on their hands—and on their landlords' rent rolls—the enterprising business owners of the Tenderloin stepped up to the mark with the only thing that paid even better than watered-down booze: women. Overnight, boarding houses became brothels, saloons sprouted upstairs knocking-shops, and even some of the finest hotels in Buffalo were transformed into high-class houses of assignation, where the better sort could schedule their shenanigans.

Thanks to John Raines, there would now be plenty of liquor awaiting the Pan-American guests, even on Sundays. But now the enterprising flesh-peddlers of the Tenderloin found themselves confronting a different kind of shortage—a dire shortfall of women. Even the most adept prostitute could service only so many men in an evening, and it wouldn't do to keep impatient, randy gentlemen waiting in a cathouse parlor for too very long. That tended to lead to fistfights and police raids, and without a penny earned to show for any of it.

But how to recruit enough women to serve the needs of all of those men? There were a few peripatetic whores, of course, but those tended to be out in western boomtowns in Alaska and Colorado. New York City wasn't about to donate any of theirs. And while there were a few coded entries in the want ads—for "massage artists" mainly—that could supply a handful at best, not the hundreds that would be pressed into service during the Pan.

There simply weren't enough willing women. And that left the unwilling or the unwitting—the most elusive prey of all, and one hunted by specialists known as cadets.

Thousands of young women had already begun to arrive in Buffalo, attracted by the promise of employment at the Pan-American. Country girls seeking their fortunes in the big city, recent immigrants, abandoned wives with mouths to feed, and those single ladies whose monthly bills simply exceeded their paltry wages—all were fair game. Every day, trains and steamers brought scores of new, fresh faces, eager for a toehold in the big city. What most of these hopeful young women didn't know was that—with prices of everything inflated by the coming Exposition—a shopgirl's wage of five dollars a week wasn't nearly enough to keep body and soul together.

The cadets would be waiting to offer them another option.

⌒

"ENGLISH" GRACE HARRINGTON RAN a high-tone bordello at 291 Ellicott Street, right across from Popcorn Charley's flagship property, The Alzora Hotel. Other than for her geographic moniker—whose origins were a mystery—Grace's brothel didn't have an enticing name like The Alzora; in fact, it didn't have a name at all. Everyone knew it as Grace Harrington's place, or simply Grace's place—and that was enough, because gentlemen who knew quality knew that English Grace ran the best, the youngest, and the most attractive whores in Buffalo.

Grace and Charley had an affinity—meaning that they enjoyed a warm friendship, shared business interests, and an occasional roll in the hay. And between them they had something even rarer: trust. It was well to be guarded in their line of work, but as time had passed each had found in the other a worthy confidant.

One slow, bleak afternoon in late March, Grace was relaxing in Charley's bed. Things didn't get going until sundown in the Tenderloin, and so afternoons were the time for shopping, running errands, or horizontal refreshment.

"Charley," Grace said to Charley, who was sitting on the edge of the bed, smoking a cigarette, "how many more girls do you think you'll need? For the Pan?"

He turned around and shrugged. "As many as I can get," he said, thoughtfully picking a shred of tobacco from his tongue. "But for the places I run now, at least six more, I'd say."

"Uh huh," Grace said, holding out her hand for Charley's cigarette. She took a draw and handed it back. "I need only one—but someone gifted. One of my steadiest girls may or may not last through the Exposition. She's wearing down."

"Which one?" he said. "Olive?"

"Yes. Can you use her?"

Charley sat back against the iron bedstead. "Yeah, I can take her off your hands."

"Don't pretend you're doing me any favors, Charley. She'll be a fresh face around this place. She's just getting a little long in the tooth for mine."

Men came to Grace's place not only to get laid, but explosively, and in style. She had no need to offer crusty sandwiches, ancient pickled eggs, or even watered-down beer. Instead, Grace served cognac in tiny snifters to keep everyone well-behaved. Her establishment was done up in high Victorian décor, appointed with velvet couches and Oriental rugs, heavy curtains, and chandeliers—and kept spic-and-span, top to bottom. Grace kept two full-time chambermaids busy dusting, waxing, sweeping, and shining every surface in the two stories, and even in the basement. They also tidied up the working girls' rooms after each client had departed.

The girls, too, were clean and well-kept. Grace provided comfortable living quarters, fashionable-if-gaudy clothing, and medical care so that the usual occupational hazards—disease and pregnancy, both dangerous and highly unprofitable—could be kept more or less at bay.

Grace's level of whorecraft demanded beauty and poise, the two things that wore away quickest of all among working girls. When one began to look a bit threadbare, she'd have to leave Grace's place for other houses with lower standards, like The Alzora. Unless a girl with exceptional ability and smarts could start a house of her own, it was a one-way staircase down, one punishing step at a time. And at the bottom was a tiny crib in The Hooks or, worse, walking the streets.

Fucking is surprisingly hard work. Some mistakenly believed otherwise, that whores had only to lie there inert while a man got his business done. If a man wanted apathy, though, he'd be at home banging the wife. In an establishment like Grace's, a working girl who didn't *work* at giving a man a good time would not last two weeks. They had to fuck, of course, but they had to fuck *well*—well enough that men would return and, in time, become regulars.

Since each client differed in personality and preference, too, each required an individual touch. Grace's girls were trained to be actresses as much as they were purveyors of sex, and each night's performance had to be at least as good as the night before's. If they failed, everyone in the flesh trade knew that there would be no curtain calls.

"Who do you have as cadets these days?" Charley asked after a protracted silence.

"Just the doctor," Grace replied. "You?"

"Mullen and Potluck."

"Charley, you're never going to bring this place up with those two plug-uglies. I'm surprised they don't scare all the girls away."

"Look, I'm doing fine. Not an idle minute around here most nights. Why should I pay more and make less?"

"Up to you. I just think you could stand to class this place up a little."

"If you've got suggestions, I'm all ears."

"Get yourself a woman cadet," Grace said. "An old lady or a smart-looking young one. Nothing in-between. But one who knows the business from the working end."

"Anyone in mind?"

"You can have Lotta Norton, if you want her. I won her in a dice game with George Haley."

"You didn't!"

"Oh, but I did. He was shaking Klondike like a man with an ague, and I called him out on it. He said he'd let me have Lotta if I bested him. Which"—Grace said, reaching for Charley's cigarette again—"I did, because I know his racket. But she's the kind of cadet that's best for the country girls. I've never had any luck with those."

"Say, thanks a million," Charley said. "What do I owe you?"

"Just keep putting that thing of yours to work the way you just did, and we're square."

"It will be my pleasure, dear. Tell Lotta to come by, and I'll put her to work right away, too."

"Very funny. Don't go sampling the merchandise, boy," Grace said.

"Aw, come on, Grace," Charley whined. "How'm I supposed to know if she's got the right feel for the job if I don't give her a trial?"

Grace rolled her eyes. "All right, but make it once and done, or else I'm not sending any more help your way. I mean it. Just one poke."

"Just one poke," Charley said, crossing himself.

FOR SOME, CADET WAS a full-time job; for others, a sideline that brought in extra income in satisfying chunks. And there were cadets for every level in the pecking order. But the job was the same, if the patter differed. A cadet had to possess three things: a winning personality; a kind of intuitive empathy for others, particularly for their troubles; and an utter lack of scruples.

The cadet's job was to winnow out likely girls from the train stations, sidewalks, and even churches—a task called cutting out, after the cowboy skill of separating an individual cow from a herd. This meant identifying a girl who looked lonely, or sad, or downcast—or perhaps simply confused, looking for direction in a new city or in the teeming railway station. The cadet would then offer assistance, which could be a listening ear, a small loan, the promise of a job, or even temporary lodging until such time as the mark got her feet on the ground.

Thus, the very best cadets were either charming young men, very old women who reminded young ones of their own mothers, or fashionable and pretty things who looked like they had the world by the tail. The dumpy, underfed, or unwashed need not apply.

Once the mark had accepted the cadet's offer of assistance, there followed a period of grooming. This could be brutally short or—for the English Grace class of ladies—involve as much as two or three months of cultivation and training.

In the former case, in 1896 two sisters from Toronto, in Buffalo on a lark, lost their pocketbook somewhere in the Tenderloin. Quite by chance, Popcorn Charley—who was just then staffing up after the passage of the Raines Law—spied the girls weeping disconsolately on the sidewalk, introduced himself as one of Buffalo's leading hoteliers, and offered them suitable lodgings lest something terrible befall them in a strange city and without resources. The grateful young ladies went sniffling into the closed carriage of this apparent Samaritan, only to reappear some four years later, thoroughly used up, in an Arizona mining camp.

In the latter case, the prettiest and the most promising would be given lodgings, taken dancing, or perhaps even enrolled in secretarial school. Only after innocently racking up a substantial debt to the cadet would the trap spring shut. Then, unable to pay what they owed, the hapless young lady would be whisked away to the cadet's brothel, stripped of her street clothes in favor of gaudy silks and lacy finery that she could never wear onto the street, and told that there was but one way to work off her obligation. The street clothes and any personal items were locked away in a special room, quite safely, and could only be recovered when the girl squared her account. Mail to and from the new prostitute was monitored and either censored or, more often, confiscated; meals were taken in the house; and for the benefit of friends and family appearances were maintained that she was still gainfully and legitimately employed as whatever she had been in her brief taste of freedom.

A lot of girls never did regain that freedom, but were consumed by disease—persistent, nagging gonorrhea or the dreaded and incurable syphilis—or by drugs. The monotony, infamy, and despair that many prostitutes felt about their trade was assuaged by cocaine, morphine, opium, chloral hydrate, hashish, or all of them, taken by mouth, nose, needle, or rectum. But with oblivion came other risks: addiction and, ultimately, being turned out into the street to hustle for their next fix. That never ended well. Usually the morphine fiends froze to death in winter doorways or died in convulsions from tetanus borne by a dirty needle. Their husks were picked up each morning by the coroner's van, just as the daily crop of dead animals were picked up by the knacker.

In just a little more than a month, the gates of the Electric City would open, and the fun would begin. But between now and then, hundreds of impressionable young ladies were about to hear the siren song of the cadet, and the only thing most of them would ever know about the Exposition would be what their clients would tell them. If they stayed around long enough to have a conversation, that is.

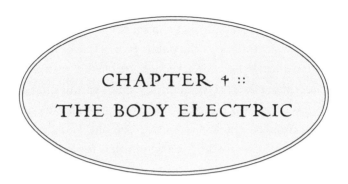

CHAPTER 4 ::

THE BODY ELECTRIC

The Pan-American Exposition
May 14, 1901
Two Weeks After Opening Day

The place was a marvel. Outside, it resembled a lavish Spanish mission, its towers and turrets dripping with filigree and painted a warm yellow. And in the Electric City, the Electricity Building was as close to the center of the universe as could be imagined—a place of pilgrimage to the altar of mankind's greatest invention, electric power.

Hordes of visitors shuffled in lockstep through a rabbit's warren of exhibits and demonstrations. More than a linear mile of corridors wound between rows of giant dynamos, motors of every size and type, spools of wire, switchgear—in short, charting the whole nervous system of the body electric. And located in the very navel of this great palace of progress, under an enormous glass dome that flooded the atrium below it with sunlight, sat the Bell Telephone Company switchboard.

Six pretty women, or operators, were perched on high chairs in front of the switchboard—a long, black panel resembling a huge pegboard. Each young lady would answer a call, flip a switch, plug a corded cable into one of the hundreds of holes in the pegboard, and spin a small crank. Then, announcing that call connected, the operator would ring off and answer the next call. A lady with a clipboard strolled back and forth behind the operators, assisting them as necessary.

Helen was so attractive and vivacious—and possessed of a clear and soothing voice—that after her month-long training course was complete, the Bell Telephone Company had chosen her as one of only six operators pretty enough to serve as the public face of the growing company. This half-dozen lovely Bell Girls, though, perched at their switchboard in the atrium of the Electricity Building, could handle only a minority of the thousands of calls placed to and from the Pan each day. Several times their number—the less attractive, the old, and those with bad teeth or grating voices—worked in a windowless room in the rear of the giant building.

Once an hour, one of the six favored operators would disconnect herself from the panel, step to the edge of the raised platform on which the switchboard sat, and spend fifteen minutes chatting with visitors, answering questions about just what she had been doing with all those plugs and wires, and drumming up interest (among rural folk, in particular) in obtaining a Bell telephone system. And—at least unofficially— these elite Bell Girls were expected to be appropriately flirtatious, so long as they avoided creating any disgruntlement among wives or sweethearts.

Helen enjoyed this part of the job most of all. No matter how engaging some of the callers were, staring at a panel of blinking lights and rows upon rows of jacks was monotonous. So when her turn to speak would come, she fairly jumped up from her stool to make every one of her fifteen minutes count. She loved meeting people from places she'd never heard of, and probably would never go, and sharing with them the marvels of the Bell Telephone system, which could allow someone in Buffalo or Boise to converse—live!—with someone in Brooklyn or Brazil.

Usually there would be a little knot of at least twenty people eager to ask a question or—in the case of most of the younger men—tell her how pretty she was. Some would ask her to join them for an ice cream float, and a few of the boldest ones for a beer at the German beerhall. On this Monday, though—which was always the slowest day of the week at the Exposition—Helen leapt from her seat to find only one person standing against the velvet rope. He was a burly fellow, late thirties perhaps, with a pugilist's nose, reddish hair, and slightly blotchy skin that made him look older and rougher than most of the young dandies who tried to catch Helen's eye.

"You're awfully dexterous," the fellow said with a soft Scottish brogue, as she approached with her demonstration card in hand. "Has anyone told you that you have very graceful hands?"

She'd heard that line several times before. "It's only a matter of practice," she said cheerfully, if slightly by rote. "It's not so difficult as it looks."

"With hands like yours, you'd make an excellent nurse," the man said.

This was a line Helen hadn't heard before, and in two short weeks she'd heard almost every one of them.

"Pardon me?" she said. "A nurse?"

"Aye, I said you'd make a good nurse. You have a kind manner about you."

"Why, thank you for saying so, sir," Helen said. "Are you visiting us from Scotland?"

He chuckled. "Scots people are never anything but visitors. But I am indeed a Highland lad by birth, although I've been here for going on fifteen years now. My Scottish friends tell me I sound like an American nowadays. But I think they're just trying to hurt my feelings."

Helen smiled. "Well, don't let them do it. My name's Crosby—my grandmother used to tell me that her parents were both from Scotland."

He nodded. "Aye, there are quite a few Crosbys in Scotland. Do you know which part they hailed from?"

"That I don't know, sir," she said.

"Ach, it's no matter. But I hope you won't call me sir, because I certainly haven't been granted a peerage, and I don't expect to be. My name's Grand. Doctor George Grand."

She put out her hand, and he shook it with a meaty palm. "So you're a doctor," she said.

"A surgeon, actually."

"Well, that explains why you know so much about nurses."

"Now don't say that too very loud," he said, giving her a wink. "You'll give people the wrong impression. I said only that I think you'd make a good one."

"I'll take that as a compliment."

"But seriously, Miss Crosby—have you ever considered becoming a nurse?"

"I certainly admire what nurses do," Helen said, "but I would have no idea how to go about becoming one. Nor do I have the kind of schooling required."

"Then perhaps today is your lucky day," Grand said. "The hospital I'm affiliated with has recently begun a nurses' training course—with scholarships, too, for the most promising girls. After two years of practical experience, you get a diploma, and you can work anywhere you please. There's a great need for nurses these days, as you might know. Unless of course you'd prefer to keep working for the telephone company, that is. There's a future in that, too, I'd expect."

Helen had thought about what would happen to her after the Pan-American: long hours in a windowless room like the one the homelies sat in, seeing nothing other than the panel in front of her, and having no conversation save the briefest one necessary to complete a call. No excitement. She leaned toward him.

"In confidence , I wouldn't say that being a telephone operator is my life's dream. It's a stepping stone."

"Then lend me your clipboard," he said, flapping his fingers. She handed it to him, her pencil dangling from a string she had neatly tied to it. Clipped to it was a blank form on which she could write down the questions she'd received and the names of anyone interested in a Bell Telephone Exchange. She received five dollars for every solid lead.

He took the pencil and scribbled something, then handed it back.

"If you find yourself intrigued, Miss Crosby, all you have to do is call." He gestured to the giant switchboard behind them. "And I know you have access to a telephone."

She glanced at the clipboard. On it he had written:

Dr. George H. Grand
Riverdale Hospital
Lafayette Street, Buffalo
Telephone Bryant 595

"That I do, Doctor Grand," she said. "I'll give it some thought."

"I hope you will. You won't regret it, of that I'm sure."

CHAPTER 5 ::
RIVERDALE

R iverdale Hospital looked much like any other tidy Buffalo duplex: three stories of cheerful yellow brick squared off against Lafayette Street. But it was unusual in that it was private, for women only, and small—housing only thirty patients. And it was unique in being the sole property of a woman, Dr. Louise Crandall.

Dr. Crandall had started the place on a lark fifteen years ago, but in doing so she had accidentally found a niche. Most Buffalo hospitals were everything Riverdale was not—large, impersonal, and dirty. And unlike most hospitals, which hired the same old medical graduates from the same few medical schools, there were no sinecures at Riverdale. Each year, Dr. Crandall announced the coming year's appointments to the medical staff. If doctors met her standards, they stayed. If they didn't, they went, without apology.

When George Grand had arrived from Scotland, aged twenty-five, with nothing but a carpetbag and a freshly minted medical degree, he had spent his first few years bouncing from hospital to hospital. Then, quite by chance, he heard about Riverdale. Dr. Crandall had taken a liking to the young Scot and offered him a year's contract. He'd shown promise, and she'd renewed his contract year after year. Now, at age forty, he had become a valued part of her staff. That said, Dr. Crandall was not unaware of Dr. Grand's two weaknesses: whiskey and women.

George had always liked to drink, but for years he had been kept in check because in New York State it was nearly impossible to get a drink on Sundays, his day off. Grand was a loquacious, sociable fellow, and sitting alone in his room getting loaded was not his idea of a good time. With the Raines Law, all that had changed, and now every Sunday Dr. Grand would get started early and finish late, cruising the Tenderloin's booziest spots: the White Elephant, the Potluck, and the Mohican. Unfortunately, under the influence of alcohol, Dr. Grand's normal affability quickly drained away. He became petty, surly, and combative—a big man with a chip on his shoulder. Once, when he'd shown up for work on Monday sporting a black eye, Dr. Crandall had given him a stern lecture.

Yet if a man had to have a vice, a taste for liquor was generally considered preferable to an inability to resist the charms of the opposite sex. A male doctor in a woman's hospital had to be especially careful about appearances, maintain a polite distance, and, above all, keep his hands to himself. In recent months, Grand had begun to pay a bit of attention to a very fetching young member of the nursing staff, Anne McClellan. At first, Nurse McClellan welcomed it, and after a couple of months, there was talk that the two might become engaged to marry.

Quite abruptly, however, some sort of ill-feeling erupted between Dr. Grand and Nurse McClellan, and there had been loud arguments between them on the sidewalk. It came to a head one morning when George arrived for his morning rounds and passed by Dr. Crandall's office.

"A minute, George?" Crandall said, waving George into her office.

He plunked down across from her. "Yes, Doctor?"

"George, you know I'm not one to beat around the bush. Nurse McClellan came to me yesterday and lodged a very serious complaint against you."

The blotches on Grand's face turned very red. "I don't understand."

"She came to me and said that an uncle of hers had died and left her a small legacy."

"So I've heard," he said.

"She went on to say that she used some of the money to repay a loan you'd made to her. Is that true?"

"That's right. I've been helping the girl with her tuition. Until recently she's not had two nickels to rub together."

"I wish I had known about that, George," Crandall said. "I can't have our staff engaging in financial transactions among one another. And as you well know, we offer tuition assistance to girls in need."

"I was merely trying to help the lass. I can't believe she'd lodge a complaint about me for doing her a good turn."

"That wasn't the subject of her complaint. She said that when she gave you the money to repay the loan in full, you became very angry. She said you took her by the shoulders and shook her, George. Is that true?"

"She's lying," he said quietly.

"Lying about what part?"

"She paid me back, yes."

"Did you become angry with her?"

Grand took a deep breath. "I *was* angry, Doctor, but only because she was more than a little snippy when she gave me the money. After all the assistance I'd provided, I expected a wee bit of gratitude. But in any case, I didn't lay a finger on her."

Dr. Crandall put her hands flat on her desk. "George. You know I like you. You're a fine surgeon. And I'm not taking Nurse McClellan's part over yours. But where there's smoke, there's usually fire. Suffice it to say, I will not have you behaving in a way that brings discredit on my institution."

"Now, Doctor—"

Crandall held up her hand. "Let me make this very plain." She counted on her fingers. "No more lending of money to the nurses. All conversations you have with them here will be of a professional nature only. There will be no displays of anger. And if you wish to drink, you will do so only in moderation, and away from this hospital and its staff. Do you understand?"

"This is an ambush," George said. "And I must—"

"*Do you understand?*"

Dr. Grand looked down at the desk. "Yes, Doctor. I understand."

"Good."

"I'm very sorry. It won't happen again," he said quietly.

"Please see that it does not. I'm sorry to have to be unpleasant, but I do not intend to have a second conversation of this nature."

"Nor would I want to have one."

"Then we are agreed. That's all I have, George. You may go."

George managed a weak smile and left Dr. Crandall's office, seething. That goddamned snooty bitch, he thought. I'd like to do a lot more than shake her by the shoulders.

～

AT 7:10 THE NEXT morning, Grand was waiting outside the front door of Riverdale Hospital.

"A word, Annie?" he said as Nurse McClellan emerged from the night shift, blinking into the morning sunlight.

She looked over at him, startled. "Doctor Grand," she said, spitting out the words. "Surely you will recall that I told you to leave me alone."

"And I'd like nothing better. But we need to clear the air first."

"There's no clearing necessary," she said. "It's been a very long night, and I have nothing further to say to you."

The 7:00 p.m. to 7:00 a.m. nurse's shift was particularly trying. There was usually only one doctor on staff, and that often only a medical intern. After twelve hours of running between beds, preparing and administering medicines, taking down notes, and emptying bedpans—and all of it on weary feet and in a rigid, starched uniform—even a young, energetic woman like Anne McClellan was worn to the bone.

"I'll walk with you to the streetcar," George said.

"No thank you," she replied, and stepped quickly away from him. He caught up with her and gripped her forearm, hard.

"I *said*, we need to talk."

"You are hurting me," she said, wrenching her arm away. "Leave me alone, or I'll scream!"

"You ungrateful little cunt," he snarled. "You have a lot of nerve to go to Crandall and complain about me. I'll make you sorry you ever saw my face."

"Believe me, I'm already sorry," she said. "You're nothing but a dirty old lecher."

"That's a laugh. You didn't seem to mind when I was balls-deep in you, girl."

She stood back as if she'd been slapped.

"And don't forget that I have some *very* colorful letters from you," Grand continued. "I'm sure Crandall would find them very interesting."

"Do what you want. I'll survive."

"Maybe you will, and maybe you won't."

"I'm leaving now. If you take one more step after me, I'll find a policeman."

"Don't waste your time," Grand said. "I have no further interest in the likes of you."

Nurse McClellan trotted away down Lafayette Street.

"Just remember!" Grand yelled after her. "I don't forgive, and I don't forget!"

She didn't respond, but a passerby scowled at him.

"If you have something to say, chum, say it," Grand barked at the man, who waved his hand at him and kept going down Lafayette Street.

"GEORGE?" DR. CRANDALL CALLED to him later that day as he tried to hustle by her office unnoticed.

He skidded to a stop and leaned into her doorway. "Yes, Doctor?"

"Nurse McClellan turned in her notice this morning."

"Is that so?" Grand said.

Crandall studied his face. "Yes, it's so."

"Did she give a reason?"

"She did not."

"She always was a flighty one," Grand said.

"Be careful, George. And don't tell me you don't know what I mean by that."

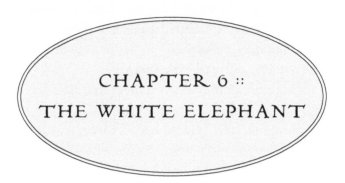

CHAPTER 6 ::
THE WHITE ELEPHANT

After weeks of long hours at the switchboard, both of Helen's
skirts were shiny with wear, and every one of her three shirt-
waists was getting thin at the elbows. So she borrowed a crisp
shirtwaist and pleated skirt from one of her fellow Bell Girls.

Her friend had asked if she were dressing up to meet a fellow, and
Helen had demurred with a Mona Lisa smile. She thought it better to
keep any report of her investigating a nursing career from reaching the
Bell Telephone people, who might discharge her as undependable, if
they knew. But what is life without some risk? she thought. And Dr.
Grand seemed like a man who could be very helpful. He was older and
more experienced—if her father had lived, he'd be only a little older than
Grand—and was already an established doctor working in a respected
institution.

She met him at Alt Nürnberg, a recreated German village on the
Exposition's festive Midway. In fine weather, the cozy duplicate of the
old town square of Nuremberg provided tired visitors a place to rest and
dine *al fresco*. The food was excellent, and the beer as close to the real
thing as Buffalo had to offer, but it was known to be the most expensive place in the Exposition, second only to the rooftop restaurant in the
Electric Tower.

Dr. Grand was sitting at one of the many tables in the busy square.
He waved when he spied her, and she smiled and threaded her way over
to him. He called over a waitress in Bavarian costume.

"Two mugs of lager," he said, and the waitress hurried away. "Big ones!"

"Perhaps I ought first to have asked you if you had to go back to work today," he said in a stage whisper. "The Bell System might not approve of beer."

"Today's my day off," she said. "And I like beer."

"That makes two of us! And the beer here is very good indeed. I've been to Germany many times, and this place reminds me of my traveling days."

"How fascinating," she said. "I'd love to see Europe someday. And so many other places, too. I think that's what I like best about the Pan. Not only does it have all these little villages, so many of the people I meet are from other countries."

"It's good to broaden the horizons. Most young people don't do it while they can. I traveled all over the world as a ship's doctor before settling down in Buffalo."

"How exciting!" she said. "I'd love to have adventures like that."

"Then you are as wise as you are beautiful, Miss Crosby."

She blushed. Fortunately the beer arrived and she didn't have to respond.

He raised his mug. "To new adventures!" he said, and they touched mugs. She sipped hers demurely and laughed when he told her she had suds on her upper lip.

"My, I need a napkin."

"Allow me," he said, reaching across the table. He wiped the suds off her lip with his forefinger. His hands were large and seemed strong, but his touch was so light it tickled, and she giggled.

"I hope no one saw that," she said.

"You really are from a small town," he said with a smirk.

"I suppose I am. City life is so different."

"It is. But you're catching on quickly."

"Sometimes I wonder. I feel very much like a fish out of water, still."

"Miss Crosby, may I offer you a word of advice? Well-meant, of course."

She raised her eyebrows. "I'd value that, Doctor Grand."

"Please call me George. And here's my advice. The best thing in life we can learn is how others see us."

"That's very intriguing," she said.

"Then it leads to a question. How do you see yourself?"

Helen thought for a moment. "I suppose I see a girl who isn't very experienced in the ways of the world. Perhaps too cautious, at first, and then suddenly too impulsive."

"That's very perceptive," he said. "Would you like to know how I see you?"

She sat back and took another little sip of beer. "I'm a little afraid to."

"You have nothing to fear from me. As I said, I've been many, many places in my life so far, and I have yet to meet someone quite like you."

"But Doctor—George—you only met me a few days ago, and very briefly."

"That's true. But I'm a very good judge of character, Miss Crosby. As a doctor, one has to be. Patients will rarely tell their doctor the things he needs to know to be of greatest help."

"I've been guilty of that myself sometimes," she said.

"As have we all. And—to come to my point—what I see when I look at you, and talk with you, is a young woman of unusual ability. Talent."

"I don't have any talent," she said. "I don't play an instrument. I don't speak other languages."

"But you enjoy good beer," he said jovially. "That's a start." She laughed.

"I mean it, though," he went on. "It's why I knew immediately that you'd make an excellent nurse. You have—how to say it—a kind of personal magnetism, and an air that suggests you could take care of people. Give of yourself for others' sake."

"How very interesting," Helen said. "I suppose I didn't see that in myself."

"You have a very comforting way about you."

George ordered some food and two more mugs of beer, and while they ate and drank, they laughed about the other people in Alt Nürnberg, some of whom looked like they couldn't tell one end of a fork from another.

"See?" he said, pointing. "*These* are country bumpkins. You're not anything like them."

"George, shhhh," she said. "They'll *hear*."

"It might do them some good to see themselves as others do."

She worked up her courage at last. "I wonder if you could tell me more about the nursing academy? Particularly how I might apply and how much it might cost."

"Application is easy. Since I work there, I'd make the application on your behalf. The only sticky part, since you're new in the city, is that they require a second reference from another doctor."

"Oh," she said. "You're the only doctor I know here. I could perhaps write to our family physician back in Hamilton?"

"No, it has to be a local doctor. Licensed in New York State, you know."

"I see," she said, pushing her food around with her fork.

"Now, don't be downcast," Grand said. "Give me a few weeks, and I can perhaps prevail upon one of my colleagues to provide a reference. But I'll have to have known you a little longer, because of course he'd ask."

She brightened. "That would be very welcome, George. Thank you. But what about the money?"

"The nursing course is a year long, and my understanding is that it costs about two hundred dollars, plus books. You'd need about a hundred dollars to get started. Maybe one-fifty."

"A hundred dollars," she said. "I don't have anything like that much. But I can save up a little at a time. I'm living with my sister now, and so I haven't any rent to pay. With what Bell is paying me, I could probably save four or five dollars a week."

"Hmm. The only problem with that plan is that the next class starts in September. That's only three months from now, and you'll need five or six months to save up a hundred dollars or more. You'd miss the class."

"Of all the foul luck," she said. "Perhaps I could ask my sister for a small loan."

He drained his mug of beer. "I might have an idea."

"What?"

"Let me ask at work if they have any scholarships or other assistance available. That may make up the difference."

"Would you really?"

"It would be my pleasure. I don't like to see talent wasted."

"Oh, thank you, George!"

"You are most welcome, Miss Crosby."

"Do call me Helen," she said. "It's the least I can do to return the favor."

"You don't need to return anything. But I'll gladly call you Helen. Now then, how about this? Give me a few days to sort things out, and we'll meet again."

"I have this Sunday off," she said. "Will that work? We can come back here."

"Perfectly. But we can't come here on Sunday."

"Why not?"

"They can't serve us beer," he said. "It's against the law."

"I never heard of such a thing," she said. "But that's fine. I don't need beer."

"Ah, Helen, but your new friend George may need one. Let's meet at a place I know downtown. It's called the White Elephant."

"What a charming name!"

"It's a good spot. Would noon be acceptable? We'll take our luncheon downtown."

"My, yes. Thank you, George. Truly."

"Not at all. I'll see you on Sunday."

HELEN ARRIVED HOME THAT evening bubbling over with enthusiasm. Over dinner, she related to Eva her meeting with George Grand and the possibility of attending nursing school. Then she broached the topic of a small loan.

"I'm glad you brought this up, Helen," Eva said.

"You are?"

"I am. When you wrote to me in February—about wanting to stay with me—I thought it might be for a few days or a week. Now it's been more than two months that I've had to defray all of your expenses. Free room and board, streetcar fare, and so on."

"Eva, you *have* been very generous. I hope you know how grateful I am."

"Gratitude doesn't pay the bills," Eva replied tartly. "And moreover, Helen—to be quite forthright with you, I've started seeing a new fellow recently."

"You have? Why haven't you brought him by so that I can meet him?"

"He comes by in the daytime," her sister said. "And he prefers privacy."

"I would never be a third wheel," Helen said. "Why, I'd introduce myself, and he'd introduce himself, and I'd say how happy I am that my sister is being courted by such a fine gentleman. Then I'd retire to my room."

Eva sighed. "It's not going to be like that. He doesn't want to meet you."

Helen was flabbergasted. "What kind of man wouldn't want to meet your sister?"

"The *kind* of man he is, Helen, is *married*."

The color drained from Helen's face. "I see," she said softly.

"Yes. And he wants to remain married. He's very successful in business, and he has a nice house and three children. So he can't have anyone knowing too much about him and me, or it could get back to his wife. And that would cause a scandal."

"I understand," Helen said. "But Eva—I am a little surprised that you'd enter into such a relation with—"

"There are a lot of things about city life that may surprise you," she said. "Since I got here three years ago, I've been living hand to mouth. Unless I find a husband—and that doesn't seem imminent—without the help I get from my *friend*, I'd be on the street or back in Hamilton. And I'm not sure which is worse."

"Hamilton," Helen said.

"Then while I am very sorry to do this—I'll have to ask you to find other lodgings as soon as possible."

Helen sat back in her chair. "But Eva, what they pay me at Bell isn't nearly enough to support myself just yet. Rent alone would consume every penny I make."

Eva crossed her arms. "Then you'll either have to find a new position, or a generous friend."

"How long may I have to find something suitable?" Helen said weakly.

"I am thinking one week," Eva replied.

"One week? However will I—"

"Helen, I know it's not much time, but there has to be a limit. It would be equally hard if I said two weeks, and I can't risk losing my new fellow. I wish things were different."

"I do, too," Helen said. "But I'll figure something out. And I *am* grateful."

ON SUNDAY, DR. GRAND was waiting for her at the trolley stop on North Division Street, not far from the restaurant.

"Don't you look lovely," he said, as Helen stepped down from the car.

She thanked him, hoping that he wouldn't notice that she was wearing the same borrowed outfit as she had at Alt Nürnberg.

"Our luncheon spot is just down this way," he said. They walked down Division a short block to Main and turned left. Within two blocks they arrived at a place with red and white awnings stretched across the broad glass front. On the big windows was lettered:

THE WHITE ELEPHANT CAFÉ.
FINE FOOD & DRINK – FULLY LICENSED.
LADIES & GENTLEMEN WELCOME.

"And here we are, milady," George said cheerfully, opening the door.

"George," she whispered as they were seated, "is this place safe?"

"Why, of course it is. I come here all the time."

The White Elephant was, predictably, done up in a shabby carnival motif. Emerging from the rear wall, flanked by swinging doors leading to and from the kitchen, was a life-size, papier-mâché elephant, painted a blinding white and sporting two outsized tusks. One of the tusks had been snapped in two, and the broken end propped up against the elephant's head. Mainly the place looked like what it was—a somewhat seedy watering hole.

She looked around nervously as a piano player took his seat at an ancient instrument. "Surely—"

"You have to learn how to relax," George said. "Don't you trust me?"

"You're right," she said. "Of course I do. Please forgive me."

A man in a beat-up derby approached their table. "Why, if it isn't my favorite Scottish doctor!" he said cheerfully, in a mock-Scots accent. "Good to see you again!"

"Well, hello, Garvin," Grand said, shaking his hand. "Good to see you, too."

"Who is *this* lovely young lady?" Garvin asked.

"Miss Crosby is considering becoming a nurse in my hospital," George said.

Garvin leaned over toward Helen, a little too close. "You would make an *exceptional* nurse, if you don't mind my saying."

Helen smiled shyly.

"Say," Grand said, "we'd like to order some drinks. Can you send someone over?"

"Of course. And they're on the house."

"I couldn't possibly," Grand said.

"Doctor Grand, it's the least I can do after everything you've done for me."

"Well then, I thank you kindly. We both do."

Garvin shook George's hand again and waved a waiter over. He whispered in the waiter's ear, smiled, and went back to the nether reaches of the White Elephant.

"And what can I get for the two of you?" the waiter said.

"I'll have a beer," George said. "My friend here will have a whiskey highball. A good, strong one, too." He smiled and nodded at the waiter, who winked back.

"I do rather like this music," Helen said, tapping her foot.

"This one's called 'Whistlin' Rufus.' You can dance a polka to it."

"How fun! Say, how is it that Mr. Garvin knows you so well?"

"I got to know him when one of his girls was unwell," George said. "I nursed her back to health, and Garvin's treated me like a prince ever since then."

"Good for you! Poor little dear, how old was she? His girl."

"I'd say about twenty-five."

"My," Helen said. "Mr. Garvin doesn't look nearly old enough to have a twenty-five-year-old daughter."

"Clear conscience, I suppose," George replied. "Say, do you enjoy dancing?"

"I do, even though I don't get many opportunities."

"Then we have another thing in common," George said as the piano player took up a new tune. "What do you say to taking a spin to this one? It's Scott Joplin."

"I don't know how to dance to anything this fast."

"I can teach you in two shakes of a lamb's tail," he said with a grin, standing and holding out his hand. "Miss?"

She took his hand, and learning to dance to a quickstep did turn out to be easier than she'd imagined. After the tune was finished, they dropped into their chairs, laughing. Their drinks had arrived, and George raised his mug.

"To the most beautiful soon-to-be-nurse in Buffalo," he said.

Helen smiled and took a sip of her highball. Her smile faded as she set the glass back down.

"Too strong?" he asked.

"No. I mean, it is strong, but it was something else. I don't mean to be a wet blanket, but I don't think I'll be able to pursue nursing quite yet."

"What's changed your mind?"

"My sister. She wants me to find my own lodgings, and that'll mean . . . well, it's going to take me longer than I thought to get on my feet."

"I see," he said. "How very disappointing."

"It is." She took another drink of her cocktail, a bigger one this time.

"Then let's have our luncheon, and another cocktail or two. I find things sometimes look clearer after a little alcohol."

Over the next two hours, Helen and George enjoyed six dances, two very long discussions of what modern medicine held in store for the twentieth century—and, for Helen, three more highballs. George seemed always to have a full mug of beer in front of him.

"George—" she said, her hair falling down around her face, "I think I've had far too much to drink."

"You're just not used to it. You've only had two, I think."

"I've had *four*," she whispered drunkenly, counting on her fingers. "One, two, three, *four*. I think."

"I think your count might be off, little lady. But I will say you're an awful lot of fun once you've had a few."

Helen laughed. "You really think so? A little Canadian country girl like me?"

"I think you're a barrel of monkeys. Canadian ones."

"I'm not," she protested. "People always tell me I'm too serious. Look at me—as much fun as I've been having, this whole time I've been worrying about finding new lodgings."

He ran his finger around the rim of his mug. "You know, Helen, I told you that alcohol would inspire me. I may have a solution to your little problem."

"What?"

"A good friend of mine has a flat that he wants to rent out to Pan-American visitors."

"There are so many of them," she said, "but they're all so dear. Rents in Buffalo are sky-high because of the Pan."

"I know. But that's because most people want them for a day or two, or a week at most. But if I approached him and said you wanted to take the place for a couple *months* . . . I think he'd give us a good deal. A very good deal."

She giggled. "How very good a deal? I could afford free."

He shrugged. "I'd guess he'd let me have it for ten dollars a week."

"My heavens! I don't even make ten dollars a week, George."

"I know. But here's the best part of my idea. Let me pay him for the flat and give you a chance to save some money. You can pay me back once you're in nursing school and making a decent little stipend."

"I couldn't possibly, George," she said, pushing back her hair. "My grandmother said, 'never a borrower nor . . .' Now what exactly *was* the rest of it?" She laughed.

"Perhaps you can tell me what grandmothers know about such things? Helen, I make excellent money, and I'm not married yet. Not that I haven't been looking, of course."

"Then you ought to be saving your money for Miss Right," she said tipsily. "Not spending it on me."

He lowered his voice. "Who's to say they're not one and the same?"

She giggled and put her head in her hands, trying to come up with a clever reply, and failing.

"Helen," he continued, "think about it. What do I have to spend my money on? Investing it in your future would give me a lot more pleasure than putting it in the bank."

Helen thought about Eva. She's getting help from her beau—and he's *married*. George is single, at least. It certainly wouldn't be scandalous to take help from a single man.

"I don't know," she said.

"Tell you what. When do you have to leave your sister's place?"

"By next week."

"When's your next day off?"

"Not until next Sunday," she said.

"That's too late. Tomorrow, tell the Bell people you're unwell and can't make it to work. Then meet me at the Delamore Apartments at ten. You can have a look at my friend's flat, and then you can make up your mind."

"I don't know how to thank you, George."

"You can buy me another drink, for starters," he replied, throwing up his arm.

THE DELAMORE APARTMENTS WERE convenient to everything, clean, and safe. Helen was pleased to observe several young ladies who seemed to be living there independently.

George worked the key in the lock and threw open the door to apartment 26A. "Welcome to your new home! Much nicer than the White Elephant, isn't it?"

"My, it's simply beautiful," she said. "But—"

"Well now, will you look at that?" he said, pointing.

In the front parlor of 26A, a bottle of champagne was sitting open on a lovely table in the center of the room.

"Champagne?" Helen said.

"It's a little welcome celebration. I decided I wasn't going to take no for an answer."

"But George," she began.

"No buts, now, Helen. I mean no disparagement here, but your sister has put you into a very tight spot. And in good conscience I can't stand by and see you turned out. If you want to find another place, that's up to you and I'll take no offense. But in the meantime, at least I'll have the satisfaction of knowing you have a decent roof over your head."

She looked at his blotchy face, his big hands, and suddenly felt guilty. Perhaps because he's not so young anymore, and a little rough-looking, I'm not seeing his good heart. Remember what he said about seeing myself as others do—surely many would think me rather ungrateful.

"Then if you won't take no for an answer," she said, "I'll have to say yes!"

"*Yaldi*! Then a toast is in order." Grand pulled a chair out for her, poured two glasses of champagne, and handed one to Helen.

"To new beginnings!" he said, raising his glass.

"To my generous benefactor." She sipped her wine. "I don't claim to know much about champagne, but this is very good."

"You'll quickly develop a taste for it, if you let yourself," he said.

She looked around the flat. "It truly was my lucky day when you visited the telephone exchange, George. I keep thinking I'm going to wake up and find that this is all a dream."

"Then we'll have to make sure you never wake up," he said.

She laughed and held up her glass. "This really does go to one's head, doesn't it?"

"I think in my case, it's the company that's making me a bit dizzy."

"What a charming thing to say," Helen said, and Grand refilled her glass.

She took a deep drink of the champagne. "George, I can't tell you how much more hopeful I feel. I've been so very worried."

"Ah, Helen, take it from an old man. Youth is the time to be carefree."

"You're not an old man, silly."

"I will say, you make me feel young, Miss Crosby."

After another two glasses, Grand stood and extended his hand. "May I? Time for a little tour of your new flat."

She got up a little unsteadily, supporting herself on the table. "As soon as the room stops spinning," she said, laughing.

Helen took his arm, and he walked her into the kitchen. Then they examined the view from the windows overlooking Linwood Street. "It's so lovely," Helen said. "It's like paradise."

Next they peeked into a large bedroom, furnished with an iron bedstead, a washstand, an armoire, and a Persian rug.

"Do you know," she said almost to herself, "that my little room in Hamilton was only a quarter of this size, with a teeny, little bed and . . . well, that's all."

He came up behind her and put his arms around her waist. She was startled, but thought that to pull away from him would seem rude.

"You're far from all that now," he whispered into her hair. "You're safe at last."

She turned around, her face an inch away from his. "I could kiss you for that."

"What's stopping you then?" he said, and kissed her.

Helen kissed back, but then lost her balance. He grabbed her around the waist and pulled her to him.

"You know what I want?" he said.

She blinked at him, trying to focus her eyes. "No," she giggled.

"I think you do. And once again, I don't plan to take no for an answer."

"Well, then," she said, pushing up against him, "I suppose I'll have to say yes."

It was well past dusk when Helen awoke to find the counterpane laid neatly over her and a cold wetness between her legs.

"George?" she said.

"I'm out here," he replied. He walked into the bedroom and sat down on the edge of the bed.

"I have a headache."

"You had quite a snootful," he said.

"What time is it?" she said, sitting up with the sheet pulled up to her neck. "My sister may be missing me."

He made a snide face. "Wishful thinking."

"Maybe so," she said. "I just wish things were different."

"And they are. You're here with me now. And I'm happy about that."

"George?" she said.

"Yes?"

"I think . . . we got a little carried away."

"Now why would you say a thing like that?"

"But we've only just met, and—I don't know what your intentions toward me may be."

"My intentions are only of the best, my dear," Grand said. "To help you get established and into nursing school."

"I believe you," she said. "I meant—after that."

He laughed. "Are you being serious now, girl?"

She looked down at the sheets. "Please don't laugh at me, George," she said softly.

"Oh, my dear, I wasn't laughing at you. I was laughing only because you are so charmingly old-fashioned sometimes."

"I don't think it's old-fashioned to be concerned about my reputation."

"Your reputation?"

"Yes. Now that we've been intimate."

"That we have," George said. "Twice."

"*Twice?*"

"After the first time, you wouldn't let me be until we did it again."

She blinked back tears. "My, what kind of girl must you think I am?"

He whistled softly. "I can tell you, if you like. The kind of girl you are."

"Please, no. I feel foolish enough already."

He shook his head emphatically. "I was going to say—you're a *prodigy*."

"A prodigy?"

"You said you hadn't any talent. Trust me, lass—you were dead wrong about that."

CHAPTER 7 ::

KAMA SUTRA

Early June 1901

May passed into June. George saw Helen each day without fail after they both came home from work. They spent their evenings quietly, at first: talking, drinking champagne, taking long walks in the park near the Delamore, and going out for supper. George always paid the bills to allow Helen to save money for nursing school.

He also began taking her shopping. Dr. Grand took obvious delight in dressing his young girlfriend to the nines, and she had to admit—when she permitted herself a coy glance in the mirror—that she was beginning to look like a very fashionable city girl. And one whose perfect face and figure turned envious heads almost anywhere they would go.

Her brusque eviction from her sister's house on Oak Street began to fade into memory, and now seemed like a blessing in disguise. While Eva may have been rough about it, she had given her sister some very good advice—find a generous fellow who could help establish her in a very big and very expensive city. George's support and encouragement made it possible for her to enjoy her new life *and* put away money for her future, instead of forever pinching pennies and worrying herself to death.

He asked for little in return, too, except of course for the one thing Helen's grandmother had long told her was the main preoccupation of men.

At first their intimate relations were straightforward and traditional.

Then, one evening, George brought with him to the Delamore a pretty, little book bound in green leather. It was a very expensive—and very illegal—copy of Sir Richard Burton's translation of the ancient but still infamous lovemaking manual, the *Kama Sutra*. The Comstock Law of almost thirty years before had made the possession of lewd material a criminal offense.

George smiled as they sat and drank, watching Helen pore over the pages of the scandalous book with a mix of astonishment and horror.

"George, this book is said to be *obscene*. Where did you get this?"

He laughed. "Never you mind. But it's not half so bad as people make out."

"Then why have people gone to jail for owning it?"

"Because the laws are stupid."

"Maybe, but I don't plan to break any of them." She closed the book and slid it over to him.

He opened the book to a page near the front. "Start reading out loud," he said, handing it over.

She frowned at him, but read:

> *A perfect woman should be beautiful and amiable. She should*
> *have a liking for good qualities in other people, and a liking*
> *for wealth. She should take delight in sexual unions and be*
> *of equal with a man with regard to sexual enjoyment. She*
> *should always be anxious to acquire and obtain experience*
> *and knowledge, including a knowledge of the Kama Sutra.*

"Now then," George said, "does that strike you as obscene? It seems like good common sense to me."

"Well, *that* part wasn't obscene."

"Here's what we're going to do," he said. "Each evening, you'll read aloud from our new book, and we'll try everything in it at least once. We'll work through the whole thing together."

"You're very naughty, George," she said, leafing through the book. "I don't even understand most of this."

"Give me an example."

She pursed her lips and scanned the page. "Here's one. It's a whole section called 'sucking a mango fruit.'"

He laughed. "The mango fruit is that lovely, juicy thing between your legs, Helen."

"Oh my heavens," she said. "People really *do* that?"

"I think we've just found our starting point," he said.

IT TOOK THREE WEEKS to work through the basics—the various positions of the body, the physical requirements of lovemaking, and, most important of all, the mental attitude required to be a good lover. George was an excellent teacher, although Helen didn't like to think too much about where her beau had acquired such broad knowledge. But she was his now, and she decided that she might as well profit from his experience—and from the sometimes shockingly explicit instructions contained in the *Kama Sutra*.

Some of the lessons made her more than a little self-conscious. Pleasuring herself in front of him, in particular, was difficult—at first. But he made her keep at it, egging her on like a coach, and in a week, she could finish herself off either quickly or slowly, as he instructed, while looking directly into his eyes. Whatever remnants of country-girl shyness she'd carried around for twenty-one years dropped away quickly after that.

The book became more challenging as it went along. The section on pain—biting, scratching, and striking—wasn't as much to her liking, but George assured her it was all part of the course. "You'll not like every part of nursing school, either," he would say. "But to get your diploma, you have to take the whole course."

On one of these uncomfortable occasions, he throttled her half into unconsciousness, whispering hoarsely into her ear the whole time. This frightened her terribly, and she slapped and scratched at him in fury, until at last he let her take a deep and ragged breath.

He had only smiled, and strangled her again, this time pinning her neck against the bed with one strong hand, while stimulating her with the other. If she had had any spare air, she would have screamed when she climaxed. It felt better than anything she could have ever imagined feeling, a combination of panic and pleasure, a state hovering somewhere between death and life. After that, she gave herself up entirely to whatever pleasure the book—and Dr. George Grand—prescribed.

It was when they came to the chapter on "Potions and Intoxicants" that the trouble began.

THEY WERE WALKING TOGETHER along Delaware Avenue, near Summer Street, when Grand stopped in front of a corner druggist.

"Helen," he said, "you know how much you like champagne?"

She laughed. "Of course. Maybe a little *too* much, but yes. Why?"

"We have to start our chapter on potions, but the ones in the book are all ancient things and impossible to obtain. We have many modern things that would substitute, though."

"Like what?" she asked.

"*Cannabis indica*. Cocaine. Morphine. Chloral hydrate. Surely you've heard of them."

"Yes, naturally. Though I certainly haven't used any of them. They're for dope fiends."

"How very quaint," he smirked. "They don't do any such thing. I'm a doctor, and I administer them every day. My patients certainly aren't all dope fiends."

This seemed eminently reasonable to her. "I guess I could try something, if you'd like."

"I think you'll like it," he said. "Tomorrow we'll get started with something interesting."

GRAND SHOWED UP THE next day carrying his medical satchel.

"Time for some fun," he said, setting it on the table. "Strip down."

While Helen was undressing, he opened the satchel. He took from it a smaller case, a number of bottles, and what looked like a miniature version of an insect sprayer. Helen looked on curiously in the nude.

He opened the little case first. In it were a half-dozen little vials, each filled with tiny pills, two glass syringes, and several gleaming steel needles.

"George, I didn't know needles would be involved. I'm afraid of needles."

"Girl, you want to be a nurse, and you're afraid of needles?"

"When they're used on me, yes."

"Fine, then. We won't be starting there, in any case. Let's see you try a little powdered cocaine first."

He pulled the stopper from a little bottle of white powder and shook some into his cupped palm. He held his hand under her nose. "Sniff it up. Good and hard."

She did as instructed. "Whoa!" she said a minute later. "I feel as though I could fly!"

"I thought you might like that."

In fifteen minutes, the high subsided, and he gave her the bottle.

"Here's your homework," he said. "Cocaine is interesting because you can sniff it, you can inject it, you can smoke it—or you can even put it into your private parts."

Helen giggled. "You can't!"

"Shall I show you?"

"I don't know about that," she said warily.

"After all this, you still don't trust me," he pouted.

"I do trust you, George. I'll try it, if you say so."

"Good girl. We'll do this in the bath."

She padded into the bathroom, singing to herself, and he followed with his medical kit.

"Just sit in the tub." He took the little insect sprayer thing out of his kit. "Now observe and learn, Nurse Crosby."

While Helen watched from inside the bathtub, Grand took the remaining powdered cocaine and mixed it into a glassful of water. This solution he then poured into the bottle attached to the insect sprayer. He turned to Helen, who was waiting patiently.

"Here we go," he said cheerfully. "Bum in the air, if you please. High as you can."

She went down on all fours, her face against the cool porcelain.

"This is so embarrassing," she mumbled.

"Trust me. It'll be worth it."

She grunted as he inserted the nozzle into her anus. He pushed the handle and sent all the cocaine solution into her.

"Jesus," she groaned. "What—"

"Just hold it in there for a minute."

"I don't think I can," she said.

"You can do anything you put your mind to."

"Oh *fuck*," she said as the cocaine hit her.

"Keep holding it," he said, lifting her body out of the tub and setting her on the toilet. "Now you can let it go." He knelt next to the toilet as she expelled the liquid in a gush.

"How do you feel now?" he asked, kissing her.

"Oh, I'm so very high. I've never felt this good before."

"Dry yourself off, then. I'm going to carry you to the bedroom and give you the fucking of your life."

CHAPTER 8 ::
A CLOSE SHAVE

For the next two weeks, every other night Grand introduced Helen to a new drug. When she came back down, he'd interview her on what she'd experienced and tell her how much and what he'd given her. Chloral hydrate was the first.

Grand poured her a cocktail, and from a small, brown bottle carefully put five drops of a clear liquid into it. He stirred it with a finger.

"Drink this," he said.

"Are you sure it's safe?"

"After all the cocaine you've had, you'll find this rather mild, I predict."

Helen drank down her highball and waited.

"Everything's going blurry," she announced after a little while.

"Perfect. Now just relax and drift with it."

She stretched out on the bed, nude, and dozed off for an hour. Grand went for a stroll outside and had a cigar. When he returned, Helen was still sleeping. He ran his eyes over her body, congratulating himself once again on having landed such a beauty when she stirred and stretched.

"George," she said, smiling. She ran her hands over herself. "I like that look on your face. Do you like what you see?"

"I've never seen a more beautiful lass," he said, and quite honestly.

She yawned. "Umm, I feel so relaxed."

"That's the chloral," he said.

"Tomorrow's my day off," Helen said. "Do you have to go to work in the morning?"

"I do."

"I wish you could stay with me tonight."

"I wish I could, too," Grand said. "Why don't you do some shopping in the morning?"

"All right. And I have to do something about my hair. It's a fright."

"Speaking of which, you might want to trim yourself up here, too." He ran his fingers over her bush.

Helen covered her face with her hands. "I'm so embarrassed. I try to keep things tidy down there for you."

"It's easily fixed," he said, getting up. "Stay right there."

Grand returned a few moments later with his straight razor, brush, and mug. "We'll take care of it right now, before I go."

She sat up, looking at the blade. "I use little scissors."

"For a trim, that'll do. But this time, we're going to take it all off."

"Why?"

"Because it's the way all the New York actresses keep theirs."

"Oh," she said. "Well, just be careful."

He laughed. "I'm a *surgeon*, girl. I won't cut anything that doesn't need cutting." He swirled the brush around in his mug and whipped up a frothy lather. "Lie back and open up."

Helen opened her legs, and Grand began applying the lather. She giggled. "That tickles."

"Stay still now," he said, touching the razor to her skin. She felt the *skritch-skritch* of the blade moving downward, then over, and then tiny, quick strokes coming back along the edges. He opened her labia with the fingers of his left hand and carefully scraped off the tiniest hairs along their edges.

When he had finished, he leaned back and examined his handiwork.

"Smooth as a baby's bottom," he said, folding his razor. "Beautiful."

Helen sat up and examined herself. "It certainly looks different."

"You were a very good girl. You stayed nice and still."

"I will admit I was a little nervous at first. But you were very gentle."

He ran the back of his hand over her sleek *mons veneris*. "The blade can be cruel or kind. It depends entirely on the person holding it."

"Do I look like a New York actress now?" she said, sitting up on her elbows, crossing her bare legs, and giving him a coquettish smile.

"You look a sight better than most of those jades," he replied. "I'm thinking maybe I could be a wee bit late to work this morning, after all."

"I knew I could make you stay."

HELEN FOUND THAT THE drugs fascinated her, and Grand encouraged her to use them liberally. Strychnine, in small doses, made her horny, which she liked. Opium gave her vivid dreams. Morphine made her forget. Tincture of cannabis under her tongue she found very relaxing. Laudanum and paregoric were constipating, but an enema—with a little bit of cocaine added—took care of things and sent her into the clouds.

She was high on coke one evening when Grand seemed to remember something. He dug around in his medical kit and found a vial of tiny, white tablets. He shook one into his palm.

"See what you think of this one," he said. "Hold out your tongue."

She obliged, and he placed a single tablet on it. "You can swallow now," he said.

"It's bitter," Helen said. "What is it?"

"It's atropine. Belladonna."

"What does it do?"

"You'll find out soon enough."

Within a few minutes, she lay down on the bed. "I feel very peculiar," she said.

"How so?"

"Hot. And my heart is going awfully fast."

"All normal," he said. "Anything else?"

"I can't focus my eyes," she mumbled.

He examined them. "Your pupils are dilated. Normal."

"Get away," she said, waving her hand at nothing.

"What do you see?"

"They're everywhere," she whispered. "Don't say anything or they'll see us."

She swatted feebly at the air a few more times, then uttered a little cry. "I'm dying."

Her body had gone quite stiff, as though she were tensing every muscle. The tendons of her shoulders and arms, taught as bowstrings, stood out from her skin, and the muscles of her back drew her body into a backward curve.

Grand ran his hands over her rigid neck, down over her breasts, and the tight muscles of her thighs.

"So beautiful," he murmured to himself. "Like a statue."

With unblinking eyes staring at Grand, Helen tried to say something, but her mouth just opened and closed slowly with a croak.

"It's textbook atropine poisoning, my dear," he said calmly. "Nothing to fret about. You'll be like this for some hours, so I'm going to go. But I will check on you in the morning."

Her eyes protruded urgently, and a little foam appeared at the edges of her mouth as she tried to implore Grand to stay.

"Sweet dreams, dear," he said, and shut her door quietly behind him.

HELEN WAS STILL ANGRY when George arrived the following morning. She was sitting at the parlor table in her dressing gown.

"What's wrong?" he asked, seeing her scowl.

"You almost killed me with that atrophy shit," she said.

"Atropine. Not atrophy."

"Whatever. I couldn't move a muscle until early this morning."

"That's the effect it has," he said. "There's no cause to be upset."

"You poisoned me!"

"I did no such thing. I'm a doctor, Helen, in case you don't remember. I know what kind of dose is too much. You had one little pill. You'd have to take three times as much as that to be poisoned."

"You always have an answer for everything. I don't want to do that again."

"Nor do you have to. But you can say you've had the experience."

She pouted for a few minutes in silence while George had a cigar.

"Will you forgive me yet?" he asked, sitting down with her.

"What I'd like to know is—how long are we going to keep at this? I'm terrified I'm going to miss my time of the month, George."

"Are you using your whirling spray afterward?"

"Of course I am, but that's not foolproof. What happens if . . . I don't even want to say it."

"Come here, child," he said, holding out his arms.

"I will not. And *child* is exactly what I'm concerned about. You've made me no promises—"

"We're having a little fun to pass the time until you enter nursing school. That's all."

"Nursing school's not until September. You mean to tell me that for another three months or more, you're going to fill me full of come?" She sniffed. "I'll be pregnant for sure. Then what?"

"Now, Helen, please—"

"And I read in one of those dirty magazines of yours that if a woman has a climax when she's being seeded, that opens up some kind of pathway for the—whatever the hell it is. And makes it even more likely to become pregnant."

"You have had countless orgasms," he said sagely. "I've never seen a woman come harder than you do. I swear, it's the gift of God."

"George, you're not taking this seriously. I need to know your intentions, or I can't—do this with you anymore."

"You can't do what? See me?"

"No. Have intimate relations."

"Is that right, now?"

She folded her arms. "Yes, it is right. If you won't buy the cow, you can't have the milk for free. Not forever, anyway."

Without saying a word, he stood and stripped the belt from his trousers.

"What are you doing?"

"Bend over the chair and show me your bottom," he said.

"I'm not about to let you—"

He grabbed her by the hair, threw her down on the table, and pulled her dressing gown over the small of her back.

"Don't you dare," she protested. "This isn't funny."

"Do you see me laughing?" He drew back the belt and let her have it.

She yowled. "That fucking *hurt*! Stop!"

"Not until you apologize," he said. "For threatening to abandon me."

"I'm not going to apologize."

"Then you'll have to be chastised."

He hit her again, twice, three times, raising red welts on the soft white skin of her buttocks. She was sobbing when he tossed the belt aside.

"Now tell me you want me to fuck you," he said.

"I won't," she said, struggling to stand up. "Let me go!"

"I will not. You *belong* to me, missy. Now do what I say or I'll get the belt again."

"Fuck me," she gasped weakly.

"Beg for it."

"Fuck me, George. I need it."

He undid his trouser buttons, squared up behind her, and seized her hips. "Look at that beautiful pussy, will you? It's just begging to be fucked." He put himself into her and slammed up against her livid buttocks. She clenched her fists in pain.

"That's how you like it, isn't it?" he grunted. "Tell me."

"I love it like that," she said, her face hitting the table.

It was over in a minute, and then she sagged down onto the floor, weeping softly.

"Ah, now don't cry, girl," he said. "You know I love you."

"That wasn't *love*," she sniffled. "People who love each other don't hurt each other."

"Love?" he said. "What the hell do you know about *love*?"

"I know what love is," she said.

"You can be an arrogant little bitch, you know," he snarled. "Well, get this through your thick head. I'm the only one who has ever loved you, and ever will."

He buttoned up and, without another word, left Helen sobbing on the floor of her lovely flat.

THE NEXT DAY, ON schedule, Grand arrived at Helen's apartment at the Delamore, but this time with a companion, a very tall, broad young man with a thick neck—a football player's build. The fellow was nattily dressed and had dark brown hair—though the hairline was slightly receding, even though he could not have been out of his early twenties—and a very thin, very carefully trimmed mustache outlining his upper lip. The two men hung up their hats and sat down in the little parlor.

"Why, George," Helen said, surprised, "I didn't know you were bringing a friend with you."

"I do hope I'm not intruding," the young man said.

"Not at all," Grand replied. "Helen, allow me to introduce Leland Davis Kennecott. Lee is one of my interns at Riverdale, working under my supervision. Lee, Miss Crosby."

"Hello, Doctor Kennecott," Helen said.

The young man chuckled. "I'm not quite yet a doctor In another year, perhaps. In the meantime, I hope you'll call me Lee."

"Then please call me Helen," she said. "May I get you two a cocktail? I bought a bottle of martini cocktails and one of highballs at Spinks's this afternoon."

"I'll have a highball, if Doctor Grand here will permit it," Lee said with a light laugh. His voice seemed too thin and high for such a big man.

"Of course. We're off duty. I'll have a martini, dear," Grand said.

Helen poured the drinks, and the three talked and drank. Helen's nervousness faded away after a highball, and Lee was easy to talk with.

"You may recall, Helen," Grand said, "that we'll need to find you a second reference for your nursing school application. Since Lee has graduated medical school, and has only to finish his internship, I thought it would be well for the two of you to get acquainted."

"Oh, George," Helen said, her face lighting up, "it's so good that you remembered. I so want to keep moving ahead."

"Doctor Grand said you were beautiful," Lee said, "but I think he was understating it."

Helen blushed. "George is very kind. As are you."

"Now, be careful, Lee," Grand said. "Don't steal my girl away!"

Lee laughed. "Nothing to fear, Doctor."

"May I inquire where you attended medical school, Lee?" Helen asked.

"At the university here. Buffalo is my hometown, and I intend to remain here."

"Good for you. As much as this city is growing, it will surely need more doctors. Do you have a particular area of interest in medicine?"

"I should think surgery," he said. "It's an exciting field. There are so many advances now, with the X-ray machines and antiseptic medicine."

"No shoptalk, Lee," Grand said. "We'll bore the little lady."

"I find it very interesting," Helen said. "It's a wonderful time in history to be entering the medical field."

"Indeed it is," Lee said. He took out his watch and then glanced at Grand.

"Helen, dear, you and Lee are almost the same age," Grand said. "It must be refreshing to talk with someone other than an old man like myself."

She forced a laugh. "You're not old, George."

"Older than he is," Grand said. "A young thing like yourself does need companions of her own age. And Lee is so busy taking orders from me that he hasn't seen a lady in months."

Helen refilled their glasses. "George," she said, "perhaps it would be fun for the three of us to attend the theatre tonight? There's a new play with Madame Modjeska at Shea's Garden."

"I'm sorry, dear," Dr. Grand said. "I told Lee that we'd stay in."

"That's fine. I can prepare something for our supper. But I'll have to go to the market first."

Grand rubbed his hands together. He glanced over at Lee.

"Helen, I hope you won't mind, but I told Lee a bit about the fun we've been having with our book."

She blushed deeply. "Whatever do you mean, George?"

George got up, went into the bedroom, and came out holding the *Kama Sutra*. "This book," he said, tossing it onto the table between them.

She swallowed hard, mortified. "George—I don't—Lee, I am so terribly sorry."

"It's fine, Helen," Lee said, leaning over the table and taking her hand. "Doctor Grand wanted to tell me more about you so that I can provide a good recommendation."

"Exactly," Grand said. "You mustn't feel self-conscious."

Helen looked down at the table and Lee's hand resting on hers. She wanted to pull it away. His hand felt cold and clammy, a dead man's hand. But she was afraid of offending him. George would say that she'd spoiled her chance if she did, and would be angry.

"Shall I perhaps arrange a little cheese for us?" she whispered.

Lee patted her hand. "I'm not hungry. And man does not live by bread alone."

"No indeed," Grand said.

"I suppose," she mumbled.

"Lee has told me that he'd like to find a girl like you one day," Grand said. "Naturally, I said who wouldn't. You're one in a million. I'm the luckiest man in the world."

"I think that about you, too, George. That I'm the luckiest woman."

"I know you do. But then I thought—in this modern age of ours— why ought I to be so selfish, and keep you all to myself?"

Helen looked up, confused, into the two faces smiling at her.

George picked up the *Kama Sutra* and flipped to the back of the book. "I don't know if you realized it, dear, but there's only one lesson remaining." He slid the book over to her and pointed to the page. It read:

> *Many men enjoy a woman that may be betrothed to one of them, either one after the other, or at the same time. Thus, one of them holds her, another enjoys her, a third uses her mouth, a fourth holds her middle part, and in this way they go on enjoying her several parts alternately.*

She looked up fearfully at Grand. "I don't understand, George."

"I think you do," he said, gesturing to the bedroom. "And I don't mind in the least. Two young people having a little fun."

Lee stood. He seemed immense, at least six-feet-two and solid. He extended an enormous hand in Helen's direction.

"George, you really can't mean for me . . ." she said, with a look of panic.

"Helen," Grand said, frowning, "you're *embarrassing* me. Now please do as I ask, and show our guest a little hospitality."

"I feel that I may be sick," she said.

"I am so very sorry, Lee," Grand said. "She gets like this every time we try something a little new. Dear, let me give you a tonic to calm your nerves."

"I don't want a tonic," she said, her voice warbling strangely. "I want to leave."

"Lee, what symptoms is the young lady presenting?" Grand asked.

"I should say hysteria," Lee said.

"I'm not hysterical," Helen protested.

"Correct, Lee," Grand said. "Antisocial behavior. Moodiness. Helen, you wouldn't even recognize yourself now. I haven't any alternative but to administer a tonic to ease your nerves."

Grand retrieved his medical kit. From a small vial, he shook out two small white pills into his palm. He placed them in the bowl of his cocktail spoon and crushed them into powder with his thumb. Then he added a little of his martini to dissolve the powder.

"What's that?" Helen asked, her voice shaking.

He ignored her and drew the solution from the spoon into a hypodermic syringe. "Extend your arm, dear."

"I don't want that," she said, wrapping her arms around herself. "George, you're frightening me!"

"Lee, some assistance please," Grand said flatly.

Lee jerked Helen's arm out straight, turning it so the soft belly of her forearm was facing upward. She struggled briefly, but Kennecott was so strong that it was futile to resist.

Grand introduced the needle into one of the pale blue veins on the inside of her forearm and depressed the plunger.

Lee let go of Helen's hand, and with an angry scowl she pulled her arm away. Then, in a few seconds, her face went slack.

"What—what is that?" she whispered.

"Now isn't that much better?" said Grand, smiling. "Lee, what do you observe?"

"Almost instantaneous shift in mood. Indicative of a state of euphoria."

"Good, good," Grand said. "Well done. And how are you feeling, dear?"

Helen looked up at them, her eyes glassy. She smiled wanly. "I don't know."

Grand took hold of her face and brought it close to him and Lee.

"Pupils contracted," he said. "Lee, from a pharmacological point of view, what does that indicate—so far as intoxicant?"

"Morphine, I'd say," Lee replied.

"Excellent! That's correct. A full two grains, to be precise."

"Two grains, three grains, four grains more," Helen giggled, drooling a little out of the corner of her mouth.

"Now, Lee, you mustn't wait too long, because the euphorical state is short-lived, and can quickly be followed by a narcotized sleep."

"Yes, Doctor," Lee said, standing up again and helping Helen rise woozily from her chair.

"Will this truly make you happy, George?" she said, her head lolling to one side.

"It will make all of us happy, my dear."

"All right," she said, her head dropping onto her chest. "Will I get my referral?"

Lee was about to speak when Grand cut him off. "Don't be so selfish, Helen. It's rude. Do as I've taught you, and squeeze every last bit out of him." He looked at Lee. "Better get to it, lad. She's drifting away."

Lee nodded and led Helen into the bedroom adjacent. There was silence, then the soft rustle of clothing, and a sound perhaps like a kiss. Then the bed creaked, once.

Lee appeared in the open doorway a moment later, naked and trying to cover with his hands a very full erection. He leaned into the parlor to close the door.

"My most sincere apologies," he said. "In my haste, I neglected—"

Grand smiled at him. "No need. Leave it open, why don't you?"

WHEN HELEN AWOKE, SHE was alone. Her bedroom was pitch-dark, and the apartment was silent. She held her breath and listened for the sound of voices in the parlor, but there was nothing.

"George?" she said to no reply.

She got up, put a dressing gown over her nakedness, and peeked out into the parlor. It, too, was dark and empty. She shook her head, wondering if it had all been a dream. But there were the cocktail bottles and glasses on the table, and the familiar wetness between her legs dispelled any notion she entertained that it had been a phantasm.

Helen walked into her bathroom and urinated, then gave herself a whirling spray. That made her feel a little better, but only slightly. She wandered back to her bedroom again and turned on the gas. The room brightened, and she sat down at her dressing table, looking at her image in the mirror.

The memories were coming back, in bits and pieces at first, and then the puzzle filled itself in. She now knew *what* had happened, but she couldn't fathom *why*. George—who was to be her husband one day—had *loaned* her to someone else, someone not even a friend, really.

The face in the mirror looked back at her, expressionless and pale, the face of a corpse. She opened her dressing gown to examine herself, and between her breasts was a dried stickiness. She touched it with a finger and sniffed. Her highballs, she thought. She must have gotten sick at some point, but when? Surely not when Lee was . . . she turned her thoughts away from that, tried not to remember his big body pressing on hers. At first she'd tried to push him away, but the morphine had made her weak and sluggish, and he'd entered her. After that, all she could remember was trying to push him up and out a little to ease her fullness, and that her struggle had seemed to excite him all the more.

She thought back to the day she'd won the job at the Bell Exchange, how happy she'd been. She remembered the earliest days with George, how proud and pleased she'd been to be seen on the arm of a doctor twice her age, that a little slip of a thing like her could win such a prize. Now, though, only two months later, she felt like something priceless had been stolen from her. Not her virginity. She had told George otherwise, but she'd given that away when she was fourteen, to a handsome young boy in Hamilton.

When she'd stepped off the train at Buffalo, she'd believed she could make something of herself. And she had: a plaything for George and, worse, for whomever George willed. She'd tried to tell herself that it was the way George loved, an older, more worldly man, who had seen South Africa and France and so many other things, and who knew the ways of lovemaking.

And in truth, it had been exciting, for a while. But a line had been crossed. Being fucked by a stranger—even to please George, even for a referral to nursing school, and even with a good jolt of morphine to loosen her up—was simply beyond the pale.

I have been weak and wrong, she thought, and now I'm paying for it. But George has been something worse than weak—he's been *wicked*, and he ought to pay, too. She wrapped the dressing gown around herself again and made up her mind.

She would never see Dr. George Grand again. It was over.

:: PART TWO ::

FEAR

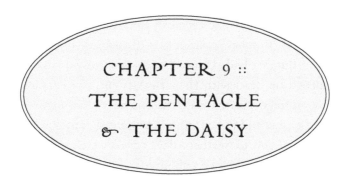

CHAPTER 9 ::
THE PENTACLE
& THE DAISY

Late June 1901

Early the next morning, Helen mailed an indignant farewell letter to Grand. As she was doing so, Detective Cusack was examining the body of Dirty Legs Lizzie down on Vine Alley. The body was barely cold when the newspapers announced the gruesome details. The headline screamed:

SATAN STALKS THE TENDERLOIN!!

The article itself was brief.

> *A woman was found murdered in the Tenderloin early this morning, her throat cut, and with a five-pointed star carved into her flesh. The five-pointed star, or 'pentacle,' is well-known among séance sitters and Tarot card shufflers as a symbol of the Devil and of the black arts.*
>
> *The murdered woman has not been identified, but it is suspected that she is among the Tenderloin's many fallen women.*

Lizzie was never properly identified; her body was handed over almost immediately to the Anatomical Board for dissection by the up-and-coming students of Buffalo's medical school. It saved the city the cost of a burial in the potter's field, and corpses were in high demand. Everyone, except Lizzie, made out in the bargain.

A single murder in a city the size of Buffalo—even a weird one like the Pentacle Murder, as it came to be known—wasn't going to raise too many eyebrows, and certainly wouldn't rattle any cages in city hall. While the "Butcher" epithet was disturbing, unlike the Ripper the so-called Butcher had claimed but one victim. So long as no other whores turned up dead with their throats cut, the Pentacle Murder would be soon forgotten, as would the Butcher.

Mayor Lennox and Police Superintendent Ball took some comfort in that. They had only to weather a day or two's worth of lurid headlines, and then everyone would forget about it and move on to whatever new shitstorm was raging, hopefully far away from Buffalo.

Unfortunately, they had only two days of peace before the Daisy Murder.

THE SECOND VICTIM TURNED up at the very southeast corner of the Tenderloin, in a burned-over part of Michigan Street. The corpse had been rolled into a drainage ditch that ran along the rear of a vacant lot just south of Swan Street. This was streetwalker territory, and the murdered woman was dressed in the faded gaiety of once-colorful silk. No respectable woman would wear such a getup outside a brothel, except for those unfortunates who had reached the bottom rung of their profession. In this case the deceased had both literally and metaphorically died in the gutter.

On Sunday morning, an Italian bootblack, a recent arrival in the neighborhood, was coming home from early mass. Glancing down into the ditch along Swan Street, he noticed what he thought was a bedsheet—a nice one—caught on a tangle of branches. Every penny counted, and bedsheets could be washed. Anything free was worth a little trouble. So he eased down into the ditch and yanked on the corner of the thing, only to realize that he was pulling on the mucky hem of a dead woman's skirt.

His first inclination was to get the hell away. Being the man who discovers a dead woman usually meant falling under the shadow of suspicion, and who needed that? He didn't know her, and couldn't bring her back, but she could bring him all manner of trouble. The words of his priest were still fresh in his mind, and he knew that God would not want him to go on his way without first summoning help. So he walked down to Michigan and Seneca, where there was always a cop or two lolling about, swinging their sticks.

A lackadaisical patrolman reluctantly followed the Italian back to the drainage ditch, confirmed that his hoped-for bedsheet was indeed a skirt, but was not convinced that the woman inside it was dead and not simply shit-faced. He proceeded to haul her out of the muck and onto the slope of the ditch, but when he flipped her over and saw a bloodless half-moon carved across her neck, he had to agree that she was, in fact, quite dead.

Again, Detective Cusack was summoned, but this time rumor traveled faster than the call box, and when he arrived at the crime scene there was already a gaggle of reporters waiting at Michigan and Swan.

"Why can't you guys just let me do my job?" Cusack groaned when he saw the familiar faces of the crime beat reporters.

"It's our job, too, Cusack," said Sam Martin, a wise-ass photographer for the *Buffalo Illustrated News*. Although the reporter was a thorough pain in the ass, even Cusack had to admit that Martin had a kind of sixth sense for crime.

"Yeah, yeah," Cusack said. He pulled away the woman's muddy shirtwaist and examined the neck wound. It looked to be remarkably similar to that he'd seen on the first victim: deepest under the left ear and tapering down to a superficial skin wound by the time the blade had contacted the right clavicle.

With Sam Martin and his goddamn camera hovering over his shoulder, Detective Cusack pulled up the woman's skirt enough to take a quick look at her pussy. Martin leaned in to snap a picture, but Cusack put his hand over the man's lens and shoved him away. "Don't be a pervert," he said.

Martin's photograph may have been foiled, but word-pictures couldn't be prohibited, and before this latest corpse had even been laid out on a slab at the morgue, the wires were buzzing with the story that this one, too, had a symbol carved into the flesh above her private parts. This time it was what looked like a small flower, perhaps a daisy, with five petals. A pentacle, and now a daisy.

There was no longer any way to deny it. The Buffalo Butcher was a most unusual killer, and one who—like the infamous Jack the Ripper himself—was clearly down on whores.

Now the papers had more than enough reason to go all in. The *Buffalo Enquirer*, as usual, led the charge.

A SECOND FLOWER PLUCKED IN THE CITY!!

Modern-Day 'Ripper' Stalking the Tenderloin?

Sunday morning, a second murdered woman—also with her throat cut ear-to-ear—turned up in a diversion ditch near Michigan and Swan Streets. There seems to be a pattern emerging, as both this and the recent death in Vine Alley featured some of the same hallmarks.

This woman, like the first, was a known streetwalker, exsanguination ended her life, and another small symbol was found carved into a private area. This time it appeared to be a five-petaled daisy. This after the equally mysterious appearance of a pentacle—widely known to be a symbol of Satan himself—was cut into the flesh of the first victim.

It ought to be clear to all now that a modern-day Jack the Ripper is stalking the Tenderloin. The question is: Can the city and the police stop him?

That was bad enough, but when even the staid *Courier* piled on with unusual gusto—

SECOND WOMAN BUTCHERED

Police Baffled
Pan-American Threatened?

—it struck a nerve in city hall. *The Pan-American threatened?* In any normal year, a couple of dead whores would have been ignored, and everyone knew that the *Enquirer* loved spinning tales about the gory goings-on in the Tenderloin. But a respected newspaper suggesting that attendance at the world's fair might be dampened sent a shiver of fear up the collective spine of the mayor and city council. What if the Butcher decided to turn his blade on some hapless out-of-town boob who wandered into the wrong part of the city? The Exposition's goose would be cooked, once and for all.

In a vain attempt to hush it up, the mayor placed a call to the *Courier*'s editor-in-chief, but he received only a polite and slightly sarcastic response. Not only did murder—for fuck's sake, a second *Jack the Ripper?*—sell newspapers, but with tens of thousands of visitors in the city on any given day, there were plenty of fresh grist for the fourth estate's money mill.

"God damn it, Bill," Mayor Lennox ranted at Police Superintendent William Ball, shaking the *Courier* in the air. "You do realize that this is going to take the Pan straight down the crapper! What the *hell* could go wrong next? As if it's not enough that the weather's been shit and we've had gangs of pickpockets working the Midway."

"Mr. Mayor—"

Lennox shook the newspaper in Ball's face. "Don't 'Mr. Mayor' me, Bill. We've got someone the papers are calling the *Buffalo Butcher* on the loose. The president of the United States himself is supposed to be here in a couple months. Jesus Christ, with my luck someone will shoot him. You watch."

"No one's going to shoot the president," Ball said. "Calm down. Get mad at God for the weather, if you like—I don't have a damn thing to do with it. As for the pickpockets, they're like lice. They go anywhere there are crowds. And I've got every one of my detectives and half of my men looking for this Butcher fellow. We'll catch him."

"He's killed two women already," Lennox said, putting his head into his hands.

"They're not, precisely speaking, *women*," Ball said. "They're *whores*. It's a dangerous job. They do get murdered from time to time, you know."

The mayor clenched his fists. "I *knew* we should have cleared out the Tenderloin before the Pan opened. The Anti-Saloon League, the temperance assholes, all of them were chewing on me to do it. But no—you told me to leave it be."

Ball tapped his finger on the mayor's desktop. "Look, we've had this conversation a hundred times. If I'd driven every saloonkeeper and whore out of the 'Loin, first off there'd be no one living there. Second, do you think they wouldn't just set up shop someplace else? As it is, they're confined to an area that I can keep in some kind of control. Raiding them is like poking a stick into an anthill. And you know it."

"Fuck," the mayor said, his head still in his hands. "Just *fuck*. Will you *please* tell me you'll find this son of a bitch Butcher?"

"We're doing our best," Ball said. "But the longer you keep me here, the less time I have to find him."

"I'm out of time, Bill," the mayor said. "I'm going to have to make a deal with the papers to keep this quiet."

"Good luck with that."

CHAPTER 10 ::
NASTY, BRUTISH,
AND SHORT

Technically speaking, the Daisy Murder wasn't even in the Tenderloin. It happened half-a-block above Broadway, north of the uppermost boundary of the red-light district. But a short five minutes' walk east would put one into some of the worst of it—the black-and-tan saloons clustered around the intersection of Michigan and William—and only a slightly longer stroll south would put a thrill-seeking pedestrian in the middle of Vine Alley.

The fact that the Butcher had ventured outside of the Tenderloin proper—even by a half-block—rattled the entire population of the district's demimonde. Since vice was effectively tolerated within the boundaries of the Tenderloin, surely a killer of low-class prostitutes had more than enough prey available without trespassing on other parts of town where law and order were expected and maintained. But since more papers were sold outside the Tenderloin than inside it, the reporters had an opportunity to scare the bejeezus out of everyone. Those who lived in the district already knew that life was nasty, brutish, and short, and didn't need another reminder.

To be fair, the Tenderloin was worse than the rest of the city only by a matter of degree. With only primitive sewers, open drainage ditches, and more horses than people, the entire city of Buffalo—with the exception of the Pan-American grounds, where the opinions of out-of-towners were at stake—reeked. The stench was bad at any time of year, but in the summertime it became eyewatering, and in the confines of the Tenderloin could be suffocating.

Daily, tons of horse manure and barrels of urine were deposited on and between the cobblestones of the vice district, but no street sweeper ventured there. From behind the bars, rivulets of vomit, stale beer, and the ripe, fruity smell of rotting garbage crept down the alleyways and into the thoroughfares of Michigan, Broadway, and Division. From there it would be at the whim of the whirling lake breezes to distribute the Tenderloin's perfume throughout Buffalo.

On the crooked sidewalks, numberless used-up wads of plug tobacco and blobs of sputum were impossible to dodge; people simply gave up and hoped that the stuff would wear off their shoe soles by the time they stepped across their thresholds. Cigar and coal smoke mingled with the smell of cooking from the restaurants and lunch counters.

Clattering hooves, the shouts of teamsters, drunken singing, and ragtime piano grew louder or softer, but were never entirely absent. Nor were the sounds of angry voices, arguments, the breaking of glass, and sidewalk scuffles. The barking of stray dogs—usually a leading part of the Tenderloin's cacophony—had recently subsided, however, after no less a light than the grandson of the founder of the Erie Canal had waged a war on stray dogs.

There had been a rabies outbreak the year before, and a new one could not be tolerated in the Pan year. Thus, a half-dozen dogcatchers' wagons plied the streets of the Tenderloin—if only because the 'Loin's rabid dogs might escape to bite someone in the better parts of the city. Catchers could net as many as sixty unlicensed dogs a day, with each captive dog paying out a small bounty. The canines were duly deposited at the dog pound on the Terrace, near the Erie County Morgue, and given a forty-eight-hour stay of execution. After that, they were stuffed into a four-foot-square wooden box, filled with illuminating gas. Death would come within a minute or so, and in 1901, the year's quota was five thousand dogs. They would exceed it easily.

Stray cats were usually caught and cooked by the Chinese restaurants along Michigan Street, but about a hundred cats a year were also gassed at the dog pound. This was almost always on application from pet owners who had no further use for their feline friends.

After a few hours in the Tenderloin, most visitors were exhausted from the continual assault on their senses. For those who would spend their entire lives, however long or short, in the district, it was simply home.

CHAPTER 11 ::
THE GOOD SAMARITAN

After sending her farewell letter to Dr. Grand, Helen stayed mostly in her apartment, skipping work, sniffing cocaine in her dressing gown, and dreading George's reply to her letter. But as the hours turned into days without any response, she fell into a cycle of expectation and disappointment.

It became a ritual. Toward three o'clock, she would wait nervously for the afternoon mail. As the hour swung slowly around, and her anxiety mounted, she would need *something* to steady her nerves, and would give herself a cocaine enema. That did the trick, and for the endless half-hour before the mail delivery, she could forget.

Then the mail slot would bang open and shut with its abrupt, metallic sound. That would put an end to her dreaming, because it never disgorged anything from Dr. Grand.

As the afternoon sunlight gave way to shadow and dusk, Helen reassured herself that she would surely receive his reply in the evening mail. She sat in the gathering dark and waited, but when the mail slot barked again, there followed only more silence from George.

After a few days of this fraught routine, Helen grew weepy and despondent. He wouldn't even dignify my letter with a response, she thought. She missed him, too, as difficult as that was to admit. And she had been so certain that her sharp letter would provoke an equally sharp response. Whether dismissive or pleading for forgiveness, either one would have given her a kind of sustenance. Instead, he had fed her only cold indifference.

She began spending hours face down on her bed, half-stupefied and blocking out the daylight, but still there was no escape. Even the smell of her own breath in the feather-down pillow would conjure a memory—one that made her want to feel him, or anyone, inside her again, if only to fill this terrible emptiness.

A WEEK PASSED WITHOUT even so much as a line from Dr. Grand. Helen fell ever deeper into a funk, leaving her apartment only briefly, either to purchase a few groceries or—more frequently—venture into the Tenderloin to buy dope. Sometimes—if she were high enough—she could manage to listen to music on her Victrola, dancing by herself to a dozen of the records George had purchased for her.

She was putting an enormous quantity of the drug up her nose and, more often, up her ass. But the high didn't seem as high as it had, the relief shorter-lived, and her nose had begun to bleed. She began to wonder if she were being cheated, sold adulterated goods. And she noticed the eyes on her as she strolled the perimeter of the Tenderloin, not going in too far, but far enough that surely there were those who wondered what she was up to.

And she was running short on funds. With the cocaine failing to help her find oblivion, she used her last two dollars to purchase a little envelope of morphine and a tidy little leather kit containing a hypodermic syringe and three steel needles.

On her way home, she passed a little knot of no-count loiterers sitting on a concrete stoop—the only remnant of a building that had burned, fallen down, or been knocked over to discourage squatters. She smiled to herself, expecting the usual wolf-whistles. But this time, one of the men called out.

"Now what is the Bell Telephone Girl doing in a place like this?"

She froze.

"Hey, Bell Girl, come on over here and sit on my lap, will you? I have a connection I want to make."

Helen broke into a run and stopped only when she got back to the Delamore.

⌒

IN THE SAFETY OF her flat, Helen was stewing over just how she'd been recognized, when there was a sharp knock on the door.

Helen opened her door to see a man, standing there, hat in hand.

"Good afternoon," she said. "May I help you?"

"I hope so. I'm Mr. Beck, and I own this flat."

"Very nice to meet you," she said with as much good cheer as she could muster. "I simply love living here."

"You are Miss Crosby, then?"

"I am."

"And do you have my rent?"

"Why would I have your rent?"

"Um, because you've been here for two months, and I haven't received payment."

"I don't understand," she said, trying to keep her smile from fading.

"Do you find this humorous, Miss Crosby?"

"Oh no, not at all. It's just that Doctor Grand has been helping me with my lodging, and—he's out of the city just now. I'm sure that's why the rent is past due."

Beck sighed. "Doctor Grand told me when he engaged this flat that you would be responsible for the rent."

"He's supposed to be paying you, sir," she said, feeling weak in the knees.

"I haven't received a nickel, Miss Crosby. Now, since it's your name that's on the lease, you are responsible for the rent payments. If Doctor Grand has been helping you with them, that's none of my concern."

"Of course not," she said. "How much does he—do I owe?"

"Two months at twenty dollars a week, plus the twenty-dollar security. That makes a hundred and eighty dollars."

"Good heavens," she said. "I don't have a hundred and eighty dollars."

Beck was getting red in the face. "And I'm very sorry to hear that, but I have a long list of other people who would love to take over this flat."

"Can you wait until Doctor Grand returns?"

"When will he be back?"

"I'm not sure," she said.

"This is becoming very frustrating, Miss Crosby. I'll give you until tomorrow, but that's the extent of it. You'll have to leave if I don't have payment in full by midday."

"All right. But you'd think you'd have a little more compassion for a girl who's new in town."

"Just because you're the Bell Telephone Girl doesn't mean that you don't have to pay your debts," he said testily.

"I will pay you somehow. You are the second person today to call me the Bell Telephone Girl," she said. "I do work for them—off and on, lately—at the Pan. But I can't for the life of me imagine why people would be calling me by that name."

He raised his eyebrows. "You must be the only person in Buffalo who doesn't know. Look inside the front of the new telephone directory. Now I bid you a good day, Miss Crosby."

"Good day, Mr. Beck."

"I'll be back tomorrow, you understand?"

"I do, sir," she said, and closed the door before he could say anything else.

Rent past due? Bell Telephone Girl?

She went over to her table and put her head in her hands, wanting to wish it all away. Her little leather kit was sitting there. She opened it, removed the glass syringe, and affixed to it one of the gleaming steel needles. Then she crushed two tablets—one grain in total—mixed the resulting powder in water, as she'd seen George do, and drew it into the syringe.

Where do I put it, I wonder? She thought, looking at her arm. I'll never find a vein without help. Then she remembered something George had told her once, that some addicts shot up behind their knees. She stretched out her leg, winced as she stuck the needle into the soft little mound of flesh, and depressed the plunger.

It was heaven.

AFTER THE MORPHINE HAD worn off, Helen took the streetcar over to Oak Street to make a last-ditch plea to her sister Eva. She walked the half-block from the trolley stop to Eva's front door, climbed the steps, and rapped.

Eva answered and then, to Helen's surprise, almost seemed to want to slam the door in her face. But at last she held it open partway.

"What do you want, Helen? This is not a good time."

"I just wanted to say hello. It's been a while. Are you well?"

"Hello. I'm well enough."

"May I come in? It's hot out here."

"I'm expecting my friend in less than a half-hour, Helen. You have to be gone before he arrives." Eva opened the door, and Helen stepped in.

They sat in the little kitchen. A new telephone directory was sitting on the table.

"You've become famous," Eva said, tapping the book. "Page four, if you haven't seen it."

Helen flipped open the book to see—on pages four and five, actually—two photographs of her, taken at the Bell Exchange at the Pan. There was a day, early in the Exposition, when her supervisor had asked her to demonstrate for a crowd of rubes from Ohio or some such place the right and wrong way to hold the telephone earpiece and how far from the mouthpiece to speak. Apparently someone at Bell had taken photographs of her, and now they had been printed in the very front of the annual Buffalo telephone directory. And the photographs were exquisite—as beautiful as she was in life, they made her look even more so.

"My word," Helen breathed. "I remember when these were taken, but I never gave them permission to use them."

Eva shrugged. "They probably don't need permission. You work for them."

"Part time," Helen said.

"I wouldn't feel too badly if I were you. Everyone's talking about those pictures. You look beautiful, and apparently men all over the city are tearing out these two pages. To God knows what purpose. I don't even want to consider it."

"That's certainly unexpected," Helen said. "I will contact the telephone company immediately and demand that they withdraw it."

"Good luck with that," her sister said, looking at the clock. "Before you go, though, there's something else. I was going to destroy it, but since you're here." She took an envelope from her pocket and handed it over the table.

Helen looked at the envelope, which was addressed in the hand of George Grand. "George wrote to *you*?"

"Read it. I have to say, it's extraordinary."

Helen pulled out the sheet of notepaper—Riverdale Hospital stationery—and read:

My dear Miss Crosby:

As much as it pains me to write to you, since there is a matter relating to your sister, I felt honor bound to share with you some distressing events of recent date.

Your sister and I, as you may know, were engaged to marry.

"*Engaged*?" Helen said. "We've not been engaged. I've been asking and asking about that. George said we could be married when I complete a course of nursing instruction."

"Well, he seems to think you were engaged," Eva said.

The letter continued:

Recently, however, Helen has engaged in behavior unbefitting of someone who intends to be my wife. She has engaged in intimate relations with one of my interns—a younger man than myself, to be sure, but one for whom Helen will never be anything more than a passing fancy.

Even thus stung, I cannot find it in my heart to blame Helen, but honor requires that I announce my obligation to her to be at an end.

That being the case, I shall expect Helen to return the gifts I gave her and repay me the sums I have advanced for her lodgings, clothing, shoes, and other items. An itemized list is enclosed. The total is $400.

You will understand that my pride, however wounded,
prevents me from addressing this to her myself. Thus, I will
be very grateful if you will share it with Helen.

Yours very sincerely,

George Grand, MD

Helen felt as though the floor might be dropping out from under her feet and plunging her into some deep abyss. "This is simply—false, Eva," she stammered out at last. "It's a pack of lies."

"What part of it?"

"Well . . . all of it. We were never engaged. And as for this intern he talks about . . ."

"Yes? Do you deny this man's existence?"

Helen could not very well reveal the shameful way in which Grand had taught her things, made her love them, crave them, and then had compelled her to give them to another man, while he himself sat listening to them rut.

"No—I don't deny he exists . . ."

"And did you have improper relations with him? Or is that also false?"

"Eva," Helen pleaded, "please don't admonish me. Doctor Grand has abandoned me, and my rent is due and payable tomorrow. One hundred and eighty dollars, Eva."

"I don't know what's coming next with you, Helen," her sister said. "One hundred eighty. Four hundred. I can't even keep it straight anymore. But as I said before, I don't have anything like that kind of money. And frankly, if I did, I would sooner throw it in the sewer than give it to you."

"Then may I ask to stay with you here again? Just for a few days, that's all."

Eva stood. "Helen, I'm afraid that life has some hard lessons in store for you. You had a good friend in Doctor Grand, and you squandered it."

"You can't possibly understand how beastly he's been to me," Helen said.

Eva tapped on George's letter with her forefinger. "There are two sides to every story. Now I really do have to ask you to go."

Helen got up slowly, trying to control her breathing. "As you wish. I don't blame you. I think, though, I might do differently if our places were reversed."

"I'm fairly certain that we'll never know," Eva said.

"I won't trouble you again. I hope things go well for you, Eva."

Helen left her sister's house, resisting the urge to run as soon as she set foot on the sidewalk. Under the punishing force of the sun, though, her tiny store of resolve finally drained away, and at the corner of Genesee and Ellicott, she sat down wearily on a bench situated in a tiny, triangular green space. She began crying softly, at a loss for what to do next. Suddenly she didn't even want to return to the Delamore, where there were nothing but memories and a big bill waiting for her.

Helen hadn't thought to bring a parasol, nor had she eaten anything, and in the midday heat she was beginning to feel dizzy and weak. I'd better get home before I faint, she thought. Like it or not. Surely I can figure *something* out, if I can just quiet my head.

She was about to struggle up and get to the trolley stop when a closed carriage rattled up and stopped in front of her little park.

"Now, what's the Bell Telephone Girl doing sitting out in this heat?" a voice said.

"Go away," she said, sagging back down onto the bench. "Leave me alone."

"Dear," the voice called, "I'm not sure that's a good idea. You look like you might need a friend."

She looked up, squinting into the sun. The driver of the rig was a somewhat nondescript fellow in a derby hat. He lifted it and smiled.

"Do I know you?" she asked.

"Not yet," he replied. "But I've seen you in the telephone book."

"It seems everyone has," she said, holding her hand flat above her eyes against the glare.

"Surely you have a place to stay?"

Helen caught back a sob. "You can't possibly understand. But thank you."

"Do you have a name, Bell Girl?"

He does have a kind face, she thought. And God knows I can use a little kindness. "Helen Crosby," she said.

"Pleased to meet you, Helen Crosby, Bell Telephone Girl. I'm Charley Willard. Why don't you let me take you someplace you'll be safe—while you sort things out? This is a city where a young lady needs a friend."

She thought about the Delamore, the four hundred dollars, the bed on which Grand and then Leland Kennecott had had their way with her, and then looked up into the bland but pleasant face of this Good Samaritan, whom chance had put in her path.

Popcorn Charley set the brake and jumped down from his rig. He leaned against it casually. "Miss Crosby, I think I know how you feel. When I first came here, I felt very much the same way. Nothing is harder than being alone in a lonely place."

She nodded sadly.

"Look, my dear, I own a hotel, and I happen to have a couple vacant rooms. Why don't you let me put you up there for a little bit, just until you can get squared away? It'll do you good."

Helen thought about a nice hotel room and being away from the Delamore. She stood and smiled. "Thank you, Mr. Willard," she said, extending her hand to him. "I'd be very grateful."

"Then let me help you in, Miss Crosby. Or, you know—maybe I'll call you Miss Bell."

She laughed for the first time in days. "Miss Bell will do fine, sir," she said, and climbed into Popcorn Charley's carriage.

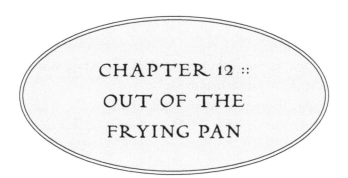

CHAPTER 12 ::
OUT OF THE
FRYING PAN

Charley installed her in the best room at The Alzora—which was not saying much, but it passed muster for a third-class hotel. To Helen it seemed like paradise. She sat down primly on a rather threadbare velvet upholstered chair and smiled at her deliverer.

"You look like you could use some sleep," he said kindly. "So you just rest. I'll have someone bring up some supper for you later."

"I can't thank you enough, Mr. Willard. You're an angel."

He laughed. "Now *that's* something I don't hear every day. But thank you all the same. Now then—surely you have some belongings I can have my man fetch for you?"

She nodded. "I have been lodging at the Delamore. There was a gentleman helping me with my rent, but then—he stopped doing that, and now I'm behind. So my trunk and few things are still at the Delamore. And the owner is very upset with me."

"Mr. Beck," Charley said.

"How do you know Mr. Beck?"

"I know *everyone*," Charley said. "Look, I'll talk with him. He's a reasonable fellow. I'll explain the situation and see if I can work something out. I'll have my man pick up your things. You'll have no more strings attached to the Delamore."

"Bless you. I can't thank you enough, Mr. Willard."

"Charley will do," he said. "Mr. Willard's my father's name."

"Fine, then. Charley it is."

He pointed at her with mock seriousness. "But remember, you're still Miss Bell to me!"

"I won't forget."

"Then you get some shut-eye, and don't worry about any of that Delamore stuff. You leave that to me."

"All right. Thank you ever so much, Charley."

"Don't mention it, Miss Bell." He grinned and shut the door gently as he left.

HELEN SLEPT FOR A long, long time, and when she awakened, there was a tray of food sitting on a little table adjacent to the bed. There was a letter desk, a washstand with a hazy mirror above it, two chairs, and that was all. She had to use the toilet, and naturally in a rather basic hotel, there wasn't an individual bath. She sat up, shook her head, and a little unsteadily went to the door. It was locked. She looked around for a key, but found none. *Probably for my own safety,* she thought, and returned to the bed. She looked under it and found a chamber pot, with a towel draped over it.

After she had relieved herself, she walked across the room to examine her new view. But her window looked out over the rear of the hotel, onto an alley jumbled with ash cans and castoff junk. *Certainly not the Delamore,* she thought, and then chided herself. *What ought I to expect? I'm lucky I have a room at all. I oughtn't look a gift horse in the mouth.*

Helen sat down and tasted some of the food on the tray— cheese and crackers, olives, a few cubes of ham, and a pitcher of coffee that had long since gone cold. But she was hungry, and it all tasted delicious, here in her cozy new room. *I wonder when I'll see Mr. Willard again,* she thought. *I do wish I had something to read, though. Maybe I ought to start reading the Bible again. Yes, that would do me some good.*

She sat for a little while longer, looking around the room, sipping the cold coffee. Then she rather suddenly began feeling morose, thinking about Eva and George and Lee. *Perhaps I ought not to have sent that* nasty letter to George. Perhaps I misunderstood the whole thing with Lee—after all, I was *very* high, and he certainly had a different memory of it in his letter to Eva. He seemed so hurt and let down. Might I have made an advance?

She wished she had a pick-me-up, a little bit of something to lift her spirits. If I could only get downstairs, I'm sure I could find a druggist nearby.

CHARLEY DIDN'T SHOW HIS face again until early the next morning. Helen passed a somewhat fitful night, and without her trunk or any apparel had to sleep in the nude, which was fine because the room was stifling hot and, of course, was securely locked. All night, she'd been tormented by strange dreams—the worst of them when she lay awake between periods of slumber. She had also felt a little sick to her stomach after the cheese and ham, and after trying to hold it for a couple of hours, in the dark had to resign herself to squatting over the chamber pot to defecate.

In getting off the pot—of all the foul luck—she knocked the fool thing over. She righted it quickly, but not before the majority of its contents had spilled onto the floorboards. The towel draped over the chamber pot was the only thing she had to clean herself—and the floor—as best she could, and now, of course, the whole room stank like a sewer. And whether it was nerves, the cocaine enemas, or simple chemistry, whatever remained in the uncovered chamber pot seemed to smell unusually pungent.

As the room brightened, Helen dressed and perched on the edge of the bed, as primly as she could manage after the chamber-pot mishap.

She sat there, abstracted, for almost an hour. Then the doorknob rattled, there was the sound of a key working the lock, and the door opened. It was Charley.

"Oh, Charley!" she said, "Am I ever glad to see you!"

"Miss Bell," he said. He seemed a little less cheerful than he had the afternoon before.

"I'm so—so sorry," she said, wringing her hands. "In the dark I made something of a mess, and I—I'll certainly clean it up, if I can get a bucket and—"

He waved his hand. "This place has seen worse. Don't worry about it."

"Did you happen to secure my trunk?" she said. "I haven't anything to wear."

"I did, and I got old Beck paid off. What an exercise that turned out to be. He drove a hard bargain."

"Oh no," she said. "How much did you have to pay?"

"Two hundred bucks," Charley said. "Half of what he said you owed, with the clothes and all."

"What does Mr. Beck have to do with my clothes? Doctor Grand bought those for me."

"I don't know," Charley said. "I suppose Grand turned over the whole debt for Beck to collect."

"It's all so horrible. But please, Mr. Willard, you needn't have the least concern at all. I'll pay you back, and with interest, too. I have a little job at the Pan-American, and today I'll find a second job."

"We can talk about that in due course," he said. "First, though, we need to move you across the street, to a friend of mine's place. Unexpectedly I got a telegram from a big group coming in for the Pan, and I can't spare this room after today."

"I completely understand, sir. I couldn't possibly expect more. Thank you. I'm sure your friend's hotel will be as nice as yours."

He smiled again. "It's a lot nicer than mine. It's probably the best one in this part of the city, in fact. But she's got room, and plenty of work. You'll make a lot more than you do at the Pan, and you'll easily be able to pay me back."

Helen jumped up. "Charley, I could just kiss you!"

He winked at her. "Miss Bell, I might just take a rain check on that. Now if you'll follow me, I'll get you all set up in your new digs."

HELEN'S TRUNK AND CARPETBAGS were waiting downstairs in the

lobby of The Alzora, sitting on a kind of low wheelbarrow. A swarthy man was waiting next to them, smoking.

"These go across the street," Charley said to him, and the man left. Charley and Helen followed. It was already hot on Ellicott Street, and busy. They dodged horses and passersby to get to Grace's place on the other side of the street. Charley rapped on the door, and in a moment Grace Harrington appeared.

"I have Miss Bell for you, Grace," he said.

"Miss Bell!" she said, opening her arms and giving Helen a bear hug. "My, you're even more beautiful than your photographs. Do come in. Charley, thank you so much."

"You bet, Grace. Bye for now, Miss Bell. I'll see you again soon."

Helen turned around and impetuously threw her arms around Charley. "I can't wait, Mr. Willard. Thank you so very much!"

She stepped across the threshold and looked around, trying not to seem too nosy. There was something queer about the place—a hotel, Charley had said, or she thought he had said, but the front room looked more like the parlor of a rather overfurnished home than it did a hotel lobby. There wasn't any desk, or clerk; no neat pigeonholes for keys or mail—only a number of velvet-covered couches, chairs, and some very fine-looking rugs and tapestries.

"You have a lovely hotel," Helen said, looking for the right compliment.

"I predict you'll be very happy here, dear," Grace said. "We have a room for you upstairs. It has its own full bath. You'll be able to clean up before luncheon and change into some fresh clothes."

"May I inquire as to how much your tariff is per night? I owe a rather substantial sum to Mr. Willard already, and I'll need to be careful with my resources."

"After what you've been through," Grace said, "you'll be my guest for now. We have a professional position worked out for you that will pay you far more than you will ever owe."

Helen bounced up and down on her toes. "I almost have to pinch myself. I wish I'd found nice people like you and Mr. Willard when I first arrived in the city."

"Charley is a sound fellow," Grace said. "Now why don't you freshen up in your room before luncheon?"

"I'd love that. Would you mind having my trunk brought up?"

"Soon," Grace said. "In the meantime, you'll find changes of clothes and fresh linens in your room. You can wear those today. Let me show you to your room."

"That will be very welcome," Helen said with a little bow.

Grace led Helen up a carpeted, curving staircase to the second floor. It was very quiet, as if the place were entirely vacant, or everyone was sleeping until an unseemly hour. The corridor was paneled in dark wood, and the walls were hung with somewhat louche scenes that seemed to Helen in slightly poor taste for a public hotel.

At the end of the corridor, Grace unlocked a door and let Helen into a large bedroom with tall ceilings. The room was furnished with a big canopy bed, which was covered with a silk bedspread in a brilliant shade of magenta. There was a tall armoire against one wall, a large window hung with floral brocade curtains, a very lovely dressing-screen with a Chinese scene, and a doorway leading into a bathroom.

"It's wonderful," Helen said.

"This will be your new home, Miss Bell," Grace said. "Take a bath, rest a little, and you'll find your new clothes in the armoire. I'll come up and collect you just before luncheon."

"That can't come too soon! I'm so very hungry."

Grace looked her up and down. "You could stand to put on a little flesh, but even so, you are still the most beautiful girl I think I've ever seen. And quite a celebrity!"

Helen laughed. "I never thought that my little job at the Bell Exchange would be anything other than anonymous."

"With a face and body like yours, dear, you couldn't be anonymous if you tried. You are truly a specimen. Well then, I should leave you to yourself, Miss Bell."

"You don't need to call me Miss Bell, you know. Helen Crosby is my name, and you may call me Helen."

Grace studied her for a moment. "No, I think Miss Bell is better. You see, I know a little bit about that gentleman who was paying for your lodging. Doctor Grand."

"You do?"

"I do. He can be spiteful, and he won't be happy that we foiled his little plot to bankrupt you, you know. So it will be best if you could lie low, as the saying goes, for a little while. Just in case Doctor Grand comes looking for you. Men like him sometimes do."

"Heavens, I'd not thought of anything like that," Helen said. "Thank you for sheltering me, madam."

Grace gave an odd smile. "No need to call me madam. Grace, between us. With the other guests, we tend to be more formal. Then it must be Mrs. Harrington."

"I fully understand," Helen said.

"Good. Well, then, welcome again. And I'll see you at luncheon, looking splendid, I'm sure."

Helen smiled and bowed again. Grace left, and Helen heard the key work in the lock.

GRACE TROTTED ACROSS THE street to The Alzora, where she found Charley lounging in the lobby, reading the paper.

"Well?" he said, looking up. "How did I do?"

"Charley Willard, I am going to fuck your brains out for this one. She's a *prize*, I say. A prize. How much did Grand charge me?"

"Eight hundred," he replied. "He said she's the best he's ever had. Bar none."

"Coming from that old rake, that's saying something. And how much do you want on top of that?"

"I'll take ten percent of her earnings. That one's going to pay back over time."

"You're a smart man, Charley," Grace said. "I tell you, I'm feeling so grateful that I'm going to let you have a free one with her."

"You won't get jealous?"

"I might," she said, touching his face with her forefinger. "But fair is fair."

"You're a peach," Popcorn Charley said.

"Tonight will be her big debut. I'm going to send messengers out to a few of the best regulars. They will never believe it—the Bell Girl? They'll think I'm putting them on."

"She starts tonight? You're not letting any grass grow under your feet."

"Eight hundred bucks, Charley, plus her room and board. She's got to start earning her keep. Anyhow, I just wanted to thank you again. I've got to get busy."

Grace was halfway out the door when Charley called after her. "Oh, Grace," he said.

"Yes?"

"In her things at the Delamore, I found a hypodermic kit and an enema bag."

"Now how about that?" Grace said. "Our little Miss Bell is naughtier than she looks."

⌒

HELEN TOOK A NICE, long soak in her new tub, which was provided with a delicately scented floral soap—not the cheap stuff, either. When the water cooled, she toweled off and opened the armoire to dress for luncheon.

There were several dresses in the armoire, and some rather fine silk underthings, too. She took one of the dresses off the hook and examined it. It was beautifully made of silk taffeta, but exceedingly frilly and of a deep maroon shade that might be suitable for a dress ball. And its daring neckline was certainly not made for going about in daylit streets. How queer, she thought. I suppose for one luncheon indoors, it'll do. But I do hope they bring up my trunk soon.

She slipped on the silk underclothes, so fine that they ran like water over her skin, but so sheer as to be almost transparent. There was a swan bill corset in the armoire, an underbust one, which pushed her breasts up and almost out of the taffeta dress. The whole ensemble may be a little *much*, she thought, but it is very flattering. It's nice to feel dressed up for a change. If only George could see me now! He thought he'd put me in the poorhouse!

She looked at herself in the mirror. Her large, dark eyes seemed to disappear in the shadows cast by the huge armoire and the canopy bed, making her face mysterious. Even in the brightest part of a summer's day, the heavy brocade curtains and the richly embroidered furniture kept the opulent bedroom in a permanent, seductive twilight.

I wonder what kind of position Charley and Grace have arranged for me, she wondered, preening. Unless it's dancing girl, though, I won't be doing it in *this* dress!

At a quarter to noon, there was a gentle rap on her door, and she rustled over to it, before remembering that it was locked.

"Yes?" she said.

"It's Grace. May I come in?"

"Why, of course."

The lock clattered and Grace stepped in. She took a look at Helen and stepped back. "What a stunner you are. You look simply marvelous."

Helen did a little happy twirl on the carpet. "Thanks to you. Though I'll need my street clothes before too long."

"Don't fret so much about your street clothes," Grace said, taking Helen's hand in hers. "It's better for you to avoid the street for a while. Let things calm down with Doctor Grand. Inside this house, you're dressed quite appropriately."

"I suppose you're right. Now I hope you're not here to tell me there's no luncheon. I'm famished!"

Grace patted Helen's hand. "Not at all. We'll all be sitting down very soon. I just wanted to go over your new duties before we do, since you'll be meeting the others who do the same kind of work."

"Oh good. I'm eager to hear what type of position you've arranged for me. I'm hoping to become a nurse, but I can do most anything."

"Excellent," Grace said. "That's the spirit! Your job is simple—to make my other guests feel at home here. Make them feel special."

"That doesn't sound much like work," Helen said.

"It really isn't, you know. It's much like what you've been doing at the Pan-American. Greeting people, making them feel welcome."

"That sounds delightful. And I'm very good at putting people at their ease, if I do say so myself."

"So I understand. Each evening, beginning at nine o'clock, you'll come down to the parlor, looking like the beautiful Bell Girl you are,"

Grace said. "You'll talk with the guests, dance, have a few cocktails. Flirt with them a bit. You know how men are."

"It sounds like fun," Helen said. "I'll be a kind of hostess, then?"

"You might say that. The only difference, really, is that after making them feel at home downstairs, you'll come back here to extend a special *kind* of hospitality." She tilted her head toward the bed.

Helen's stomach sank, and she thought she was going to be sick. "You're joking," she said with a wan smile, managing a hopeful chuckle.

"Trust me," Grace said, "it's the easiest work there is. My girls here have only to put on a little show four times a night."

"Your girls?"

"Yes. I have five of them now, counting you. You'll meet them all downstairs, and I have no doubt you'll get along famously. Oh, and by the way—they make a lot of money, my dear, doing nothing more than showing men a good time."

Helen swallowed hard. "Do you mean to say that these girls are *prostitutes*?"

"That is such a pejorative term, and one invented by men. I prefer *belles de nuit*. And you are going to be the best of all the belles—*the* one and only Miss Bell. You see?"

"But I . . . I can't do *that*," Helen said. "I don't mean to sound rude, but I'll have to find some different kind of situation right away. May I please have my trunk, so that I can leave?"

Grace looked at her patiently. "You owe me a thousand dollars, Miss Bell. You're not getting your trunk until you pay me back in full, with interest."

"I owe you *a thousand dollars*? For what?"

"Charley and I paid all your debts," she said. "Lodging, clothing, shoes. And we had to pay Doctor Grand for finding you and training you."

"For *training* me?"

"Do you think I'd shell out a thousand dollars if he hadn't? Miss Bell, I've been in this business a long time, and I can tell just by the way you move that you are *special*."

"Nonsense," Helen said. "I'm just a regular girl. You don't want me here."

"Don't sell yourself short. Let me tell you something—and I hope you'll take it as a compliment—George Grand swears that no one, but *no one*, can fuck as well as you can. And believe me, he would know."

"What a *monster*!" Helen said, stamping her foot.

"We've all got a monster in us. Grand just got eaten up by his. But he does know talent."

"Well, I don't care about any of that. I didn't come to Buffalo to become a whore."

"Poor dear," Grace said. "I hope this won't burst your bubble, but in America, all women are whores."

"What a preposterous thing to say!"

"Is it? Think about it, Miss Bell. You know firsthand that—without a man's help—single women can't *possibly* make ends meet. And do married women have it any better? Of course not. They depend on their husbands for every red cent, and earn it all on their backs. At least we whores, to use your rather horrible word, are honest about it. We do it for good money, and, best of all, the men go away afterward."

Helen looked at the floor. "Doctor Grand said we would be married. He deceived me. I would never have done—any of that, otherwise."

Grace put her finger under Helen's chin and lifted it.

"Dear," she said, "don't be so downcast. All women may be whores, but all men are liars, which is much worse. Old Grand just gets paid for doing what comes naturally to him. So why shouldn't you?"

"That evil, evil man," Helen muttered.

"Miss Bell, you needn't spend another second thinking about him. You're free now."

"Free?" Helen said with a small, bitter laugh. "I'm a *prisoner*."

Grace's eyes narrowed, and she reached out and slapped Helen's face, hard.

"What's that for?" Helen yelped.

"To knock some sense into you."

The clock on the wall chimed noon.

"Time for luncheon," Grace said.

"I'd rather starve."

"Miss Bell—"

"Don't call me that! My name is Helen Crosby."

"Not anymore it isn't. Now either come downstairs and be pleasant, or after luncheon I'll sell you on. It'll take me two calls, and I'll make a tidy profit in the process."

"You can't *sell* me. I'm not a slave."

Grace shrugged. "Enough of this unpleasantness. I'll be going downstairs now. I'll allow you five extra minutes, because you're new—and because you need to rouge that other cheek. But I'll be watching the clock. Five minutes, or you'll find out what happens to girls who fuck with me." She turned to leave.

"Wait," Helen said, trying to slow her breathing. "Mrs. Harrington, please. This is all . . . I don't know even what's . . . what's *involved*."

"Honey," she said with a warm smile, "as I said, it's the easiest thing on earth, and especially since you already know how to please a man. Tonight you come down the staircase at nine o'clock, sharp. Chin up, shoulders back, and those beautiful tits of yours pointed straight out."

"What then?"

"Some of my very best clients will be bidding for your first time. It's all very discreet, though, not like a cattle auction. The highest bidder buys you a cocktail or two, and then you bring him here for an hour, and no more. Oh, and you get paid. A lot."

"How much?"

"Ten percent of whatever I charge, to be held on account against what you owe me. If at any point you want spending money, just say so, and it will be charged against your account. Your room and board are provided. You get two new outfits every season. Laundry service, doctors, and dentists are also provided at no charge to you. Clients pay for your cocktails during working hours. If a client tips you, or buys you a dress, or a piece of jewelry—and *my* clients do such things—those are yours to keep."

"And what happens when I have enough to pay off my debt?"

"Your street clothes and other things will be returned to you, and you are free to go. But I'll predict you won't want to leave, because other than the old biddies on Delaware Avenue, no woman in Buffalo lives as high as you will. *The Bell Girl*? You'll make us both a fortune."

Helen was silent.

"You work six nights a week, nine o'clock until you've seen four clients. That's your quota, same as the other girls. Wednesdays are off, but you must be back here by midnight. At first, you will require a chaperone if you leave the house, just until I know I can trust you. If you betray that trust, the consequences will be severe and much to your detriment."

"A few final oddments," Grace went on. "Strictly no street drugs are permitted, on pain of eviction. If you want drugs, you must purchase them from me, and such purchases are deducted from your earnings. My drugs are hospital grade, not full of all the shit the dope peddlers put in them. Which is, by the way, why you've been having nosebleeds and shat yourself over at Charley's. You've probably put a half-pound of borax up your nose and ass."

"My God," Helen said, horrified.

"No call to be embarrassed. I don't mind if you have a few bad habits, so long as they don't get out of hand. No smoking, though, end of sentence. No man likes kissing an ashtray."

"Grace . . . Mrs. Harrington—please," Helen said. "I don't think I can do this."

"Yes, you can. And in return I'll take very good care of you, because it's in my interest to do so. You'll be well-fed, clean, well-dressed, nice hair, sound teeth, fresh breath. And you'll find that my clientele is the very best. All you have to do is be your charming and beautiful self."

"*Charming*," Helen sniffed. "It's a little more than *charm*."

"Doctor Grand may be a liar, but he knows better than to lie about talent," Grace said. "And he swears you have it. Might as well put it to good use."

Helen looked at the rug, which had seemed so nice just fifteen minutes before.

"We've kept the others waiting far too long," Grace said. "Which is rude, and that I cannot abide. Now are you coming with me, or not?"

"I thought you wanted me to rouge my cheek?"

Grace slapped Helen on the opposite side of her face. "There. Nice and even."

Helen stepped back and stared at the madam.

"I can tell you understand," Grace said quietly. "However you treat me, that's what you'll get in return, Miss Bell. Now, shall we?"

Helen followed Grace to the door and into the corridor. As she closed her bedroom door, she took a deep breath and put her shoulders back. Goodbye for now, Helen Crosby, she said to herself. Perhaps we'll meet again one day.

~

DOWNSTAIRS, SEATED AROUND AN oval dining table and looking none-too-amused, were four other young ladies, all dressed in styles similar to Helen's. They put on convincing smiles and stood when Grace entered. When Helen stepped into the room, though, every expression turned to one of amazement.

"My apologies, girls," Grace said. "I was taking a little additional time with our new sister."

"Hello," Helen said.

"You can sit next to me, dear," Grace said, taking her place at the head of the table and ringing a little bell. "Girls, please don't stare so." Summoned by the bell, two waiters entered with trays and began serving the ladies roast beef and potatoes.

"Has anyone ever told you that you look exactly like the girl in the telephone book?" a redhead in a bright green dress said.

"That's because she *is* the girl in the telephone book," Grace said. "Girls, meet Helen Bell."

"Hello, Miss Bell," all four said in unison.

"Miss Flower," she said to the redhead, "you begin. Tell Miss Bell about yourself."

"I'm May," the redhead said. She laughed, seeing Helen's puzzlement. "Yes, May Flower. Because I'm from Boston. As you probably know, we all got new names when we came here."

"Very pleased to meet you, Miss Flower," Helen said. "Your hair is beautiful."

"Thanks," May said. "Some men love it, others don't. It's one way or the other."

"Thank you, May," Grace said. "Next."

A very buxom brunette spoke up. "I'm Alice Star. Star because I come only at night." Everyone laughed.

"Very pleased to meet you, Miss Star," Helen said.

"I'm Olive Moon," a slightly pudgy blonde girl on the opposite side of the table said. "And Alice stole my line."

Helen laughed. "You're funny."

"And you're gorgeous," Olive said.

"The girls do like to laugh," Grace said. "Men like that, by the way. Their wives are all a bunch of sad sacks."

The last girl to introduce herself had long, black hair tied up in a ponytail. "I'm Raven. Just Raven. I'm Indian, if you can't tell."

"You're very beautiful," Helen said, and Raven nodded at her.

"Thank you, girls. Now eat before it gets cold."

Helen was out of excuses, and so took a small bite of her roast beef, which was tender and excellent. She glanced around, thinking that prostitutes must be the kind of women who shovel down their food, but all of the girls ate daintily and with excellent table manners.

"Mrs. Harrington, may I ask a question of our new sister?" Olive asked.

"You may, dear."

"Miss Bell, have you done this sort of work before?"

"You don't have to answer that, Miss Bell," Grace said.

"Oh, I don't mind. No, Miss Moon, I haven't. But I'm looking forward to giving it a try," Helen said.

"She was trained by Doctor Grand," Grace said with a note of pride.

"You poor thing," May said. "That's how I got here, too. Believe me, this is nothing compared to *him*."

"Miss Flower."

"I'm sorry, Mrs. Harrington."

"Girls, tonight in honor of our new arrival, we'll have all our best gentlemen in the house. So I will expect you to be at your best, too. That means a thorough bath this afternoon, enemas, and douches. No food, drugs, or drinking after luncheon, except a cocktail or a little coke right before we open, if you like. Understood?"

"Yes, Mrs. Harrington," they said.

"Yes, Mrs. Harrington," Helen repeated.

Soon after Helen had returned to her room from chatting with the other girls, Grace rapped on her door again.

"You did brilliantly at luncheon, Miss Bell," Grace said. "I was very proud of you."

"Thank you."

"So I have a little something for you." Grace held out an envelope. Helen looked inside. It was half full of snowy powder.

"Cocaine?" Helen asked.

"Yes, and the good stuff," Grace said. "On me. Consider it a welcome present."

"Thank you. I'm sorry I was so surly earlier."

Grace studied Helen's face. "Why the sudden change of heart? You wouldn't be putting me on, would you?"

"I'm afraid I don't have a very good poker face," Helen said. "I have to make the best of things. So I'll work hard and pay off my debt, and then I can pick up where I left off. What other choice do I have?"

"I'll take you at your word, then. But don't try to deceive me, Miss Bell."

"I am doing my very best, ma'am, under the circumstances."

The madam nodded. "Then we will see you at nine tonight, Miss Bell. Look your very best."

"I wonder, Mrs. Harrington, whether Mr. Willard happened to find a little leather case over at the Delamore? It's nothing—"

"Yes, your syringes. I have them. You may have them back."

"Thank you. And may I purchase some morphine?"

"You may, but I want you to be careful. We don't need you becoming a slave to it. Every once in a great while only."

"Yes, ma'am."

After Grace left, Helen shook a little of Grace's powder into her palm and sniffed it up. She watched the pendulum of the wall clock marking the time, back and forth, back and—

Not quite a minute had passed when the high came on, roaring and invincible, like nothing she'd experienced. She shook her hair free, pins clattering to the floorboards, and danced. She laughed out loud, gloriously. For more of this stuff, she thought, I'll fuck a horse if I have to.

A t two minutes to nine, Helen sniffed up some cocaine and sat down on the edge of her bed to wait. In two minutes, a hundred twenty seconds, she'd walk down the staircase as Miss Helen Bell. And then, soon after, she'd be back here, on this bed.

No use trying to wish it away, she thought. I've certainly done my fair share of fucking, and everything else, too. At least I can get all paid up, put aside some money, and start over. For now, I have to.

Then she heard someone unlock her door, just as the clock began chiming, counting nine. She stood and smoothed her skirt, feeling the cocaine's courage. I'll show them, she thought. Remember the *Kama Sutra.*

"May I present—Miss Helen Bell!" Grace announced when Helen appeared at the top of the staircase, wearing her silk dress, long gloves, and with her hair done up in a perfect Gibson Girl swirl. Helen looked down to see a parlor full of men, most in evening dress, applauding. She stepped lightly down the stairs and took her place by Grace's side. She made a graceful curtsey.

"Thank you, Mrs. Harrington," she said. "And a good evening to all!"

Men began clustering around her, each trying to say something wittier than the one before. She laughed and flirted, meeting their eyes or averting hers as the mood took her.

After a few minutes, Grace put her hand on the small of Helen's back. "The gentleman at the bottom of the staircase is Mr. Jones. You may go upstairs with him now."

Helen nodded, and then brushed through the group of men to where Mr. Jones was standing. He was in his mid-fifties, perhaps, prosperous-looking, with grey hair and a slight paunch. She gave him a bright smile. "Mr. Jones?" she said, offering her hand.

"At your service, Miss Bell," he replied, kissing it gently before leading her upstairs.

"I'm right down this way," she said when they reached the landing, and then guided him to the back of the house.

While she was downstairs, someone had been in her bedroom, put the gas on low, and pulled the coverlet down halfway. There was a pitcher of iced cocktails and two glasses sitting on the writing desk.

Helen stepped close to Mr. Jones and put her hands on his chest. "You're very handsome."

"And you're exquisite," he replied.

"How shall we get better acquainted?" she asked, not really certain of how this ought to begin. "A cocktail, perhaps?"

"No thank you," he said. "But I'd like to watch you drink one."

"You would?"

"I would."

She poured herself a cocktail and took a sip, looking at him coquettishly.

"Not like that," Jones said. "Tilt your head back, so I can see your throat when you drink."

She took a mouthful of the highball and threw her head back, taking three swallows to make her neck pulse. When she looked at him again, his hand was down the front of his trousers.

"Wouldn't you prefer me to do that for you?"

He shook his head. "I'd prefer it if you would take off your dress."

She stripped off her gloves, stepped out of her dress, and was about to unfasten her corset when Jones shook his head again.

"No?" she said.

"Leave that on, if you please."

"Then let me help you out of your—"

"No, thank you. If you would lie down, I'd be grateful."

Helen lay down on her bed and watched him slip off his suspenders and step out of his trousers.

"Would you tilt your head back again," he asked, "so that I may see that lovely neck of yours?"

"Why, of course," she said, and threw back her head. He bent over her and kissed her throat, and then pressed his hand against the side of her neck, feeling her pulse.

"So beautiful," he murmured. "May I penetrate you now, Miss Bell?"

"You may, Mr. Jones," she said, opening her legs. Her underthings were standard-issue—open at the crotch—and he squared himself on top of her.

He slipped in, quite smoothly, and Helen was surprised at how good it felt. She let her thoughts roam as he began to move. The coke had mostly worn off, but still—it felt good.

Jones continued to kiss her neck. "May I squeeze it a little?" he whispered.

"My neck?"

"Yes."

"So long as you're gentle," she said. "And don't leave marks."

"Oh no," he said. "I only want to feel your heartbeat."

He went back on his knees, put his hands around her throat, and squeezed. She felt her face getting warm.

"Is that too much?" Jones asked.

"No, but no more than that."

"You're very beautiful, Miss Bell. Thank you for your indulgence."

He seemed very earnest, even a bit shy. She caught a look at the clock. Thirty minutes gone already, but he didn't seem to be in any rush.

Helen thought of a way to move things along. "Mr. Jones," she said, remembering a particular evening with Grand, "I have an idea."

"Yes, Miss Bell?"

"How would you like it if I squeezed *your* neck?"

He looked startled.

"I only want to do what you might like," she said.

"Yes, I'd like that, then."

"Let's switch places."

He pulled out of her, and she let him lie down in her place. Then she straddled him and lowered herself down on his cock.

"Good so far?" Helen asked.

"You feel wonderful. Do you find me exciting, Miss Bell?"

"Can't you tell, Mr. Jones? I'm wringing wet."

"Yes," he murmured. "You're so warm."

"And now the real fun begins. I'm going to choke you, Mr. Jones. If it's too much, just shake your head, and I'll stop. But if you don't, I'm going to do it harder. Harder is better, if you can stand it."

"Oh my," he whispered.

She started to rock her hips back and forth, the way Grand had shown her, and put her hands around Jones's throat. "Ready?"

He nodded, and she squeezed. She felt him try to push into her. He likes it, Helen thought. So she squeezed again, this time harder.

"Too much?" she asked.

He shook his head.

"You mean stop?"

"No," he wheezed. "Harder."

This time she gripped hard, and he coughed. But he didn't shake his head again, and now she was enjoying it, feeling a strange, warm sensation, the thrill of having this man utterly in her power.

His face turned red and soon, a shade of purple that Helen thought couldn't be healthy. She knew she should probably let up. But she was excited now, too, riding him hard and thinking again of Grand—how he'd nearly killed her, but how powerful her climax had been.

Suddenly Jones went limp, and Helen was afraid he was dead. She took her hands away from his throat. There was a momentary pause, and then he gasped and drew in a huge breath.

"Mr. Jones," she said, rolling off of him, "I hope that was not—"

"Miss Bell," he said raggedly, "God bless you."

She smiled and glanced at the clock. Nine-forty.

"I'm happy you had fun," Helen said. "Next time I'll know exactly what you like."

He sat up and nodded weakly, then got up and pulled on his trousers again. She wriggled back into her dress and caught sight of herself in the mirror. I'll have to fix my hair and tidy up, she thought.

Mr. Jones finished dressing. His high collar covered the marks she had left on his throat.

"It's truly been a pleasure, Miss Bell," he said hoarsely. "You are everything Grace said you were. And more."

"The pleasure was all mine, sir."

"I hope you will accept this as a small token of my gratitude," he said, holding out a twenty-dollar bill.

"It would be my honor," she said, taking the bill.

"Then until next time."

When the door had closed behind him, she got out of the dress again, gave herself a quick douche, washed her face and put some fresh rouge on, and then tidied her hair. It was ten-fifteen when she was ready to go downstairs again. Four men had seemed like nothing at all, but they weren't exactly a chorus line. Each one required some brief seduction, the appearance of not being rushed, and then the act. Dress, undress, perform, douche, and tidy. Repeat.

It's not quite so easy as Grace made it out to be, she thought. But twenty dollars, plus ten percent of whatever he paid her for my first time—in an hour and a half? That's more than I made in a month at the Pan. And the men were ogling me there, too. Here at least there's no pretense, no need to be coy. And I'm not Helen Crosby, but the mysterious Miss Bell.

She preened in the mirror a little more and was surprised to feel eager to get back downstairs.

AFTER HER FOURTH CLIENT had departed, Helen was spent. Three of the men had tipped her. With Jones's twenty and the three others, she'd made forty dollars on top of her cut of Grace's take. It had taken until almost two-thirty in the morning, though, and it would have been three if her last client hadn't had only enough time for a quick handjob before getting back home to his wife. No wonder these girls sleep until noon, she thought.

After each client, she had hurried downstairs, put on a fresh smile, and after some chitchat and another cocktail, Grace had whispered in her ear, and then it was back upstairs. She found that in the time she'd been flirting in the parlor, someone had entered her room, checked and ironed the bedclothes—after number two the sheets had been changed altogether, because he'd pulled out and gone everywhere—and the pitcher of cocktails refreshed.

Physically speaking, it hadn't been particularly exciting. She'd found her mind wandering much of the time, thinking about how to play her role, or watching the clock. Choking Jones half to death had gotten her going pretty well, but even then she hadn't climaxed, though it seemed close a couple of times. The handjob was novel and interesting, like a magic trick; oddly, that was something Grand had never asked for. The other two were straight up intercourse, rather boring, and neither man had been able to last very long. After that much sex, she might have been sick to death of it, but instead she felt a little frustrated. She touched herself tentatively, but things were too sensitive down below to finish.

Helen drew a hot bath and slipped into the tub, luxuriating in the feeling. She dozed off and was dreaming of something when she thought she heard her door open and then close again.

"Is someone there?" she said to no answer.

My imagination, she thought. The bathwater had cooled, so she got out. She looked at herself in the mirror, raining onto the tile. I don't *look* any different, she thought.

She toweled herself off, wrapped a dressing robe around her, and went out to her bedroom. On the bed was a small cloth bag with a note pinned to it. It read:

> *Well done, Miss Bell.*
> *G. H.*

Helen smiled and opened her present. Inside was her leather syringe case, a brand-new enema kit, and a vial of morphine tablets.

HELEN COULD SMELL LUNCHEON wafting up the staircase, and as noon approached, she dressed and trotted downstairs. As she rounded the newel post, she almost collided with Grace.

"Miss Bell," Grace said. "How are you today?"

"I'm well, thank you. And yourself?"

"Also well. I trust you found my little present last evening?"

Helen smiled. "Yes. And I am very grateful."

"Good. You cleaned up last night, by the way. Everyone loved you."

"Really? How much did I make?"

"You cleared almost fifty dollars, I think. Jones gave two hundred dollars for your first time. And I don't know what you did, but when he came down afterward, he said from now on he wants to see only you. So you have your first regular."

"Will he pay that much each time?"

"Oh no, that was special. Twenty-five or thirty dollars is the usual rate. Will you be ready for tonight?"

"Yes, although I am a little sore," Helen said.

"After luncheon, take a long, warm soak. I'll send up some vinegar to put in the bathwater. Then two or three times before nine, douche with some of the vinegar and maybe some witch hazel. In a week or two, you'll be used to it."

AT LUNCHEON, THE GIRLS asked Helen a hundred questions about her first night's work.

"What did you think of it? Was it what you expected?" asked Olive.

"Miss Bell, you are under no obligation to indulge idle curiosity," Grace said.

"I don't mind," Helen said. "I suppose I found the men to be much kinder than I expected them to be."

"You're used to Grand," May said. "He's a brute. You won't run into many like him."

"Every once in a while," Raven said, "you'll run into a real shitbird."

"Raven, mind your language," Grace said.

"I'm going to call you MP," May said.

"Whyever would you do that?" Helen asked.

Grace frowned. "Don't, Miss Flower. It wasn't funny the first time I heard it."

"*Please*, Mrs. Harrington."

"It's all right," Helen said. "I'm curious, if nothing else."

May grinned. "One of your clients, when he came back down, went over to Grace and said, 'I'll tell you, she's got a magic pussy.'"

Raven rolled her eyes, and Helen blushed.

"May, you're embarrassing Miss Bell. You wouldn't like it very much if we called you something like that," Olive said.

"Let's hope it's the right kind of magic," Raven said, "because we're going to need it. Surely Miss Bell is aware that two of our kind have had their throats cut already."

Helen hadn't been in any condition to obtain or read a newspaper, so her answer was no, she wasn't aware of any such thing.

"You don't know about the Buffalo Butcher?" Alice said incredulously. "It's been all over the newspapers. He kills girls like us and cuts symbols into their bodies."

"How horrifying," Helen said. "What kind of symbols?"

"The first one was a pentagon," Alice said to Helen's puzzlement.

"Penta*gram*," Raven said wearily. "A star with five points."

"It's the symbol of the Devil," May said.

"I've had quite enough of this morbid talk," Grace said, rising from the table. "And I suggest you girls find a more pleasant topic of conversation." She left and walked into the rear of the house.

"The second one had a little daisy cut into her skin," Olive whispered.

"That's a far cry from the symbol of the Devil," said May. "I wonder what significance that has?"

"Grace has a book on floriography," Alice said. "That might give us a clue."

"What's floriography?" Raven asked.

Alice seemed very pleased with herself. "The language of flowers. Every flower has a meaning—a symbolic significance. You know, as lilies are used for mourning."

She got up and scanned the shelves in the corner of the parlor. She returned with a thick book and began paging through it. "Daffodil . . . dahlia . . . here it is," she said. "Daisy. Let's see what it says." Alice ran her finger down the page. "It says here that daisy symbolizes purity, innocence, and true love."

"Well, at least he's got a sense of humor," Raven said.

"It does seem a rather odd mark, given the victim," Helen said. "It's probably his way of poking fun."

"What kind of person would know the language of flowers?" Raven wondered. "A florist?"

"A florist, certainly," said Olive.

"Florists don't seem like the murdering type," Helen said.

"Bell," Raven said, "wait a while. You'll find out that if there's one thing you can never tell about a man, it's what type he is—until he gets you alone."

CHAPTER 14 ::
THE FERN

Two weeks passed, and as her new life required, Miss Bell carefully locked Helen Crosby away in some secret place, along with her street clothes.

Helen found that she liked the other girls. It was well to be somewhat guarded around Grace—she was the boss, after all—but with the other ladies Helen found the kind of social outlet she'd been craving with her sister and then, disastrously, with Dr. Grand. Olive, May, and Alice were all generally gregarious young ladies, and seemed to accept their lot with a wry sense of resignation. If the three of them had a motto, it would be that *things could always be worse.*

Raven was the exception. The Indian girl was cool and reserved, and while there could be no doubt that she was beautiful, poised, and—judging by the number of her regulars—unusually gifted in bed, she kept herself at arm's length from the other girls. Toward Grace she was deferential, but not obsequious; if anything, she seemed to carry around a barely disguised resentment for the madam. But like the others, she would never dare challenge Grace openly, lest she be sold on to The Hooks.

Most of the girls would sneak down individually in the late morning to spirit back to their rooms a little something to tide them over, but unless a girl was feeling unwell, taking luncheon as a group was one of the house rules. It was at luncheon that Grace would brief them on the evening's clients—anyone especially notable, an alderman or the like— or someone possessed of unusual tastes that needed catering to. Then the girls would decide which one of them would be best-suited to the task.

Also at luncheon, Grace would share with the girls the newspapers, which in their somewhat cloistered existence were their only source of something approaching uncensored and unfiltered information about the world outside. Helen's musical and precise voice soon got her unanimously elected as the news reader. She was able to select the articles and read them aloud to the rest, and Grace seemed to enjoy listening as much as did the other ladies.

As July rolled into August, at one such luncheon the papers broke fresh bad news with their usual good cheer. Helen held up the front page for all to see, and then read:

BUTCHER STRIKES AGAIN!!!

Fallen Woman Almost Decapitated

Tenderloin in Uproar!

"'Another fallen woman—'" she began.

"*Fallen woman*," Raven sniffed.

"For every *fallen* woman there are a hundred *risen* men," May said.

"Say, that's funny!" said Olive. "Where did you hear that one?"

"Golly, you must think I'm a complete idiot. I made it up."

"That is pretty good," Helen said. "May I continue?"

The girls fell silent again and Helen resumed:

> . . . *but this time not a common prostitute—*

"I'm sorry, but I pride myself on being an *uncommon* prostitute," Raven said to general laughter.

"Girls, will you please allow Miss Bell to continue without interruption?" Grace admonished.

Helen started again:

> . . . *this time not a common prostitute but a woman suspected of arranging liaisons with prominent local men, was found murdered early Tuesday morning near the intersection of North and Michigan Streets.*

Helen paused, knowing that the girls would want to discuss the location.

"Stone's throw from here," May said. "That's right over near the hospital."

"It says as much here," Helen said, and resumed:

> *The woman was found with her throat cut, not far from the ambulance barn associated with the General Hospital. By the time detectives arrived on the scene, the woman was long dead, having been dispatched, it is believed, the evening before.*
>
> *Two Polish boys playing a twilight game of hide-and-seek stumbled across the corpse. The boys, Pete Domanski and Michael Cieslewicz, were playing hide-and-seek around a disused section of trolley line running behind the barn, when one of them crouched down next to the tracks. In a patch of weeds not two feet from his hiding spot was the woman's body. He and his friend then summoned the police.*
>
> *The victim bore similar marks to previous recent murders: a deep gash across her throat, but also several additional cuts and bruises, indicating that the woman put up a desperate struggle for life before succumbing to her wounds. This unfortunate, like the others, had been incised a design that detectives identified as either a fern or feather.*

In a small inset box, there was an artist's rendering of the symbol.

> *This brings it to three murders believed to be performed by the same hand, that of the man who has come to be known as the Buffalo Butcher.*
>
> *No comment had yet been received from Mayor Lennox nor from the Common Council at the time*

this newspaper went to press. It is expected that more information will become available by the evening edition.

Helen carefully folded the paper and set it down next to her. "Well, what do you make of that?"

"This is getting bad," Olive said. "Three ladies now, and presumably by the same hand. The first two were streetwalkers, and that's awful risky, but this one was a call girl. High class."

"You know," May said, "they could be right. It could very well be Jack the Ripper himself."

"He stopped killing a long time ago," Raven said. "And he was in London."

"Not that long ago. Ten or fifteen years?" Helen said.

"And a few days on a fast steamship, and he's in New York," May added.

Olive pointed to the rendering of the fern. "Why a fern, I wonder?"

"Could be a feather," Raven said.

"It's a pretty ragged looking feather, if you ask me," May said.

Raven frowned. "Well, it's a pretty ragged fern, too."

"I'm really scared. I'm afraid to go outside," Olive said.

"Go in the company of one or more of your sisters, Miss Moon," Grace interjected. "A man like this wants to catch women alone and unawares. And do try not to be so much of a worry-wart."

"Yes, ma'am," said Olive.

"I was hoping to do the Pan on my day off this week," May said. "I don't want to miss that. I'll never get another chance."

"Why don't we all go together?" Helen suggested.

"No thanks," Raven said. "Five whores at the Pan. They'll think we're setting up shop on the Midway. Imagine, the five of us in *these* getups." She looked down at her bright lavender dress whose neckline dived almost to her navel.

"I'll let you use your street clothes on Wednesday," Grace said, "if you all go together, and don't get yourselves into any trouble."

"You would do that?" Olive said.

"Yes, my dear, I would."

"What do you say, girls?" Helen asked. "It would be so much fun!"

"You used to work there, Bell," Raven said. "Why would you care about seeing it again?"

"Well, because I was working, I really didn't see it properly," Helen replied. "And even if I had, I think it'd be fun to see it with all of you."

"When you think about it," Alice said, "imagine how much money we could make if we did set up a little concession on the Midway."

"Blowjobs fifty cents," Raven offered. "There'd be men lined up for miles. They'd kill us."

"I wouldn't blow *anyone* for less than a dollar," May said. "I hate the taste of that stuff."

"You have to time it so they shoot it back a ways," Alice said helpfully. "Into your throat. It just slides down from there."

"What does it cost here, Mrs. Harrington?" Helen asked. "Just for a blowjob."

"Ten dollars," Grace said.

"That's a bargain, if you ask me," Olive said. "It's nearly as much work, and I don't get a thing out of it."

"Including a child," Raven said dourly. "Mrs. Harrington, I hereby volunteer for blowjob duty. I'm sick and tired of being humped by four men a night."

"Four men a night is really not *that* many," said Alice.

"It's four *too* many, if you ask me," Raven said. "And in my case, almost every last one insists I do some kind of naked war dance, or some other horseshit, before they'll fuck me. Do you know how *tiring* that gets?"

"That explains all the whooping and thumping from your room," May said. "And here I thought you were just having a good time."

"I'm sorry you have to do that, dear," Helen said.

Raven looked at her, puzzled. "Oh, it's fine. Comes with the territory."

AFTER THE LATEST CRIME, and in the best tradition of public service, Mayor Lennox decided that it was high time to deflect blame from himself. So he invited a few trustworthy reporters from several of the leading Buffalo papers—the *Courier*, the *Enquirer*, the *News*, and the *Commercial*—to meet with him personally. When they were all assembled, the mayor drew himself up to his full height—five-and-a-half feet, on tiptoes.

"Gentlemen," he began, "I asked you here today to appeal to your civic sense. In this summer, our city is in the national limelight. To such a degree, in fact, that in a matter of weeks the president of the United States himself will be in our midst. And yet, for all the good going on in our city, we must acknowledge that perfection is possible only in the next world."

"Your Honor," interrupted Bill Heath, a known gadfly over at the *Enquirer*, "I'm sure everyone's time here is valuable. Do you have some statement for us about these grisly murders going on around town? People are afraid to leave their homes."

Lennox cleared his throat. "Yes, yes, Mr. Heath, naturally I do have thoughts about that. In a city of our size—more than three hundred fifty thousand souls in permanent residence, and at least another hundred thousand on any day during the Pan—one must expect the occasional crime. However sanguinary."

"Sanguinary?" Heath said. "That's an understatement. Three women have been almost beheaded."

Bernie Feldman from the *Courier* piped up. Feldman was known to be friendly with Superintendent Ball. "Does Chief Ball have a suspect or suspects?"

This was the mayor's opening. He shook his head slowly and with deep sadness.

"I'm afraid Ball seems baffled by these crimes," he said.

"How do you mean *baffled*?" Feldman said. "Are you suggesting he's not up to the job?"

The mayor stroked his chin. "I didn't say that."

"I know," the reporter said. "I asked if you were suggesting it."

"I do not believe so," Lennox said.

"Is this going to prevent the president from making his visit?" asked Mike Peters from the *News*.

"I'm sure the president has far weightier matters to attend to," the mayor said. "I doubt very much that he's even aware of local crimes."

"That's not what I hear from our Washington bureau," said Jack Kelley from the *Commercial*.

This sent a flush of fear down the mayor's spine. "Is that right, Mr. Kelley?" he said, fishing for information.

"McKinley's security detail has had concerns about his visit for some time," Kelley said. "They can't possibly keep an eye on everyone at the Pan. But McKinley likes crowds, so until now they've been at loggerheads. Now these murders have given them something else to prove their point."

"Nonsense," Lennox said. "William McKinley is safer in Buffalo than he is in the White House. He needn't have any concern, if that's what you call it."

"I think that's what most everyone calls it," Kelley said.

"So what's next, Mr. Mayor?" Bill Heath asked. "What's the plan?"

"We have every detective on the force combing the city for clues," the mayor replied. "And I'm informed at least half of the force is now in plain clothes."

"Isn't that only going to encourage crime in other parts of the city?" Feldman chimed in. "At present, the matter seems confined to the Tenderloin. But if the whole police force is concentrated there, as you say, what's to stop serious crimes elsewhere?"

"I didn't say the *whole* force," Lennox said.

Feldman consulted his notebook. "You said 'at least half,' plus 'every' detective."

"*Half* and *every*, Mr. Feldman, are colloquial approximations. Figures of speech. I don't mean them literally."

"What percentage, then, would you say? To be more precise?"

"I don't know that I can give a more precise figure," Lennox said, feeling his collar getting tighter.

"Are the rumors true that you're considering disguising women as prostitutes and using them as part of your plainclothes force?"

"That's absurd," the mayor said. Actually the question smarted a bit, because two years before the mayor had tried exactly the same thing with two very attractive female volunteers. He and Ball had soon learned that their two deputies had gone native, and in a month had earned enough from their fellow officers of the law to buy themselves half a duplex in East Buffalo.

"How soon do you think you'll run a suspect to earth?" Kelley said, piling on. "I don't need to tell you, Mr. Mayor, but my editors are hearing from leading businessmen—"

Lennox pulled out his watch and glanced at it with apparent surprise. "Gentlemen, I must apologize for cutting this a little short—"

"Odd choice of words," Heath muttered, provoking titters.

"—but I have another pressing engagement," the mayor went on, glaring at Heath. "Thank you for coming today. I will certainly keep you informed."

The next morning, Mayor Lennox arrived in his office to find, as usual, the major morning papers, all neatly ironed and sitting on his desk. With a shiver of dread, he picked up the *Commercial*—by far the most sober of the local rags—first. The headline read:

LENNOX AT A LOSS!
M'Kinley's Visit in Jeopardy?

He turned it face down and looked at the *News*.

BALL BAFFLED, MAYOR CLAIMS
No Clues to Buffalo Butcher's Identity

Lennox almost hadn't the heart to look at the *Enquirer*, which was nothing if not hyperbolic. He took a deep breath and scanned the front page.

HIZZONER'S SHARP TONGUE
Mayor 'Cuts Off' Reporters on Butcher

"Fuck," Lennox said to himself, throwing the paper aside. "Just *fuck*."

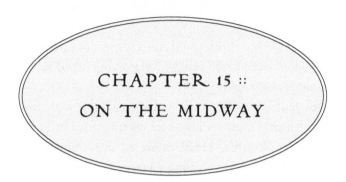

CHAPTER 15 ::

ON THE MIDWAY

On Wednesday, as early in the morning as ladies of the evening could manage, the five girls took the streetcar to the Pan-American grounds. Grace had wagged her finger at them before they left: no smoking, even while away from the house, and they, and their street clothes, had to be returned by midnight, and not a second later.

They stepped down from the trolley at the fair's Amherst Gate.

"I've lost weight," Raven said, looking down at her slightly baggy attire. "How the hell does one lose weight sitting around all day?"

"The war dances?" May snickered.

"Very funny, Flower," Raven said. "At least my clothes still fit."

"That's not very nice," Alice said. "May simply has an ample bosom."

"I have an ample *everything*," Olive said with a degree of dismay. "I thought I'd have to rip out the seams in this dress to get into it this morning."

"Of course, Bell looks stunning," May said. "I have to say, Bell, I'd give you five dollars to let me run my hands over your body. I can see your nipples right through your shirtwaist."

"Can we change the subject?" Raven said impatiently. "I'd much rather see the fair instead of talking about Bell's nipples."

"I second that," Helen said.

The girls each bought a fifty-cent daily ticket and walked into the great Exposition. They crossed the mighty Triumphal Bridge across

Mirror Lake, which reflected the shields and banners of the nations of both Americas as gondolas rippled by beneath them.

"It's magical," Olive said, looking around. "Every one of these buildings is like a fairy-tale castle."

The good people of Buffalo had raised almost two million dollars to build the Exposition. All of the buildings, however grand, were temporary—made of lath and plaster, painted and gilded, intended to last a season, if that. Only halfway through its life, though, the place was already beginning to show its age. Countless dogs pissing against the foundations of bridges and buildings had stained them a weird shade of chartreuse, and the many colorful hues of the Exposition buildings were starting to fade under what had been thus far a relentlessly wet summer.

Still, on any given day fifty to a hundred thousand visitors toured the place, spending twenty-five cents here, fifty cents there, and a dollar most everywhere. It was a very expensive vacation, when one included train fare and lodging at least two dollars a day, plus meals. Still, eight million people—one in every nine Americans—found the time and money to do the Pan.

Since each vast building—Ethnology, Music, Electricity, and so forth—was crammed full of small exhibits from thousands of manufacturers of everything from cigarettes to envelopes, most visitors quickly found the exhibition buildings frankly rather dull. The real fun of the Pan-American was on the Midway.

The Midway was a serpentine path winding through the various concessions, an outsized version of the arcade at a county fair. But at the Pan, the shitty little amusements of a local event were replaced by vast and complex immersive attractions. There was the Aerio Cycle, the world's largest Ferris wheel. There was a rocket to the moon, a visit to the land of the dead, and the nostalgic Old Plantation, recalling the supposed happier days before Emancipation.

Scattered along the Midway were little villages—like Alt Nürnberg—which recreated other countries that most people could never hope to see in person. These villages—Fair Japan, Darkest Africa, Streets of Mexico, and others—were peopled by actual natives from these exotic locales who had come to Buffalo for the summer. It was as much a lark for them as for the gawking visitors filing through, or seemed like it. But months of trying to look indigenous could become wearing. The denizens of the Esquimau Village had it the worst, forced to endure the humid Buffalo summer in full polar regalia: fur-trimmed sealskins, vast mittens, and mukluks.

Though in truth, quite a few of the Japanese and Mexicans, Cubans and Filipinos who came to Buffalo liked it well enough to remain behind after the Pan was over. Without much English, however, the men were generally compelled to take hard, low-paying labor on the Lake Erie wharves and grain elevators. The women—young or old—frequently became featured attractions at specialty brothels. The opportunity to fuck an Esquimau was not something easily passed over by the connoisseur of the recherché.

The Indian Congress—a supposed conclave of sixty different tribes of the dwindling Native American population—was particularly popular. There one could watch a sham battle, demonstrations of basket weaving, and whooping war dances. How many of the Indians were genuine Indians, though, was something of a mystery. "Winona, the Sioux Crack-Shot," billed as an Indian Annie Oakley, was rumored to be a white woman. But Geronimo himself was there, and for an additional ten cents guests could have their photographs taken with the famous warrior. Once a month, throngs gathered for the White Dog Feast at which a local dog—sourced personally from the pound by the Pan's general manager, F. T. Cummins—was slaughtered and consumed by the Indians.

Helen, May, Alice, and Olive all wanted to see the Indian Congress, but Raven refused.

"I'd rather have my eyes gouged out," she said.

"Don't be such a spoilsport," said May.

"Are you afraid you'll be recognized?" Alice asked.

"For fuck's sake, Star," Raven said, "not every Indian knows every other one."

Helen tugged at Olive's arm. "Come on, girls. If Raven doesn't want to go, let's respect her wishes. There are lots of other attractions we can see together."

"Why, thank you, Bell," Raven said.

There was some short-lived grumbling, and instead the five walked over to the Infant Incubator exhibit, where actual premature babies publicly struggled for life inside the novel devices. While they were standing their marveling at the tiny infants, one of the nurses monitoring the machines quietly draped a black cloth over one of them, disconnected it from the electric supply, and hustled it away on its casters. The crowd murmured and whispered, but didn't leave.

"Ugh," May said after they left the incubator demonstration. "Damn me if I don't need a pick me up after *that*."

Olive trailed behind the others, and after a half-minute Helen noticed she was missing. She turned to find Olive walking along slowly, dabbing her eyes with a handkerchief.

"Olive," Helen said, "are you crying?"

Olive turned away, sniffling. Then started to cry in earnest. "The little one *died*," she sobbed, "right in front of us."

Smack-dab in the middle of the teeming Midway, Helen put her arms around Olive. "It's all right, dear," she said into Olive's hair. "She's in a better place now."

"With the other angels," Olive wept. "I know, but it's so very sad."

"It's life," May said.

"Not now, Flower," Helen said, still holding Olive as disgruntled fairgoers parted around them.

They sat down on a pair of wooden benches to let Olive compose herself.

Helen consulted her guide map of the Exposition. "Olive, look! This will be fun. There's a sculptor just up ahead who makes plaster models."

"That does sound like fun," Olive said. "I'm sorry, girls. I'll be fine."

They got up again, Helen arm-in-arm with Olive, and just beyond the Fair Japan village, they saw a row of painted plaster faces strung from a wire above a concession whose sign read:

August Langenbahn's Plaster Casts.

People were lined up for a chance to have plaster casts made of their children's feet, their hands and feet, and some even were reclining in wicker chairs with the stuff smeared over their faces, breathing through small straws that poked out of their nostrils.

The five ladies stood there watching Langenbahn's patrons, laughing at their newly minted plaster hands, feet, and faces.

"I'd like to make one of my tits," May said. "I'd put it in my bookcase."

"You'd have to throw out all your books to make room," Raven said.

May sniffed. "You're just jealous."

"You do have nice tits," Olive said, trying to cheer things up.

Raven laughed. "Yeah, she does, but no one's got Bell's magic pussy. Hey Bell, why don't you have them make a cast of that so we can see if it's different somehow."

"It's not any different," Helen said.

"Yes, it is. I've seen it," said Alice.

"How did you manage that?"

"Bell was passed out on her bed one night last week, naked as a jaybird. I saw it."

"What did it look like?" Olive asked.

"Alice, be nice," Helen said.

"She shaves it."

"You *do*?" May and Raven said in unison. "Why?"

Helen blushed. "Just something a little different, I suppose. Men don't know what to make of it. It gets them all hopped-up. I don't know why."

"I'm shaving mine as soon as I get back," Olive said. "I can't seem to get anyone hopped-up these days. Maybe because I'm fat."

"Men like a woman with a little flesh on her," Alice said.

"Not lately," said Olive.

They walked along the Midway, arms linked.

"Do you think people know what we do?" Helen asked as they passed Dreamland, the Exposition's Hall of Mirrors.

"Some do, some don't," Raven replied with a shrug. "I've already recognized three men I've screwed. Of course, they were all with their wives, so I didn't let on."

"I've spied two," May said.

"I won't be going anywhere near the Bell Exchange, that's for sure," Helen said.

Alice chuckled. "Hate to burst your bubble, honey, but in case you haven't noticed, half the men here recognize *you*."

"They do not."

"I do sometimes wonder how many men have jacked off to your photos in the telephone directory," Raven said.

"A *lot*," May offered.

The girls stopped for a drink at the beer garden in Alt Nürnberg. Helen thought to protest, but then decided that the old city was charming, and she wasn't about to let Dr. Grand ruin it for her.

"I'd sure like a cigarette," May said, looking into her suds.

"Don't," Alice said. "We don't need that kind of attention."

"Night off tonight, girls," Helen said. "What are we going to do?"

"I've got to write to my family in Arizona," Raven said, and then laughed. "Boring, I know. But they think I'm a waitress, so I have to keep up appearances. Thank God they don't ever leave the reservation."

"I have to mend my stockings," May said.

"Me, too," said Alice.

"That leaves just you and me, Olive," Helen said. "I plan to get high, and I mean *really* high. Want to join me?"

"What do you have?"

Helen laughed. "Everything. Tonight, though, I'm shooting morphine. I'm not wasting any time. I want to vanish."

"Yeah, I'll shoot some with you, if you don't mind."

"My treat," Helen said. "I'll shave your beaver if you want, too."

"Fun! Yes, let's," Olive said.

"Where do you shoot it? The morphine, I mean. I don't see any marks on your arms," May asked.

"Back of my knees," Helen said. "No one looks there."

"You do know, Bell," Raven said, "that dope just wears you out faster. Don't think that Grace won't sell you off to The Hooks—if you get hooked. She's not sentimental."

Helen shrugged. "I'm already hooked. It doesn't take long. Anyone who tells you different has never shot up."

"It doesn't scare you?" May asked.

"There's only one thing that scared me. Atropine."

"What's that?"

"Belladonna. Like the eye drops, but more concentrated. Grand gave it to me once. Let me tell you, it does strange things."

"Like what?" Raven said, despite herself.

"Makes you go stiff as a board," Helen said. "You simply can't move, no matter how much you want to. Eyes go all wide, and you can't see a thing. And you have really frightening dreams and visions."

"Why in the world would you want to take that?" Alice asked.

Helen shrugged. "I didn't have much choice."

"Not that I give a shit," Raven said, "but I wish you wouldn't take that stuff."

Helen put her arm around Raven. "That's about the nicest thing anyone's ever said to me."

THE GIRLS LAUGHED AND drank at Alt Nürnberg for a couple hours, then rode the Aerio Cycle, took the Trip to the Moon, and marveled at the Upside-Down House and Bonner the Mathematical Horse. After they had a bite of supper, it was almost sundown.

"Now for the real show," Olive said. "The lights are said to be magical."

"Let's walk over to the Court of Fountains," May suggested. "That's supposed to be the best place to see them."

"I'm so fucking sweaty I may jump in," Raven said. "Fish me out before the lights come on, will you?"

"I don't want this day to end," Olive said as they sat on the edge of one of the great fountains encircling the Electric Tower, a mighty structure that was the centerpiece of the entire Exposition.

"It has been a wonderful day," said May.

"You were so fortunate to work here, Bell," Alice said. "You got to see this every single day."

Helen looked at the spouting water shooting up from hundreds of jets. "Thing is, I never really noticed it until today."

They sat quietly in intimate solitude, watching the water and the endless procession of passersby. Dusk was gathering quickly, and soon thousands of tiny electric lights, strung along the outlines of every building, began to glow. Yellow, at first, and then bright gold. Some twinkled like miniature stars; others streaked like comets across the dancing water of the fountain. Searchlights atop the soaring Electric Tower began to sweep the horizon, playing over the dark city, the great lake, and as far as thundering Niagara Falls, twenty miles away.

"It's what I hope heaven will be like," Olive said, marveling.

"It'll be better," said Alice. "Heaven's all gold and jewels. All this is plaster and paint."

Olive sighed. "I hope I get to see it someday. I'm afraid I won't, though."

Helen sidled up next to her friend. "Moon, if you're not in Heaven, no one will be. We'll all be there together."

"What about Raven?" May said. "Don't Indians go to the Happy Hunting Ground or something?"

Raven rolled her eyes in the starlight of the Exposition. "For fuck's sake, Flower, I'm Catholic."

THE GIRLS RETURNED TO Grace's place well before midnight, folded their street clothes again until the next time, and then slept until noon the next day. They lolled around, doing their mending, reading, or nothing. Around three o'clock, Olive rapped on Helen's door. Helen was still in her underwear.

"Time for our siesta!" Olive announced.

"You've spent too much time in the Streets of Mexico," Helen laughed, and pulled her friend into her room.

They sat on the bed and talked for a while, until Helen looked at the time. "Time to get naked. You're getting a shave."

"Oh goody!" Olive said, jumping up and shucking layers of clothing.

Helen wriggled out of her silk drawers.

"It's true!" Olive said, looking at Helen's crotch.

"Yup. What do you think?"

"I think it does look rather exotic that way."

"We'll soon be twins. Now lie down and let me work my magic."

She went into the bathroom and returned with her razor and soap.

"Be careful!" Olive said, staring at the bright blade.

"I'm an old hand at this. And we're not high yet. I wouldn't dare try it then."

Olive laughed and lay still while Helen shaved her. When she toweled away the last of the soap, she examined her handiwork.

"Perfect," Helen said. "Take a look in the mirror!"

Olive stood and turned this way and that in the cheval mirror. "I love it. I can't believe what I've been missing!"

"Good," Helen replied, folding her razor and setting it on the bedside table. "And now you get to have another new experience."

"The morphine?"

"Exactly! Dinner will be in a few hours, so we have just enough time to really get flying."

"What do I have to do?" Olive asked.

"Nothing. Just relax."

Olive lay down again, and Helen retrieved her syringe and small bottle from her bureau. She shook out three small pills from the bottle and crushed them in the bowl of a soupspoon and added some water.

"These soluble ones are the best," she said as Olive watched, spellbound.

Helen took up the syringe and pulled the plunger back, sucking the cloudy liquid into the glass barrel. She sat down on the side of the bed, crossed her legs—ankle on the opposite knee—and slowly introduced the needle into the soft skin behind her bent knee. Then she straightened out her leg.

"Well, hello there," she said quietly. "*Much* better. Now I'll jab you. Just relax."

The syringe was now about one-third full. Olive lay on her side, and Helen found a likely spot on the back of Olive's knee and depressed the plunger.

"Good heavens," she whispered a few seconds later. "I can see why you like this."

"It's pretty wondrous stuff," Helen mumbled. "Like I said to Raven, I know I'm hooked, but I don't care."

The two girls lay there naked on Helen's bed, cruising on the morphine. Olive threw her leg drowsily over her friend.

"Thanks for shaving me. I didn't want to say it, but I'm terrified of razors. I couldn't even look when you were doing it."

"I felt the same way, at first. I will say it's easier to do it on someone else than on yourself."

"Whew, this dope is making me so very dreamy," Olive said.

"Uh-huh," Helen said.

"May I ask you a question?"

"Of course."

"Do you think I look old?"

"No, I don't think you look old. You can't be more than thirty."

"I'm not quite twenty-two," Olive said, with a snort.

"I'm sorry, dear," Helen said.

"It's all right. I can see myself as well as anyone. But I have a feeling that Grace is going to sell me soon."

"She wouldn't do that."

"Helen, you are a breath of fresh air, but you're new. Grace does it all the time. I know I don't look good anymore. I got cysts on my ovaries after—having something taken care of—and they made me fat. And I like food too much."

"Where would you go, if Grace did as you say?"

"I don't know. I don't think The Hooks, but you never know. Whoever's willing to pay the most."

Helen lay there, drifting with the morphine. "What I don't understand," she said after a while, "is this. You've been here what, four years?"

"About that," Olive said. "I was seventeen when Grace took me in."

"So then—why is it that you haven't paid off whatever is owed? Why can't you walk out the door and do as you please?"

Olive rolled onto her side, her pupils tiny poppy seeds in a sea of green. "That's what they tell you, Helen," she said softly. "And it keeps you going, for a while. I paid off what I thought I owed in two years, and I expected my street clothes to be on my bed the day I did."

"And they weren't?"

"No," Olive said, flopping onto her back again. "Of course I asked!

But then I find out there's a long list of things they don't tell you about. Telephone, amounts over the clothing allowance, and—worst of all—the interest. You know the interest is something like fifty percent a year. You can't possibly catch up. I owed more after two years than I did at the beginning."

"How much did you owe at the beginning?" Helen asked.

"Two hundred fifty."

"Then I'm royally fucked," Helen said. "Do you know I'm in hock for a thousand?"

"I'm very sorry to hear that. You don't deserve that."

Helen sniffed. "As somebody once said to me, God forbid any of us gets what we deserve."

"Sad but true."

"Oh well," Helen said. "However long it lasts, I like it here. I like you, Olive. I hope you don't go anywhere for a long time."

Olive snuggled against Helen. "I hope not either, Helen. You've been so good to me ever since you arrived. Yesterday at the Pan. And today you cleaned me up downstairs and shared your morphine." She started to sob. "You always make me feel special. And you never ask for anything in return."

"Dear, I don't want anything in return. You're my friend, and that's enough."

WHILE HELEN WAS SHAVING Olive's beaver, Grace and Charley were sitting in the lobby of The Alzora, smoking a cigarette and killing time before things got hopping.

"How are the girls handling the news?" Charley asked. "The murders, I mean."

"They're rattled."

"I don't blame them. You know the cops don't have any ideas at all, and they'd just as soon sweep it under the rug anyhow, so long as the guy stays in the Tenderloin."

"Same old story, Charley."

"No doubt. Say, how's the Bell Girl working out, by the way?"

Grace took a drag on her cigarette. "She's a fucking machine, Charley. I've never had anyone like her."

Charley shook his head. "One thing you have to say about Grand. He's rarely wrong about talent. Hey, I almost forgot. When do I get my poke?"

"You're a pig, Charley, you know that?"

"A promise is a promise, Grace. I want to see for myself what all the fuss is about."

"Fine," she said. "I'm sure she's in her room now, high as a kite. I've never seen a girl put so much coke up her ass. She shoots morphine, too."

"Not good, Grace. You know how that goes."

"I do, but it's her life. You want me to ask if she can see you now?"

Charley adjusted himself. "I wouldn't mind, actually. Just thinking about it's got me half—"

"Shut up, Charley. You're a pig."

CHARLEY RAPPED GENTLY ON Helen's door.

She peeked out. "Hello, Charley. Long time no see."

"What's it been, Helen? Two months?" he asked, stepping into her room.

"At least. Seems like two years."

"Dog years in this business," Charley said. "Grace tells me you've really taken to the life."

Helen laughed. "I'm not so sure about that. When you're out of options, you might as well make the best of the one you have."

"Words to live by."

"I suppose. Anyhow, Grace said I owe you one."

"If that's all right with you," he said.

"Why not, when I have you to thank for all the good things coming my way these days?"

"Very funny," he said.

"I'm kidding. So what is it that you'd like?"

He shrugged. "I'm not fancy. Just straight up is fine. I don't like to pull out, though. My timing is shit."

"That's fine," Helen said. She began shucking her layers of clothing.

"Say, Helen," Charley said, stripping down, "what do you think of these murders?"

"I feel sorry for the girls who died."

"Are you afraid?"

She smiled. "Not in the least. I'm just as sorry for the girls who live."

"Aw, Helen. I don't like to hear you talk that way."

"It's nothing," she said, lying back nude and running her hands over her body. "I suppose I ought to be grateful. But this won't last, Charley. You know it, and I know it. Whether it's a razor or—something else— this only ends one way."

Charley lay down next to her. "I sometimes feel bad about you," he said, brushing back a wisp of hair that had fallen across her face.

"Why? You were only doing your job."

"I know. But sometimes it's harder than others. If I had it to do over again, I would buy you a one-way ticket back to Hamilton."

"You're a sweet man, Charley Willard. But you know, I probably would have just come back again. I'm my own worst enemy."

"Aren't we all," he said.

They lay there side-by-side.

"Grace says that you like dope."

She looked at him dreamily. "Who doesn't? You want to do some with me before we fuck?"

"Naah," he said. "It's not a good habit. You need to be careful with that stuff."

Helen chuckled. "Too late."

"You really are beautiful, Miss Bell."

"Thank you. Well, how about we get you all emptied out?"

She reached over and squeezed Charley's cock. "What's wrong? I know you like me, Charley. But I sure wouldn't know from *this*."

He propped himself up on one elbow. "Listen, Helen, I'm worried about you."

"Whatever for?"

"Look, I've seen a lot of girls come and go. They're all different, but they all have one thing in common. Not one of them takes to this life as fast as you have."

"So what's wrong with that?"

"Because you're really not the type. I think maybe—you're . . . I don't know the word. Pretending. Like an actress. But the real you—where is she? I saw her around here, not so long ago. I liked her, Helen. I really did."

She kissed him on the cheek. "Come on, Charley. I don't want to talk about all this. It just brings up things I want to forget."

"You can't forget your whole life."

"Who says?" she said, laughing. "What would I want to remember? It's all been shit. Orphaned. Fell into Grand's clutches the first month I'm in Buffalo, then got raped by his friend. My sister hates me. But I'm good at this, at least. And I like it well enough. Come on now, feel my pussy." She took his hand and put it between her legs. "You feel that?"

"Yeah, of course I feel it."

"Does it feel good?"

"Uh-huh. Beautiful."

"And look at you now," Helen said. "I knew you couldn't resist me forever."

He climbed on top of her. "Helen—"

"Shhh," she said, putting her finger on his lips. "Shut up and fuck me."

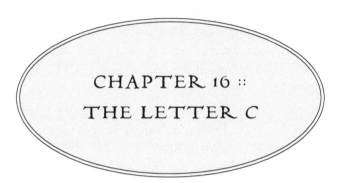

CHAPTER 16 ::
THE LETTER C

The girls were still reliving their magical day at the Pan-American when another jolt hit. There had been a fourth murder in the Tenderloin. This time the deceased was not a whore, but a nurse—although not an *ordinary* nurse.

Being a nurse was quite a favored position, if all-consuming. Nurses rarely married; if they did, they left the profession. Most young women interested in a nursing career were more attracted to young doctors than to the nursing profession itself, and it was well-known that interns and doctors took their liberties with the young members of the nursing corps. It was better to marry a doctor than to become a nurse and remain a spinster.

Mary Sweeney wasn't any recent transplant who didn't know her way around the city. She had been born and raised in Buffalo, gone to nursing school at the General Hospital, and since her graduation had been working in the Tenderloin District, mostly out of the goodness of her heart. Her parents had money, and so nursing was more a calling than an occupation. There were darker rumors about the good-hearted Mary, however.

However good their mathematics or their whirling sprays or spermicidal concoctions, prostitutes did, in fact, get pregnant, and regularly. Possibly other than contracting syphilis, getting knocked up was the worst thing that could happen to a working girl. No one, other than a few perverts, wanted to fuck a pregnant lady, and then if the baby was carried to term, any respectable house would turn the mother and child out without a qualm. Men came to brothels to get away from screaming brats and loose pussies. They had all that at home.

How to handle it, then? These weren't women of the middle-, upper middle- or upper-classes, who could generally prevail upon the unlucky sire to do the right thing and marry them. These were whores, and no one was marrying one of *those*. Accordingly, the poorest—streetwalkers and crib-women in The Hooks—took matters into their own hands, getting good and drunk and then introducing a knitting needle or hatpin into the cervix to break the water and induce labor. They might also ingest one of a number of toxic potions that were known abortifacients. All of that was risky, though, and not infrequently the mother would follow her unborn into the afterlife.

Naturally, any girl with more than two nickels to rub together would resort to a handful of risk-taking doctors who had built a highly illegal, land-office business in taking care of such problems. These doctors—sometimes even notable ones—could earn substantial pocket money providing after-hours abortions. Even these procedures were not without risk to the patient, most notably from abdominal sepsis or kidney failure from unsterile instruments.

Physicians undertook a different kind of risk: six months in Erie County Penitentiary if caught performing "unlawful operations," as they were euphemistically called. But those doctors who hadn't any qualms about breaking a few laws could make fifty dollars, easy, in a half-hour. And if they could find a decent nurse to assist with the procedure, administering ether or chloroform to anaesthetize the patient, things could go even more quickly.

Enter Mary Sweeney. Mary was what many might have called a do-gooder. Without any financial need to earn her living, she volunteered her time to a variety of Buffalo medical charities: the Newsboys and Bootblacks Home, the Home for Friendless Women, and Élodie's Refuge, a home for elderly men without means or families to help them. Somehow she drifted into the whirlpool eddy of the Tenderloin, where she started feeling sorry for the working girls. She joined forces with a couple of scofflaw doctors, thinking it was better to provide a semi-sanitary service for the unfortunate ladies of the evening then to see them sent to the Anatomical Board.

Not everyone saw it that way. In fact, most did not. And there were some religious crusaders who called her, publicly, the "Angel of Death," in parody of Clara Barton. In their eyes, killing a single Mary would be saving hundreds of children—an easy calculation.

Mary's body was found behind an old brick rowhouse near Washington and Eagle, where a couple of abortionists were known to have set up operations. What was left of her had been stuffed headfirst into an ash can, legs and feet sticking out like chopsticks. Like the others, her throat had been cut, ear to ear; but this time something else had gone on, too. She had been neatly opened from the apex of her vagina to her belly button, and her womb carefully removed. What was worse, the blood loss from this incision was far greater than that from her throat, suggesting that the organ had been removed while she was still very much alive, and that the cut across the neck was something more like a *coup de grâce*. One could only hope that the unfortunate young lady had been sedated before the cutting began.

Mary, too, had been screwed before, during, or after the event. The ejaculate—unusually copious, as before—however, was discovered in her colon, not in the vagina.

Just above the cleft of Mary's buttocks was carved a shallow but bloody letter *C*, probably cut while she was being violated.

THE LUNCHEON DISHES HAVING been taken away, Helen cleared her throat and snapped the paper open.

"Uh oh, girls. Another one!" She read:

FRIEND OF THE FALLEN FALLS!

Infamous Tenderloin Nurse Found in Ash Can

Butcher Strikes Again

Mary Sweeney, a nurse infamous for assisting in numerous illegal operations, fell under the Butcher's knife last night. Her body was found last evening by a watchman patrolling the area.

While not the typical prey of the Buffalo Butcher, Nurse Sweeney was nevertheless closely associated with the disorderly houses of the Tenderloin. Perhaps in a nod to the divine justice awaiting Sweeney for her crimes, the woman's generative organs were removed from her body by her murderer and a symbol carved into her flesh.

Helen held up the paper for the girls to see.

"You'd have to think the killer would have some surgical experience to pull off a stunt like that," May interrupted. "Cutting out a uterus in the dark?"

"Did anyone here know Sweeney?" Olive asked.

"I met her a few times," Grace replied. "But I avoided her, because she was indiscreet about what she did."

"Seems unwise," Helen said.

"She wasn't so different from Carrie Nation or Emma Goldman," Grace said. "Those women want to get arrested, because it draws attention to their cause. We don't want that kind of attention."

"Keep reading, Bell," Raven said.

Helen went on:

The mayor, for his part, is said to be convening a group of local dignitaries with a view to stopping the depredations of the Butcher as President McKinley's planned visit to the Pan-American draws nearer by the day.

It is said by reliable sources that the mayor is even considering recruiting a corps of plainclothes female agents who will pose as streetwalkers and Tenderloin jades.

"Tenderloin jades," Helen said. "That stings."

"I love that color," Olive said.

"Moon, I'm buying you a dictionary for Christmas," Raven said.

"That's a long way off," said Olive, "but that's awfully nice of you, Raven."

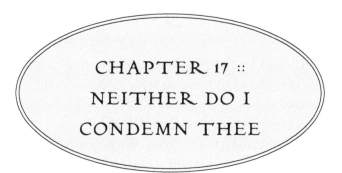

CHAPTER 17 ::
NEITHER DO I
CONDEMN THEE

"I have fucking well had it up to here with this shit!" Mayor Lennox roared when the papers appeared that morning. "Who the hell told these idiots that I'm recruiting plain-clothes whores?"

"Not I," Chief Ball said. "You know what happened last time we tried that."

"Don't remind me. What a nightmare."

"I don't know. I've never seen my men so happy."

"You know, Ball, sometimes you just aren't helpful."

"Sorry, sir."

"Oh, I'm sure you are," Lennox said. "I'm taking the bull by the horns now. I'm going to get the editors of all these goddamned rags together in this room, and I'm going to lay down the law."

Ball frowned. "I don't think they're going to care about that."

"Ha ha, Ball," the mayor said. "I've got an ace in the hole."

"You want me to stick around for the fireworks?"

"No. Better if you can say you hadn't anything to do with it. Less blame for you if it backfires, Ball."

"And more for you if it doesn't."

"Look. Just make sure that there's no more murdering before tomorrow morning when I meet with these assholes. After that, you'll be amazed at how quiet it gets," Lennox said.

"THANK YOU ALL FOR coming here so early today," Lennox said the next morning to the six men sitting at his conference table. "Do we all know one another?"

This was greeted with a good deal of headshaking.

"How about introductions, then?" the mayor said. "We'll just go around the table." He gestured to the man on his right.

"Let me guess, you're the mayor." This sent a ripple of laughter around the room.

"You got me there," Lennox said.

"Good. I'm Orin Gifford of the Anti-Saloon League."

"John Muncey, editor of the *Buffalo News*," the next man said. "Also representing the *Courier* today."

"Reverend Doctor Lemuel Morse Powell, of the Pure Light Mission."

"Jack Stevens, editor of the *Buffalo Commercial*."

"Charles Donaghy, chief editor, *Buffalo Enquirer*."

"Lodowick Jones, Anti-Vice League."

"Thank you all, and again, welcome," the mayor said. "If the members of the press wouldn't mind, I'd like to request they put their notebooks away for the present."

The newspapermen looked at one another, surprised, but after a few grumbles, stowed their notebooks.

"This morning," Mayor Lennox resumed, "we have the three most prominent reformers in Buffalo, and representatives of its four leading papers. You might think it's an unusual gathering, but you'll soon see why it is otherwise. I would like to speak with all of you about these murders that have been happening in the Tenderloin."

"Mr. Mayor—"

The mayor held up his hand. "Hear me out, gentlemen. I brought you hear this morning because it's well past time we all joined hands toward a common good. It is not lost on any of us that murders—even of common prostitutes—generate the very kind of notoriety that is bad for our city. The Pan-American is in full swing. In six weeks, or less, the president himself will come to Buffalo. All eyes, gentlemen, are on our city. We do not need a few murders giving people the impression that Buffalo is a wide-open city."

Lodowick Jones, a young man in his very early twenties, who was wearing a pink dress shirt, raised his hand. "May I comment, your honor?"

"Yes, please."

"As most of you know, I have been doing everything within my power to shut down the Raines hotels and to prevail upon the police department to do their duty and close the bawdy houses of the Tenderloin. Almost fruitlessly, I might add. These killings would not happen if we did not have a concentration of vice in which murder can take root."

"I agree with Mr. Jones," said Gifford of the Anti-Saloon League. "And I will add that if illegal sales of alcohol were curtailed—"

"Or banned entirely," said Reverend Powell.

"Mayor," said Donaghy of the *Enquirer*, "this is big news." His fellow newspapermen nodded in assent. "I've got to get my reporters on this, pronto."

"Please, gentlemen," the mayor said. "You represent the four largest papers in this city. Fully ninety percent of Buffalo's readership. If you don't print something"—he rapped the table with his knuckles—"*it didn't happen.*"

"What are you suggesting?"

"Can you come to the point?" said Muncey from the *News* and the *Courier*. "Now the three of us are neck-and-neck on this story. My reporters are going to be furious."

"It's very simple, gentlemen," the mayor said. "I want us to strike a bargain here today. In short, I'd like to ask that our esteemed gentlemen of the press do not cover any other similar murders, should any occur between now and the conclusion of the president's visit in September."

"I'm confused," Orin Gifford of the Anti-Saloon League said. "Why are Jones and Powell and I even here, if you're striking a deal with the newspapers?"

"There's something in it for everyone," the mayor replied, "and here it is. If the newspapers agree not to cover these or similar murders, I will agree that those papers will have personal access to the president during his visit. I will also agree that the current prohibition on your newsboys peddling papers at the Pan-American will be lifted, and you'll be able to sell as many papers there as you wish."

"What about the news concession holder?" Muncey asked.

"I'll make sure he's well taken care of," the mayor replied. "But with him out of the way, you'll have between fifty and a hundred thousand more newspaper-buying customers per day from now through the closing of the Exposition on November first."

"And what do we get?" Lodowick Jones piped up, his face almost the color of his pink shirt. "It seems like quite a windfall for the papers."

"If you, Reverend Powell, and Mr. Gifford—the three most visible, prominent, and respected members of the city's progressive movement— if you will all denounce the unfortunate victims, past, present, and future—if any—if you will, in essence, point out to your followers that the wages of sin are death, and that prostitutes are putting themselves willingly in harm's way—then as soon as the Pan is closed, my police will clear out the Tenderloin as utterly as Rome did Carthage."

"Speaking for the *News* and the *Courier*," John Muncey said, "you have a deal."

"*Enquirer* is in," said Donaghy.

"As is the *Commercial*," Jack Stevens agreed.

"I'm for it," Lodowick Jones said.

"Done," said Gifford of the Anti-Saloon League.

Reverend Powell remained silent, twiddling his thumbs thoughtfully.

"Reverend Powell," the mayor said after a long wait, "what say you? We are very close to unanimity."

Powell looked up. He was a peculiar-looking fellow, with thin, blonde hair parted in the center and plastered down to his skull with far too much pomade. And, oddest of all, he had no eyelashes, just lines of little nubs along the edges of his eyelids.

"The Pure Light Mission, as most of you know, is located in the heart of the Tenderloin," he said. "I minister to the very fallen women whose lives recently have been taken so brutally."

"Where is this going, Powell?" asked Lodowick Jones. "The man's going to clear out the Tenderloin. Your mission will be obsolete. Wasn't that the idea all along?"

Powell blinked his lashless eyes. "If we could make my mission obsolete by exterminating sin, I'd welcome it. But simply moving everyone sinful out of the Tenderloin means that they'll set up shop in a thousand other scattered places, and be entirely unreachable.

"Also, I cannot fail to think of what Jesus would command. John, chapter eight," he said. "I'm sure you all know the passage, gentlemen. In it, our Lord refused to condemn a fallen woman. 'He who is without sin among you, let him cast the first stone.' But today, you ask me to condemn and denounce the very people for whose sins the Savior shed his blood! And for the sake of—what, exactly? An enormous county fair? More newspaper advertising? A president who represents the rich and the powerful, and cares nothing for the weak and the poor who are my flock? And whom I love?" He paused. "I'm sorry, gentlemen, Mr. Mayor, but this I can never do. Here I stand, and may God help me."

"No more sorry than I am, Reverend Powell," the mayor said. "But, with respect, yours is but one voice. We have agreement from many others represented here."

Powell smiled gently. "That you do, sir. But as for me, I'll be content to be the lone voice crying in the wilderness. And we all know how that story ended."

"With the man's head on a platter," Donaghy muttered under his breath to Jack Stevens, who smiled.

:: PART THREE ::

LOVE

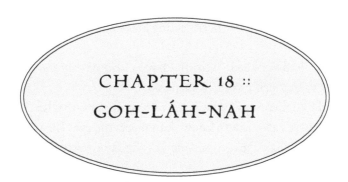

CHAPTER 18 ::
GOH-LÁH-NAH

Between the murders—creeping ever closer to their sanctuary—and an announcement at luncheon by Grace that the Pan-American demand for pussy was so great that each of the girls would have to service five men a night, Helen was dreading the arrival of the nine o'clock hour.

"I know I'm asking a great deal of each of you," Grace had said, "so while we're catching up, you will earn twenty percent of your highest-paying client each night. Instead of the usual ten."

"Pray for small dicks and hair-triggers," Raven had muttered, setting off laughter around the table.

Helen chuckled to herself. Raven. Such a beautiful girl, very smart, and so very tough. Of all of us, she'll be the one who survives.

She looked up at the clock. It wasn't yet eight. In a little more than an hour I have to be Miss Bell, she thought, so I'd better shake off this funk. I guess it doesn't matter what kind of work you do, some days you feel more like it than others. Maybe I'll go downstairs and read a book instead of staring at myself in this damn mirror.

Helen put the finishing touches on her hair, sniffed up a little cocaine, and went downstairs. She found Raven sitting cozily by the bookcase in the corner of the parlor, reading.

"Raven!" she said. "I thought I'd be the only one down this early."

"I can go upstairs if you'd prefer to be by yourself," Raven said, closing her book.

"Not at all," Helen said, sitting down on the settee next to Raven. "I'm *happy* you're here. I've been feeling lonesome all day."

"Why's that?"

Helen tilted her head. "I think I have a little case of the blues."

"What's bothering you?" Raven asked.

"I feel like there's still a lot I don't know about—this life."

"Bell, there's a lot less to know than meets the eye. The world in here is a lot simpler than the one outside. It's the same every day—sleep, eat, fuck, don't get pregnant."

"You may have a point," Helen said. "But I find it odd that I don't even know anyone's real name."

"Nor will you. It's that way for a reason. Whores aren't allowed to have a past."

"Do you mean that seriously?"

"Look, Bell. When we walked through that front door, they took our names away. Our clothes were locked up. We can get mail only if it passes inspection first. And we *certainly* don't talk about our families or our lives before. It's either too painful or it seems after a while that it may all have been a dream—so we deny it. We start believing that only *this* life is real."

"Does that bother you?"

Raven looked over at her. "Why all the questions, Bell?"

"I suppose I find you intriguing," Helen said.

"Because I'm an Indian?"

"No, I don't think so. I think it's because I want to know more about you."

"That's saying the same thing twice," Raven said.

Helen was quiet for a moment.

"I think I'd like to learn how to *observe*," she said at last. "I feel that you know how."

Raven made a little chuckle. "Be careful what you wish for."

They sat in silence, Raven examining the ornate plaster cornice at the corner of the parlor. A piece of gilt filigree had fallen off, leaving a bright white plaster scar.

"Do you mind if I ask you a question, then?" Helen said quietly.

"Depends on the question, I guess."

"Is Raven the name Grace gave you?"

Raven looked over at her and squinted, considering. "No," she said. "Raven is my real name, but in English. In our language my name is Goh-láh-nah, which is our word for *raven*."

"*Goh-láh-nah*," Helen repeated. "I have to say, I think that's even prettier than Raven."

The Indian girl gave a little smile. "You're the first person who's ever asked me that. People seem to think that even though Indians speak native tongues, we all have English names. Like Sitting Bull or Red Cloud."

Helen laughed. "You know, I'm ashamed to admit that I've never thought about that before now."

"Don't feel badly. White people are the sun, and everyone else the planets."

"Still, it doesn't seem fair."

"I wouldn't go looking too hard for fair," Raven said. "May I ask, what was your real name?"

"It's Helen Blanche Crosby. I'm from Hamilton, Ontario, in Canada. My parents died when I was a little girl, and I was raised by my grandmother. I came here to get a job at the Pan."

Raven turned this over in her mind. "Thank you," she said slowly.

"Thank me for what?"

"It's hard to explain," Raven said. "But to my people the names of things are important. They have meaning. And a lot of that has been lost."

"You mean because of white people?"

"Everyone knows that white people took our land away," Raven said. "What they don't know is that they also took even more important things. We weren't allowed to speak our language in public. We were forbidden to follow our old ways. When you take away a people's history, then they have to depend on you to tell them who they are. Or who they can become."

"That's a terrible thing. I wouldn't blame you if you hated every white person."

"What good would that do? Why would I hate someone like you who had nothing to do with any of that? That would make me no better than the people who think all Indians are savages."

"Raven, do you think you and I—in private—could be who we used to be and not who we have to be?"

"I don't know, Bell. For Indians and prostitutes, the past is a lost country. And I'm both."

"But would you try, Goh-láh-nah?"

Raven gave Helen a strange look. "Yes, I will try, Helen Crosby."

"I have only one other question," Helen said.

"Yes?"

"Would you hold my hand?"

CHAPTER 19 ::
THE SÉANCE

"Now what are you two cooking up, I wonder?" May said as she and Alice and Olive came down the staircase at eight forty-five.

Raven and Helen looked up from their settle, where they had been chatting for almost an hour, holding hands.

"There's no conspiracy here," Helen said cheerfully.

The other girls sat down adjacent to Helen and Raven. "You're not a couple of these anarchists the paper says McKinley's staff are afraid of, then," Alice said. "People seem to be very worried someone will attack him when he comes to the Pan in September."

"It's hard to imagine," said Olive. "Surely no one would hurt the president."

"They probably said the very same thing to Lincoln and Garfield," Raven said.

"There'll be a small army of cops around him," May said.

"And not one of them to spare to find the Buffalo Butcher," said Helen.

"That's because people give a damn about the president," Raven said. "What do the cops care if we all die? Less work for them to do."

"I don't know about you," Olive said, "but I'm frightened. I wish someone would find this man, once and for all."

"If anyone is going to find him, most likely it'll be one of us. I sometimes wonder if we could chase him down somehow. Like vigilantes," Helen said.

"Oh, I can see it now," Raven said. "The papers would call us the pussy posse."

The girls laughed, and Helen gave Raven's hand a squeeze.

"I have a better idea!" May blurted out. "You girls may know that I'm a member of the National Spiritualists' Association."

"Not this again," Raven said, earning a scowl.

"It's not so far-fetched," May said indignantly. "There are hundreds of thousands of Spiritualists in the United States alone. We believe that the soul and the personality go on after death, and that it's possible to communicate with the dead."

"What does that have to do with anything?" Alice asked.

"My *idea*," May said with a note of pride, "is that we hold a séance here. And ask the dead women who it was that killed them."

The other girls laughed, but stopped abruptly when they saw that May was quite in earnest.

"Aren't séances just magic tricks?" Olive asked.

"No, they're not magic tricks. Any more than MP here has an actual magic pussy."

"I really wish you wouldn't call me that," Helen said.

"It's a term of endearment," May said. "Don't go anywhere. I'm going to get the paper."

She returned with the *Courier*, and turned to page ten, the Help Wanted ads. She pointed to a tiny item in the middle of the page. There was a little box around the advertisement.

Mme CLARISSA. Spiritualistic medium without equal; séances my specialty; no better living, 142 Broadway.

"See? It took me less than a minute to find a medium. That's how many there are."

"That doesn't mean they're real," Raven said.

"Maybe some aren't," May admitted. "But séances are this one's specialty. That's a *very* good sign."

"Anyone can say that," said Alice. "For two cents a word, the papers will print anything."

May crossed her arms. "You can't just *lie* in advertising. It's illegal."

"Madame Clarissa's ad has a box around it," Olive said, trying to be encouraging. "Those boxes cost twenty-five additional cents."

Raven rolled her eyes. "You two are off your rocker. I'm having nothing to do with it."

"Don't your people believe in spirits and ghosts?" asked May, rather pointedly.

"It's different. Trust me," Raven said.

"What do you think, Bell?" Alice asked. "Is it worth a try?"

"I don't know how much of all this is true," Helen said, "but one thing I do know. If a séance will help us find out who the Butcher is, I'm in favor."

"Let's do it! It'll be fun," Olive said.

"It's not supposed to be for *fun*, Moon," Alice said. "We're on the trail of a murderer here."

"Raven, if we do it, will you join us?" May asked. "I've read that because of the five-pointed star they use, five people make the most powerful group."

"Nothing doing," Raven said. "It's stupid."

"Oh, come on. Don't be a spoilsport," Olive said.

"I'll braid your hair if you'll agree to do it," Helen offered.

Raven thought a moment. "You're on. Bell, if you'll braid my hair, I'll sit in on this silly séance."

Helen held up her finger. "On one condition, though. You *have* to take it seriously, or try to. Even if you don't believe it. If we can contact that poor woman, we all have to be behind it."

"She's right," May said.

"Come on, Raven," said Alice.

"All right, agreed," Raven said reluctantly. "If I can't get my hair braided unless I take it seriously, then I'll take it seriously."

The girls erupted in a little cheer.

"You know we'll have to get Grace's permission," Helen said. "Which one of us ought to talk with her?"

"You're her favorite," May said. "You're her rainmaker."

"It was your idea, May. I think you ought to," Helen said.

"Least you can do for getting me into this," Raven muttered.

May chuckled. "I'll talk with Grace tomorrow morning."

"Talk with Grace about what?" Grace said, walking into the parlor with a frown on her face. "Girls, it's almost nine, and you're sitting around reading the newspaper? Put that thing away, and May, wash that newsprint off your hands. It's two minutes to showtime, ladies."

"The show must go on," Helen said to Raven.

"Are you ready?"

"Ready as I'll ever be," Helen said. "Though I suppose I ought to let go of your hand now."

Raven looked into her lap, where their hands were lying still intertwined. "I suppose, unless the first man tonight wants a threesome."

Helen looked into Raven's eyes, and then laughed. "You know, that just might be a good time."

⌢

"YOU WANT TO DO *what*?" Grace said the next morning.

"The five of us want to hold a séance," May said. "To see if we can communicate with the dead girls. One of them may reveal the identity of her murderer."

Grace looked at her incredulously. "You're serious? This is something you all want to do?"

"Yes, ma'am."

"What about Raven?"

"She's in on it, too."

"Now that's surprising," Grace mused. "I wonder what—"

"MP offered to braid her hair," May said.

"Why do you persist in call her MP?"

May blushed. "It's just for a lark."

The madam sighed. "So what is it you'd want from me?"

"Just your permission to use the dining room for an hour or two."

"In the daytime, I trust?"

"Yes, ma'am."

Grace shrugged her shoulders. "If it'll make you happy, I don't see any reason to object. But let's not make a habit of this sort of thing. We are serious about our work here."

"I know, Mrs. Harrington. We just want to do something to help, if we can."

"You're good girls," Grace said. "You have my permission. But please—stop calling Miss Bell that horrible name."

"It's intended as a compliment, ma'am," May said. "Bell does seem to have *something*."

~

MADAME CLARISSA WAS A tall, rawboned woman of indeterminate middle age with deep-set eyes and a frowsy mass of hair that had been bleached to the color of egg custard. She arrived wearing a slightly shabby dress and holding a small school slate in one hand. Raven and May met her at the door.

"Thank you for coming today, Madame Clarissa. It's quite an honor," May said.

"I was called to do it," the medium said.

"You mean on the telephone?" Raven smirked.

May ignored her. "Everything is in order as you requested, Madame. Curtains are drawn tight, chairs are all in place. Right this way."

They escorted their guest into the opulent dining room, where the other three girls were already seated.

"You have a beautiful home," Madame Clarissa said. "Did you girls inherit it from your parents?"

Raven looked quizzically at her. "Do you think we're all *sisters*?"

"I assumed as much. Why?"

"You don't think I look—different—from the others?"

"I thought perhaps your mother had remarried."

"We *are* all sisters," May said, cutting Raven off.

"And your parents have passed into the spirit realm?" the medium asked, taking her place at the end of the table.

"Sadly, yes," Helen said.

"If you'd like, we can perhaps contact them."

"Good heavens," Olive said in an aside to Alice. "Mine would roll over in their graves if we did."

"Now then, ladies," Madame Clarissa said, setting the school slate neatly next to her, "one thing before we begin."

"What's that?" Alice asked.

"My fee is two dollars."

"Of course," May said, reaching into a pocket. "Here you go."

The Madame folded the bills and tucked them away. "Now who is it you wish to contact, ladies?"

"Did you hear about the woman who was murdered recently?" Helen asked. "Not far from here."

"Oh yes," Madame Clarissa said. "The nurse. It was all over the newspapers. Very unfortunate. Although of course a woman who chooses such a life must bear some share of responsibility for her fate."

Raven cleared her throat.

"I suppose," May said. "Though sometimes, I think, women don't *choose* this—that—kind of life."

"Ah well," the medium said, "I suppose it would be difficult for most of us to understand the mind of the common prostitute. But thankfully, you girls are a long way from such a life."

"About six hours," Raven said, looking at the clock.

Madame Clarissa looked confused but soldiered on. "Well then, what is it you want to do in connection with this poor unfortunate?"

"We want to ask her who murdered her," Helen said.

The Madame smiled broadly. "We Spiritualists are being called upon more and more in police work, you know."

"See? What did I tell you?" May said indignantly.

"So what do we do?" Olive asked.

"Here's how this works," the Madame replied. "You ladies will all close your eyes and join hands. I will enter my trance and attempt to summon the spirit of the fallen woman. I will ask her questions."

"Will we hear her answers?" said May.

"No," the medium said, and held up her slate. "That's what this is for. In my trance, I will receive her communication and transcribe it here. Shall we begin?" She looked around the table, and the five girls nodded.

"Good. Now close your eyes, and keep them shut for the entire séance. Join hands."

The girls complied, and Helen felt Raven give her hand a little squeeze.

"Now I will enter my trance," the Madame intoned. She began to hum in a low, droning tone. That went on for a minute or two.

"I wish to contact the spirit of the dead, um, fallen woman—killed near the hospital." Another minute passed.

Madame Clarissa suddenly drew in a sharp breath. "I am in communication with her. Poor unfortunate, we wish to know the identity of the one who took your life."

After a moment, the girls heard the scratching of the pencil against the slate, then silence.

"Are you still there, spirit?"

Another long pause.

"Spirit?"

"Ladies," Clarissa said after an interval, you may open your eyes. The spirit has departed."

The five girls opened their eyes and blinked. "What did she say?" May asked. "I heard you writing something down."

Madame Clarissa picked up her slate and looked at it, puzzled. "I'm not sure what it means." She held up the slate.

On it was scratched:

THE DOOR HAD BARELY closed behind Clarissa when May began gleefully jumping around.

"I *told* you! And no one believed me! Not one of you! And what did she do but draw the symbols!"

"Jesus, Flower, the woman admitted that she'd read the papers. Those symbol things were all over them. It's not as though she told us the man's name and address," Raven said.

"Not this time," May said. "But if we had her back, she might be able to tell us more."

"As much as I hate to admit it, I agree with Raven," Alice said. "That was a bust."

"Thanks a whole fucking lot," Raven said.

"What do you think, MP?" May asked Helen.

"She's said already that she doesn't like to be called that," Olive said. "You wouldn't like it very much if someone poked fun of you."

"As I've said a hundred times, it's a compliment. Bell has a magic pussy. Everyone knows it," May said.

Helen sighed. "And as *I've* said a hundred times, there's nothing special about it."

"I beg to differ," May said. "I've been standing in the parlor when some of your clients come hobbling down afterward. One fellow looked like his eyes were permanently crossed."

"You *do* have *something*," Raven observed.

Helen's eyes opened in surprise. "Why, Raven, that's an awfully nice thing to say."

"Yeah, well, I just want you to do a good job braiding my hair."

"Since the spirits have departed, we can go and do it right now, if you like," Helen said.

"That's all I need to hear," Raven said. "Let's go."

Raven bounded up the stairs, two at a time, hair flying out behind her.

In Helen's bedroom, Raven sat down cross-legged on the bed. "I'm ready!" she announced, shaking out her silky black hair.

Helen sat behind her and began to brush and separate Raven's hair into long bundles.

"Wait a second!" Raven said, jumping up. She started shedding her clothes.

"What in the world are you doing?" Helen asked.

"I want the full treatment," Raven said, pulling off her layers. "I like to feel the hair on my back. And you can rub my neck while you're braiding, too."

"Was that our deal?" Helen said.

"Look, you don't know how difficult it was for me to keep a straight face through all that horseshit just now." She jumped back into bed, buck naked.

"Fair enough," Helen said, snuggling up behind Raven again. She resumed brushing her hair in long, smooth strokes.

"That feels *so* good," Raven said after a moment. "You have a nice touch."

"And you have beautiful hair. It's so lustrous. It really isn't anything like white people's hair."

"It is Indian hair, no doubt about that. But sometimes I wish I had wavy hair like yours."

"No, you don't. It's difficult to keep it under control."

Helen continued plaiting Raven's hair. When she was almost finished, Raven turned to look over her shoulder.

"Helen?" she said.

"Yes?"

"Would you run your hands over my back?"

"Sure," Helen said, and softly ran her hands up and down Raven's naked back.

"Wait, let me lie down so you can give me the full treatment." She flopped down on her stomach. "Go on, now. All over. Don't miss anything."

"Good heavens, you're demanding."

Helen gently ran her hands over Raven's back, buttocks, and the backs of her legs. "There you go," she said when she'd finished.

Raven rolled onto her back. "You're only half done."

Helen smiled and slowly ran her hands over her friend's breasts and flat stomach, then down all the way to her toes. Raven closed her eyes.

"Your hands are as soft as a dove's wings," she murmured. "No man touches like *that*. They're all so rough."

Helen nodded. "I'm afraid I have to agree. And the more excited they become, the rougher they get."

"If I tell you something, will you promise to keep it our secret?"

"Why, of course I will."

"I'm scared, Helen."

"What are you scared of?"

Raven looked up at Helen, her eyes deep and black. "Everything. I never let on, of course, but being locked in my room four times a night—five, now—and most of the time with men I've never met, well, I don't ever know how that'll go. And I'm afraid someday one of them will know someone back home in Arizona. Then these *murders*."

"I think we all feel afraid, Raven."

"We sure don't talk about it much. Other than Olive, that is."

"I think if we don't say it out loud, it doesn't feel so real. But it's there, all the same."

Raven gave her a fey smile. "Thanks." She jabbed her finger at Helen. "Now remember, it's our secret. You'll be sorry if you repeat any of this."

Helen leaned over, grabbed Raven's hand and then, to the other girl's surprise, took her finger into her mouth. She closed her eyes. After a long moment, she opened her lips and let Raven take her hand back. They looked at each other.

"No one's ever done that to me," Raven said.

"I don't know what got into me. It just seemed like the thing to do at the moment. To let you know that you may always trust me."

Raven took Helen's hand and gently placed it between her legs.

"Need I remind you that this was supposed to be a hair-braiding?" Helen asked.

Raven locked eyes with Helen and closed her legs on her friend's hand.

"Raven, are you trying to seduce me?"

"I don't know," Raven said, stretching languorously. "Is it working?"

"Oh yes," Helen said, and lay down next to her.

"Has anyone asked Grace what she thinks we ought to do?" Olive said on Wednesday morning. "I don't even want to go out shopping today. Or anywhere. We can't very well all go shopping together at one time."

"Ask her, if you're so keen to know," Raven said.

"I'm not asking Grace *anything*," Olive replied. "I'm on thin ice around here. I'm fat, I'm old, and if Grace thinks I'm a worry-wart, believe me, I'll be sold to The Hooks by sunrise."

"You are not fat, and you are not old," Helen said. "No one's selling you anywhere. Grace wouldn't do that."

"These are the times when I am reminded how new you are to this life, Bell," Alice said. "Grace is the best of her kind, but even she looks at us the way trainers do horses. You slow down and don't win races, it's off to the glue factory. Just like that."

May reached over and patted Alice's knee. "You know, that's about the smartest thing you've ever said, Star. We're horses, and Grace is—"

"Grace is what?" said Grace, coming into the parlor, dressed to the nines. "Tell me, Miss Flower. Just what do you think I am?"

"I think you're very generous," May said. "And beautiful, too."

"Oh yes, that's what I thought you were about to say. And what are you girls doing all sitting around gabbing on your day off? Get some sunshine, why don't you? You all look terribly pekid."

"We're afraid to leave the house," Alice said.

"And I don't want to go shopping," Olive added.

"Mrs. Harrington, we're scared," Helen said. "The Butcher could strike anywhere."

"I see," Grace said. "Well, he's not going to be a match for five fit women. As I've said before, go in a group. You'll be perfectly safe."

"Perfectly safe," May repeated.

"It strikes me as peculiar that there hasn't been another thing printed about the killings since the day the last one was discovered," Helen said. "It was all the newspapers could talk about, and then they just disappeared."

"Charley may know more," Grace said.

"Would you call him?" Olive asked.

"I was just heading over there to see him, as it happens. That's why I'm all dressed up."

"Will you tell us if he's heard anything?"

"Of course I will. I'll be back in an hour."

GRACE RETURNED WELL BEFORE luncheon, but breezed past Olive and May without saying a word and went straight back to her private parlor, in the rear of the place.

"What was that all about?" May said.

"Good question," Olive said. "She seemed rather preoccupied."

"She said Charley may know more about the Butcher, though. Go back there and ask her."

"I'm not going back there!"

May made a wry face. "Oh, don't be such a chicken. Go and ask her."

"All right, I'll do it," Olive said, wringing her hands. She stood and walked quietly back toward Grace's parlor.

She returned ten minutes later. "Did you learn anything?" May said eagerly.

"I did," Olive said slowly. "It's pretty bad."

"What is?"

Olive wiped her eyes. "Those poor women. They never had a chance."

"Let's talk about it at luncheon," May said. "You can tell everyone what Grace had to say."

"I'm going to go shopping after all, I think," Olive said. "Grace can fill you in."

"Do you want some company?" May asked.

"No thanks. It'll be good for me to get over this fear I've been feeling."

CHAPTER 21 ::
A WORLD APART

Helen and Raven—her hair again freshly braided—came downstairs just before noon. May and Alice were already sitting at the table, chatting.

"Where's Olive?" Helen asked.

"She went shopping after all," May reported.

Grace came into the dining room from her parlor as the grandfather clock started chiming and took her seat at the head of the table.

"Ladies," she said.

"Mrs. Harrington," the four replied.

"Before luncheon is served," Grace said, "I have a brief announcement to make."

"Don't tell me our quota is going up to six a night," May said to laughter.

"Miss Flower, please," said the madam. "I wanted to tell you all that Miss Moon will no longer be residing with us."

"What?" Helen said.

"Why?" said May.

"Where has she gone?" Alice asked.

"Miss Moon has gone across the street, to The Alzora. She'll be living over there henceforth."

"The Alzora!" Raven said. "What a shithole."

"Raven, that is simply not so. Charley runs a tight ship."

"Ha!" Raven said. "Popcorn Charley runs a sex factory. Quantity, not quality. Olive will have a hole bored clean through her in six months."

"It's not a *sex factory*, whatever that is," Grace said.

"Believe me, it's a sex factory," Raven said to the other three girls. "I used to be friends with Gertie over there, before, that is, Popcorn Charley sold her to some crib over in The Hooks. She told me that at The Alzora she had to turn over ten on busy nights. Didn't even have time to wash between them. Just to make her quota she'd be riding one and blowing another at the same time."

"That will be enough, Raven."

"Am I wrong? Poor Olive knew the axe was about to fall, too. She was putting on so much face paint lately that I told her she ought to be the Indian."

"She was only twenty-one," Helen said.

"It's not a question of age," said Grace. "It was her time, that's all."

"*Her time had come*," Alice intoned. "Fucking Grim Reaper is standing behind all of us."

"Language, Miss Star. I know very well how fond you all were of Olive, but it's simply the nature of our business."

"*Were*," Raven muttered.

There was a stunned silence around the table.

Helen shifted in her seat. "What I'd like to know is how in good conscience you could send Olive away when these killings are going on?"

"Miss Bell," Grace said, "I do *not* welcome impertinence."

"I simply don't understand," Helen said, "while someone's killing us—two of them two blocks from here—how you can send Olive away."

"Give her what-for, Helen," Raven said. "And Grace—fuck with Bell and you fuck with me!"

"*Mrs. Harrington*, if you please," Grace said, her eyes glittering.

"If that's even your real name," Raven said. "But whoever you are, this is my day off, and I choose not to spend any more of it with you." She stood.

"That goes double for me," Helen said, also standing. "You ought to be ashamed of yourself."

Grace came out of her chair in fury. She threw her napkin onto the dining room rug.

"I've half a goddamn mind to sell both of you to The Hooks!"

"What's stopping you?" Raven shot back. "Do it. I dare you. See how many of your regulars you lose. Sorry to say this, girls"—she looked at Alice and May, who were sitting in stunned silence—"but we *all* know who brings in the money around here. Bell and me. Good luck, Grace."

"Get *out* of my sight!" Grace screamed, pointing at the staircase. "I don't want to see you again until tomorrow at nine o'clock. That goes for both of you!"

Raven and Helen left without a further word and trooped upstairs. In the distance a door slammed.

Grace slowly sat down again, replaced her napkin in her lap, and regained her usual composure.

"I am truly sorry you had to see that ugliness, girls," she said to May and Alice.

"It's fine," Alice mumbled. "They're just upset, that's all."

"I don't mean them," Grace replied. "I meant *me*."

UPSTAIRS, IN HELEN'S BEDROOM, Raven pummeled the bed with her fists. When she ran out of energy, she stared at the ceiling, her hands clenched by her sides, panting.

"How I *hate* that goddamn woman!" she gasped. "Hate hate hate hate *hate*!"

Helen put her arms around Raven. "Shhhh," she said. "Olive will be all right."

Raven took a half-step back and looked into Helen's eyes. "Helen, this is not only about Olive. It's all of us. We're not safe, and we won't be until either the Butcher is caught or we're all dead. And I'm not sure sometimes whether I care which one."

"I care which one," Helen said, stroking Raven's cheek. "You have to go on. If any one of us does, it has to be you."

"Why in the world would you say such a thing?"

"Because one day—if you can get away—you can go back to the reservation. No one—not Grace, not even the army—is permitted to remove you once you get there. I know it's not what you wanted in life, but neither is this."

"Come with me, then," Raven said. "We'll escape together."

"I'd like that. I would. But—as much as I'd like to escape from here, I . . ."

"But what?"

Helen smiled gently. "I'll never escape the drugs, dear."

"Of course you can," Raven said. "Lots of people do. There are *cures*, Helen."

"How in hell would I get out of here long enough to take a cure? Do they have overnight cures? Raven, think. You know I'll never have the chance to take a cure."

Tears started in Raven's eyes, but she blinked them back.

Helen sat down on the edge of the bed, studying her hands. "I'm sorry I was rough with you. I suppose I'm just frustrated."

"It's fine. But even if you give up on yourself, I never will."

"You know, we probably ought to go out. If I stay here, I'm afraid I'll shoot up," Helen said.

Raven sat next to her. "Please don't. Just this once. We'll go out together, and you'll find me so intoxicating you won't need any of that stuff."

Helen smiled. "You are that." She leaned over and kissed her friend for a long moment.

"Imagine how different things might be," Raven said, her eyes still closed, "if we'd only met each other—in some other life."

"A world apart," Helen said, looking into her lap again. "Promise me, though—if something should happen to me—I get sold or, one day, I make a mistake with my needle—will you promise me you'll get back to Arizona somehow? And *live?*"

"I refuse to think about anything happening to you."

"Fine. But will you promise me—just in case?"

"I'd do anything for you, Helen Crosby," Raven said.

"Good. Then let's go out for a while."

Raven quickly looked away, toward the dressing table.

"What is it?" Helen asked. "Is something wrong?"

"I was wondering," Raven said shyly, "before we go . . ."

Helen smiled and put her hand on Raven's cheek. "I'd do anything for you, too, Goh-láh-nah," she said.

CHAPTER 22 ::
CONNECTIONS

R aven and Helen spent most of the afternoon shopping, and
then returned home at five o'clock for an afternoon nap
before supper.

Raven woke to find Helen scribbling away at the writing desk. She
got up, leaned over Helen, and kissed her on the back of the neck.

"What are you up to, beautiful?" she whispered in Helen's ear.

"I've been trying to figure out how these all connect," Helen said,
showing Raven some papers on which she'd been drawing.

Helen tapped her pencil on the paper. "The first symbol was a pentacle. Then there was a daisy. Then there was a fern or feather and then a
letter *C*. They don't seem to have a thing in common."

"The pentacle has five points," Raven said. "And the daisy had five
petals. I wonder if that means anything?"

"It might. I think the fern had five—I don't know what you call
them. Leaves? Stalks?"

"It's fine," Raven said.

"Now the letter *C*—well, that's just a letter *C*. Nothing five about that. Even in Roman numerals it means one hundred."

"I've said it before, but Helen, you're simply too intelligent for this line of work."

Helen kissed her. "I keep thinking if only I were a tiny bit smarter than I am, I could figure this out."

"Do you think it could be any of our clients?"

"Could be, of course. But mine? Some of them may be a little *off*, but I can't see any of them as evil. There's only one man I know who's capable of this level of venom."

"Let me guess," Raven said. "Grand."

Helen nodded. "If I opened the paper tomorrow morning and saw that the cops had taken him in for these killings, I wouldn't be at all surprised."

"It makes me shiver to think that—if you're right—you were practically *living* with him."

"Thank God my memory seems to have been erased of most of that. Maybe it's the drugs, but I don't remember a lot of it very clearly. Just bits and pieces."

"That's probably for the best. Not the drugs part, though." Raven looked at the clock over Helen's mantel. "Ugh, supper's in a half-hour. I'd better go get ready."

"Yeah, me too."

Raven took Helen's face in her hands and kissed her gently on the lips. "You know, Helen, I never thought I'd know what this feels like. I thought it was all just stories, you know?"

"What *what* feels like?"

"Love," Raven said, and left Helen standing there, open-mouthed.

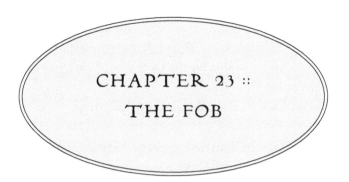

E arly every Monday morning, the ashmen came to collect the barrels of garbage stashed in the alley behind Ellicott Street. Two men, two horses, one wagon, and enough noise to wake the dead—or the working girls sleeping it off upstairs—as a week's worth of empty bottles and broken crockery went clattering into the back of the wagon, and empty barrels thundered back into place. The ashmen knew how irritating their racket was, and they took their time about it, scraping the barrels along, yelling at the top of their lungs, and generally raising hell. It was good sport in a job that afforded few other pleasures.

On the third Monday in August, the sun was just beginning to redden the sky when the ashmen rattled into the alley behind The Alzora, laughing and singing as usual. Charley's tired whores had only just groggily started wadding up cotton wool to stuff into their ears when the cacophony from the alley suddenly went silent.

Moments later, the front door of The Alzora banged open, setting the bell mounted to the top of its frame jangling like a marionette. Popcorn Charley emerged from the depths of the building, rubbing his eyes.

"Aw, what gives?" he said, nursing a colossal hangover and in no mood for the ashmen's hijinks.

"You better come around back," one of the ashmen said.

"Why?" Charley whined. "This better be good."

He shuffled along behind them around the side of the hotel and into the alley. When they arrived, the second ashman was taking an epic dump in the alley.

"*Seriously?*" Charley said. "Why is it every goddamn time you guys come, you leave piles of shit for me to step in? Can't you do it behind someone else's place?"

"*Look*, will you?" the ashman said, pointing. "You better call the cops."

Lying against the battered garbage barrels, staring blankly at the dawn, was the body of Olive Moon, the front of her dress rusty with blood.

⁓

"DON'T SAY A WORD about this to *anyone*," Charley instructed the ashmen. "I'll call the cops as soon as you're clear."

"You know, Mr. Popcorn," one of the men said, "the newspapers would give us each a dollar for a scoop like this one."

"You fucking guys," Charley said, annoyed. He dug into his pocket and pulled out a fistful of rumpled banknotes. He teased out a five-dollar-bill and handed it to the fellow.

"Divvy it up anyway you want," he said. "Now are you going to keep your mouths shut?"

The men smiled at each other. "That ought to do it," the first one said.

"Good. Now scram."

"You want us to empty your barrels first?"

Charley cocked his head. "What do you think?"

The two ashmen mounted up and clattered off down the alleyway, leaving Charley alone with Olive's corpse.

"God," he muttered. "What next?"

He ambled across Ellicott Street and collected Grace, who was also none too amused by the early wakeup call. "Do not start bitching at me," he said. "We've got to get our heads together on something."

They walked around back of The Alzora, where it was again quiet. The ashmen were long gone, and the whores had fallen back to sleep.

"Oh, no," Grace said softly when she saw Olive's remains. "Oh, no."

"Yeah," Charley said. "I figured you'll want to break it to your girls someway before it hits the papers."

"Thank you, Charley. They're going to take this hard. Everyone loved Olive. And they've been angry with me ever since I let you have her."

"She was a good girl. But I will say she wasn't happy after she came across the street to my joint. Going through the motions, you know?"

Grace put her hands on her hips. "What was I supposed to do, genius? I kept her on as long as I could, and we agreed that moving her over to you was a hell of a sight better than the other alternatives."

"That's not what I meant," Charley said. "I think she missed the other girls, that's all."

"My girls do have a special bond," she said.

"You think any of them—"

"Try not to be a complete pig, for once," Grace said. "You better call the cops. I'll stay here and wave off anyone who tries to come down the alley."

CHARLEY WENT RIGHT TO the top, telephoning Superintendent Ball at his home.

"I'm sure you have a *very* good reason for calling me at this hour," Ball said.

"One of my girls was killed last night," Charley said. "Behind my place. Throat cut—the same thing as the others."

There was a long silence on the line. "Shit," Ball said at last. "All right, I'll get Cusack down there pronto. And I'll have to tell the fucking mayor. Does anyone else know?"

"Grace, and the two garbage men who found her. That's all so far. I paid the ashmen off, but you never can tell if they'll stay mum."

"Nothing to be done about it," Ball said. "Just try to keep anyone else away until Cusack shows up."

"I'll do my best."

"Thanks for the call, Charley. I owe you one."

"Sure thing," Charley said, tucking away in an inner pocket of his brain that the chief now owed him one.

～

"SHE'S ONE OF YOURS, then?" Detective Cusack said, squatting next to the upturned face of Olive Moon. He pulled at one of the flaps of skin bordering the long slice that had ended her life and whistled softly.

"Good night," he said. "He really went deep this time. He's getting better at this."

"Better?" Grace asked. "How about a little respect?"

Cusack looked up scornfully at Grace. "Maybe I should have said confident." He stood and pulled out a pocket notebook and pencil.

"Her name?"

"Olive Moon," Charley said.

"Is that her real name?"

"Real enough," Grace said. "I think her name might have been Mc-Something. I'll see if I have it anywhere."

"Age?"

"I think she was twenty-one," Grace replied. "Or twenty-two."

"She looks a lot older than that," Cusack observed.

"Hard life," Charley offered.

"You think, eh? Either of you know anyone who didn't like her? Enemies? Maybe a man who wasn't pleased?"

They both shook their heads. "Look, detective," Grace said. "She just came over to Charley's place after four years with me. I never once had a complaint about her. Now, she wasn't the kind you'd give to a man with any—special requests. Straight-up kind of girl, meat and potatoes."

"I'm not writing that part down," Cusack said. "Charley, you know anything about her movements last night?"

"Her *movements*?" Charley said, puzzled. "Why would I—"

"For fuck's sake, Charley," Grace said. "Not like bowel movements. Her comings and goings. Where she was at a certain time. The last time you saw her alive. That sort of thing."

"I saw her last at, hmm, must have been about two o'clock," Charley said. "She'd been with someone upstairs and then she came back down to hang around."

"I'm not even going to ask what you were doing open at two in the morning," Cusack said. "Two hours after the curfew."

"Better make that slightly before midnight, then," said Charley, going up on his tiptoes to peer at Cusack's notebook. The detective rolled his eyes.

"So, you two—don't go anywhere for a while. The coroner's on his way. He'll want a statement from both of you."

"After that, though, I have to go break it to my girls," Grace said. "They have to hear it from me."

"Fine by me," Cusack said.

Grace, Charley, and Cusack stood quietly, looking at Olive. Cusack knelt down again.

"Looks to me like she put up quite a fight," he said. "Her hands are both clenched, and she's got some blood on her knuckles." He picked up Olive's left hand, unfolded the fingers, and examined it. He then picked up the right one, but this time when he opened her fist something tumbled out and onto the ground.

"What's that?" Charley said. Grace saw it, too, and they peered over the detective's shoulder.

"Don't know." Cusack picked it up and examined it. It was a gold ornament of some sort, oval, a double-sided piece mounted on a swivel. One side of the item was set with a dark green oval stone, flecked with red, and on the other was a bright red one, matching in size and shape. There was a small piece of gold chain attached to a ring on a horseshoe shaped swivel that held the item captive.

"Watch fob," Cusack said. "She must've grabbed it during the struggle."

"Good girl," Grace said. "Any initials?"

Cusack looked at both sides of the twin setting. "Not that I can see. A jeweler might be able to tell us more, though."

"I know just the place," Grace said. "Best jeweler in Buffalo, and the only place I buy my things. I'll call her now, and I know she'll see us right away."

Cusack nodded. "Good. But not until we're done with the coroner." He slipped the fob into his vest pocket.

SUPERINTENDENT BALL MET DETECTIVE Cusack, Grace, and Charley at T&E Dickinson's Jewelers, 254 Main Street. A pretty, middle-aged woman came out of the rear workshop when the doorbell rang.

"Thank you for seeing us so early, Elizabeth," Grace said.

"Anything for you, Grace. And good morning to you, gentlemen. I'm Mrs. Dickinson."

"I'm Police Superintendent Ball."

"No introduction is required in your case, Chief Ball," Mrs. Dickinson said, and Ball grinned. "I trust I'm not in any trouble."

"None whatsoever. This here is Detective Cusack. He and I were hoping to get your expert opinion on a piece of jewelry."

"I'll do my best," she said.

Ball handed her the fob. "What might you make of this, madam?"

Mrs. Dickinson put a loupe into her eye and squinted at the item. "It's not one of ours, but we do make a very similar piece. This is quite a nice one. Two very good quality stones, set in ten-carat gold."

"So you've seen something like this before?"

"Oh my, yes. Many times. These double-sided fobs are very popular nowadays. We call them spinners."

"Who would buy something like this?" Cusack asked.

"These pieces are usually gifts—to commemorate something—because the stones have symbolic significance. The stones in this one are carnelian"—she showed them the bright red stone, and then flipped the swivel over to the dark green one—"and heliotrope."

"Very interesting," Ball said. "Is it valuable?"

"Carnelian and heliotrope are semiprecious stones, unlike diamonds or emeralds, which are precious stones. But as I said, these are nice examples, and with the gold setting—I'd say a piece like this would sell for about fifty dollars. Maybe even a little more."

"So not something a working man would wear?" Cusack asked.

"I shouldn't think so, no. It's not inexpensive, and also it's too nice an object for hard labor."

"You said that the stones have symbolic significance," Grace said. "Can you tell us more about that?"

"Of course," the woman said. "Two things come to mind. Carnelian is September's birthstone, and heliotrope is March's. So you might see stones set like this to commemorate a couple of special dates."

"And the second thing?"

"It could have a more general significance, or none at all. Carnelian symbolizes endurance, and heliotrope signifies courage. So this combination is sometimes given to a new graduate embarking on a career. And sometimes people just like red and green."

"I told you this was the right place," Grace said, patting Mrs. Dickinson's hand. "Elizabeth, you know I pride myself on knowing a little bit about jewelry, but I must confess that I have never heard of heliotrope. Other than the flower, of course."

Mrs. Dickinson suppressed a chuckle. "I forget myself sometimes. Heliotrope is jeweler talk for this stone. It has a more popular name you might know."

"And what might that be, madam?" Cusack asked.

"Bloodstone," she said.

THE FOUR OF THEM left Dickinson's jewelry store in silence.

"I'll need to brief the mayor," Ball said when they were on the sidewalk. "Cusack, you and your men better start talking to everyone within ten blocks of The Alzora."

Charley and Grace walked back to the Tenderloin. "You want me to be there?" Charley asked when they arrived at Grace's place.

"That's very sweet, but I can handle it. Thanks anyway."

"Understood. Tell me how it goes."

"I'm not looking forward to it," Grace said.

Charley walked back across the street to The Alzora, and when Grace had collected herself, she had the chambermaids rouse Raven, Alice, May, and Helen and gathered them in the big parlor downstairs. Grace thanked them for coming down so early, after a late night.

"I hope this is worth it," Raven mumbled. "I was having the first dream in weeks where I'm not getting fucked."

"Raven, please," Grace said. "Girls, I have some very difficult news to share."

"Another one," said May. "I knew it."

"Unfortunately, I'm afraid so," Grace said. "Another young woman has been murdered."

The girls all started talking at once.

"Where?" Alice finally managed to shout over the din.

"Across the street. Behind The Alzora. Girls, I am terribly sorry, but it was—"

"No," Helen said, shaking her head. "No, no, *no*!"

"It was Olive."

General pandemonium broke out in the parlor. Grace let it calm down into soft weeping. Helen was stunned, silent, staring at the grandfather clock.

"The ashmen found her early this morning," Grace said.

"Her throat was cut?" Alice asked.

Grace nodded.

May wiped her eyes. "Any other mutilation?"

"I don't think so, no. Olive put up a fight, though. And she came away with the first good clue so far in this whole mess. She had in her hands a watch fob that she tore off of her killer."

"What kind?"

"A double-sided kind of thing, with stones on either side. One was a carnelian and the other a bloodstone. Set in gold."

"So much for trying to pin it on a slaughterhouse man," Alice said. "A gold fob? It could be one of our clients."

"Well, girls," Raven said, "it's been nice knowing you."

Helen slowly put her head in her hands, the first time she'd moved a muscle since Grace had broken the news. When she looked up her face was red with anger.

"You know this never would have happened if *you* hadn't sold her off!" she said, pointing at Grace. "You're responsible for this. Her blood is on your hands."

Alice and May looked down at the carpet, terrified.

"Miss Bell," Grace said coldly, "I understand you're upset. But you will *not* speak to me in that manner. This is your second warning. There will *not* be a third."

Helen stood, furious. "Fuck you, Grace." She turned and ran up the staircase, Raven hot on her heels.

"Miss Bell is understandably not herself just now," Grace said quietly.

"Yes, ma'am," May said. "I hope you won't punish her too severely."

Grace had gone quite pale. "There have to be consequences, Miss Flower. But I will take the circumstances into consideration. You two may go, if you wish."

WHEN GRACE SOFTLY ENTERED Helen's boudoir, two hours later, she found Miss Bell sprawled naked on her bed, her syringe lying next to her on the bedspread. She sat down on the edge of the mattress and shook Helen's shoulder. No response. She put her fingers under Helen's nose and felt the warm, humid breath, shallow but present. She shook the girl again, harder, and Helen slowly half-opened her eyes. She was terribly pale, and her pupils were invisible black dots.

"*What?*" Helen said, stupefied.

"What did you take, Helen?" She shook her again. Helen's skin was clammy, almost sticky.

"I don't know," Helen murmured. "Go away. I hate you."

"Morphine?"

Helen looked annoyed. "Yeah. Why should you care? Leave me alone."

"Oh, no you don't," Grace said. "I'm going to walk you up and down the stairs." She got up and opened Helen's door.

"Hey! Somebody bring us some black coffee, *now*!" she yelled down the staircase.

When she turned back to the bed, Helen had half-slipped off and was lying with her head toward the floor, breathing in a staccato wheeze. Grace pulled her the rest of the way off the bed, and she hit the floor with a dull thud.

"Jesus, girl, don't you die, too," she muttered under her breath, slapping Helen's face. A little bit of color returned.

"Coffee!!" she screamed again, just as there was a rap on the door.

"Coffee, ma'am," the porter said. "May I come in?"

"No!" Grace shouted. "Leave it there. I'll take care of it. And tell Raven that I need her, right away. Go!"

"Yes'm," the voice said, and retreated.

Grace pulled the bedspread down over Helen and got the tray of coffee from the hallway. She poured a little of the hot brew directly from the pitcher into Helen's gaping mouth.

Helen coughed and spit. "Huh?" she said.

Grace was slapping and rolling Helen to and fro on the rug when Raven arrived. "What happened?" she said.

Grace looked up at her and brushed her hair out of her eyes. "She's taken God knows how much morphine. We've got to keep her moving. Help me get her up and we'll see if she can walk the stairs."

"Oh, Helen, Helen," Raven said, getting her hands under Helen's arms.

They wrangled Helen into a sitting position, propped up against her bed. From there they heaved her to her feet, and Helen roused enough to keep her legs under her.

"Why is she naked, I wonder?" Grace murmured.

"Hmm, no idea," Raven said.

They lugged Helen in unsteady circles around her boudoir. After fifteen minutes, they were exhausted, and let Helen fall backwards onto her bed. She did seem to be breathing more evenly now, and a bit of rosy color was coming back to her face.

"The coffee was a bad idea," Grace said, panting. "Let's just rub her. I think she'll be fine now. By tomorrow, anyhow."

The two ladies massaged Helen's arms, legs, and feet until their arms ached. When they finally had to take a break, Helen was snoring loudly on her back.

"She's going to be all right," Raven said. "You can go. I'll look after her."

"She really is beautiful," Grace said, almost to herself. She turned away and blinked.

"Inside and out," Raven said.

HELEN REMAINED WEAK AND wobbly for most of a day, and to the great disappointment of ten unlucky men, missed work both Monday and Tuesday night. She was up earlier than usual on Wednesday, her day off, and came downstairs to find Grace sitting by herself in the kitchen.

"Hi," Helen said sheepishly.

"Good morning, Miss Bell," Grace said. "You're looking much better."

"I'm sorry about all that. I didn't know what to do, after hearing that news. I hope—"

Grace waved her off. "I'm not angry, and don't tell the others, but I'm not going to punish you, either. Just don't let it happen again."

"I won't. I promise. It was an accident."

"You know I don't care if you take dope, but only if it doesn't interfere with your work. And it did. You owe me for two nights' lost wages, on your account."

"I understand. Say, Grace, I wanted to talk with you about another thing, without the other girls around."

"Now or another time?"

"Now's fine, if you can. It's about that fob that was in Olive's hand. I was reading about it in the paper today."

"Yes?"

Helen tapped on the table. "I think I know that fob."

"You do? How?"

"The last time I saw Doctor Grand," Helen said, "he was wearing it. Or one just like it."

"Are you sure?" Grace said.

"I am as sure as I can be. He'd shot me full of morphine that day, but I remember that fob because it seemed like a little plaything. The whole time he was humping me, I was spinning it round and round and watching the colors."

"Elizabeth Dickinson said they're popular, though. There may be many just like it."

"I know, but think about it. Grand is always in or around the Tenderloin after he's done at the hospital. He's certainly capable of being brutal. And—there's one other thing. When I was seeing him, one night he brought out a straight razor and shaved me. Down below. I can tell you he looked pretty handy with it."

"So that's where you got the idea?"

"What idea?"

"About the shaved beaver."

"Oh God, you know about that?"

"You were sprawled out naked after you had all that morphine. It was hard not to notice."

"Cat's out of the bag, then," Helen said with a shrug. "But about this fob. If there's anyone I can imagine fitting the mold of the Buffalo Butcher, it'd be Doctor Grand. He's terrible enough to get a charge out of killing a woman."

Grace mulled this over. "I know there's no love lost between you and Doctor Grand, and I don't disagree that he has an unpleasant quality, but a multiple murderer? That's taking it a bit far, don't you think?"

"Honestly? No, I don't. But I remember that fob, I swear. And as much as I don't want to see Grand again, I wanted to suggest that perhaps you invite him over some night. We can see if he's missing a fob."

"Helen, dear, Doctor Grand is a wily old fox. I can't invite him over here for no reason. He'll smell a rat immediately. Especially if he really is the Butcher."

"All right," Helen said. "Then ask him to round up a half-dozen of his medical cronies and come here for a good time. Offer him a free one. Believe me, he'll take the bait. And if you don't want to do this for me, Grace—do it for Olive."

Grace looked at Helen, pursing her lips.

"You really believe this?" she said.

"I do. I know it sounds farfetched, but I saw that thing."

"Then I'll do as you ask. How soon?"

"As soon as you can manage," Helen replied.

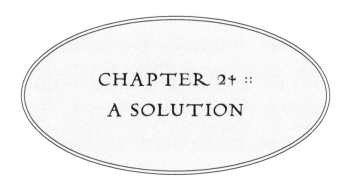

CHAPTER 24 ::
A SOLUTION

It was almost four in the morning by the time the last man of the night had departed, and Helen was slumped naked over her dressing table. She'd fallen into a dreamless sleep when her door opened, and Raven slipped in.

Raven shook Helen's shoulder.

"Helen?" she whispered.

"Huh?" Helen said.

"Please tell me you haven't taken more of that dope."

Helen sat up and shook her head. "Nothing, no. I've just felt so tired lately. It's as though I can't get rested."

"Why don't we lie down together for a while, then? Everyone's gone. The front door's locked at last."

"Thank God," Helen mumbled as Raven helped her to the bed. "What a night."

"Was it bad?"

"Rough bunch. I feel like I've been fucked to within an inch of my life. Everything's sore. You?"

"I did six tonight."

"Six? Why six?" Helen asked.

"Because, the sixth one was a free one." She seemed barely able to conceal a smile. "I got the information we wanted."

Helen propped herself up on her pillows. "About Olive?"

"Yup."

"How'd you manage that? There's been nothing in any of the papers."

"I know the editor of the *Enquirer*," Raven said. "He's one of my regulars. I sent a messenger boy to his office this afternoon to tell him that if he could answer a question for me, I had a present for him."

"Only you, Raven," she said, shaking her head.

"He's actually a decent fellow. His wife's crippled, so I blow him a couple times a month. Tonight I fucked his brains out, though. Seemed like the least I could do."

"Are you trying to make me jealous?"

"Maybe a little," Raven said with a light laugh. "Good to know you are."

"Very funny. So what did he tell you?"

"There *was* a symbol on Olive, too," Raven said, taking out a slip of paper from her skirt pocket. "I had him draw it for me."

"Let's see!"

Raven unfolded the paper. On it was drawn an odd shape:

Helen squinted at it. "What is it, I wonder?"

"It looks to me like some kind of a cap," Raven said. "Or a longhorn cow, upside-down."

"Very creative," Helen said. "It looks like an omega to me."

"Omega?"

"Yes, it's the last letter in the Greek alphabet. It signifies the end of something—like the end of the world."

"Fuck me," Raven said.

"If I had the energy, I would. This is very good detective work, my dear."

"Then you may reward me properly tomorrow, when you're rested."

"Deal," Helen said.

"Speaking of which, I'm going to go and get some rest myself. Don't take any dope tonight, will you?"

"I won't," said Helen. "Though you know I'll get the itch tomorrow morning. But I'll try to take as little as I can. Believe me, honey, I try. I just don't seem to have any willpower when it comes to that stuff."

"That's why we need to find a way for you to take a cure."

"I would like that," Helen said. "For the first time in quite a while, I feel like I have something to live for."

"Me, too. And on that note, get some rest."

"I wish you could stay with me."

"I do, too. But one more strike with Grace, and we're out." Raven kissed Helen on her forehead. "Sweet dreams."

She went out noiselessly into the corridor, toward her room.

After Raven had gone, Helen leaned back into the pillows and studied the scrap of paper and its strange symbol.

Helen was falling into a doze when the answer came to her. She sat bolt upright, shaking.

There could be no doubt of it. The Butcher was coming for them.

HELEN COULDN'T SLEEP AFTER that, and at some point near dawn, decided that her promise to Raven could be slightly relaxed, if only to get a little bit of shut-eye. So she put a few drops of chloral hydrate into the settled remains of her cocktail pitcher, drank it down, and dozed off immediately.

At nine-thirty—after about four hours of sleep—Helen threw on her dressing gown and tiptoed down the hallway to Raven's room, at the far end. She rapped gently, to no answer. She rapped again, a little more decisively, and the door opened.

"What *time* is it?" Raven said sleepily. "Is something wrong?"

"Let me in," Helen said, squeezing through the half-open door. "I have something to show you."

"Can't I have some coffee first, at least?"

"No. I've figured it out," Helen said.

"Figured what out?"

"The symbols! It came to me last night after you left."

Raven perked up. "Why didn't you say so?"

"Um, I did say so. Almost the first words out of my mouth when I walked in your door."

"If you're going to use your mouth this early, don't use it to argue with me," Raven said, kissing Helen. "Tell me what you've discovered."

Helen took a piece of notepaper and a pencil from Raven's desk. She took Raven's hand with the other and had her sit down next to her on Raven's rumpled bed.

"It's been hiding in plain sight the whole time," Helen said, poising the pencil. "Look."

She drew on the paper the five symbols carved into the bodies of the victims.

"A pentacle, daisy, fern or feather, the letter *C*, and then either the little cap or the omega," she said. "Right?"

"Right."

"And the pentacle and the daisy have five points each. As does the fern."

Raven nodded.

"So last night I was staring at these, and I thought—what if they're not what we've thought they were all along?"

"All right, fine. But what are they, then?"

"A pentacle is what? It's a kind of star."

"Yes," Raven said.

"And a daisy? A kind of flower."

"Uh-huh."

"And for the fern or feather . . . I thought about it both ways. I settled on it's being a feather—there are a lot more birds around here than there are ferns."

"I'm following," Raven said.

"Then there's the letter *C*. But what else does a letter *C* look like?"

"I don't know."

"Think, Raven," Helen said. "In the sky at night."

"Oh . . . I understand. It looks like a crescent moon."

"Exactly. So now we have a star, a flower, a feather, and a crescent moon. And the last one—the one on Olive—it's not a cap or an omega, either."

"So what is it?"

"It looks to me like the outline of a bell."

Helen looked at Raven for a long minute, and then her friend turned slowly toward her with an odd, dead expression.

"Helen," she said. "Oh, Helen."

Helen nodded and wrote:

Alice STAR

May FLOWER

RAVEN

Olive MOON

Helen BELL

"He's coming for us, Raven. He has been, all along."

"What the hell do we do?" Raven said, eyes wide.

"Before we get to that," Helen said, "there's one more thing that we may have misunderstood. The fob."

"What about it?"

"We've thought that Olive tore it off her killer in a struggle. But from what I heard, it's a pretty sturdy item. It seems that if it could be torn off, it might have been damaged, but it wasn't. So what if—just what if—the killer placed it in Olive's hand deliberately?"

"Why would he do that?"

"As a taunt. Look, you know I think that fob belongs to Doctor Grand. Raven, this is just the sort of thing he'd do. He loves to tease and taunt people. It's like a sport with him."

"But what I don't understand is why Grand would do this sort of thing at all? He's making money hand over fist as a cadet. He's a respected doctor. Why would someone like that start killing girls?"

"Because deep down, he hates us. He hates women. He doesn't care about the money—he likes doing what he does because he can take girls and degrade them. Gets them hooked on dope. And I think killing is only the next step. Besides, he's a surgeon."

"Maybe he'll come to his senses," Raven said feebly.

"Grand? Not a chance. It's going to be up to me to stop him. He'll keep killing until I do."

BACK IN HER BOUDOIR, Helen sat down at her dressing table, shaking and sweating. The itch had come back already—earlier than she'd expected—and with a vengeance.

She shot some morphine and things calmed down, but the dope made her sleepy, and she needed to think. So she sniffed a little coke to balance things out, and felt considerably better. Not high, exactly—just not uncomfortable.

Helen had thought of something else, something that she chose not to tell Raven. The order of the names associated with the symbols had to have a meaning—nothing Grand did was by accident. Olive had been the first of the five girls to die, and Helen was certain that Grand would work in reverse order, saving Helen for last. She had been his greatest achievement and killing her would provide his greatest release.

That meant that Raven would be next to feel the Butcher's blade. Then May, then Alice—then me. I can't—I won't—stand by and watch them die, one by one, she thought. I have to break his pattern somehow. But I'll have to act quickly.

:: PART FOUR ::

DELIVERANCE

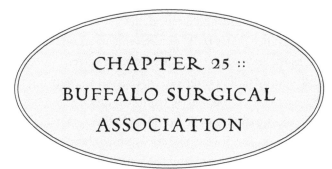

CHAPTER 25 ::
BUFFALO SURGICAL
ASSOCIATION

It could easily have been mistaken for a meeting of the Buffalo Surgical Association. Twenty of Buffalo's best surgeons—many of them household names—had been invited to Grace's place for one very special evening: twenty men, four girls, one night only.

Helen didn't care about any of that. For her, the evening had but one purpose—to see if Dr. Grand was missing his watch fob. Of course, the mere absence of a spinning fob wouldn't make him a murderer—surely a man of his stature owned more than one watch chain and fob—but it might generate enough suspicion that they could appeal to Popcorn Charley to have the cops follow him around. The police listened to Charley's occasional tips, even if they never gave him credit for them.

Helen came down the stairs last, to gasps. She was wearing a sleek, black velvet dress, perilously low-cut, and wearing a diamond necklace she had borrowed from Grace herself. With a sultry pout on her pretty mouth, her hair done up perfectly, but with two carefully selected, stray wisps framing her face, Helen's whole aspect was that of a young woman in complete command of herself.

After a fashion, that is. She'd taken a whole handful of pills, dropped belladonna into her eyes to make the pupils huge, and then— for good measure—shot some morphine. So many intoxicants would have dulled and deadened most women's appeal, but in Helen's case they helped her play the role of Miss Bell on the ragged edge between tantalizing and terrifying.

She smiled as she took her place between the other girls, and then curtseyed to the distinguished medical men.

"A fine entrance, Miss Bell," Grace whispered out of the corner of her mouth, as the men applauded this vision in velvet.

"Thank you, Mrs. Harrington," Helen said, scanning the line of men. Her heart was racing, partly from too much coke, but also from fear that Grand's piercing eyes would meet hers. But Dr. Grand was nowhere to be seen, and it was time for her first client.

Grace took Helen's hand and delicately led her over to a young man standing by the cold fireplace. "Miss Bell, may I introduce Doctor Stevens."

Dr. Stevens gave an awkward bow. "Miss Bell, you're more beautiful than even Mrs. Harrington said you were."

"That's a high compliment coming from such a handsome man," Helen said.

"Doctor Stevens is an osteopath," Grace said.

"You'll have to forgive me," Helen said, "while I've certainly heard of an osteopath, I confess I don't know what one is."

"Not too many people do, even within medicine," Stevens said, his face flushing. "It's unfortunate, but many confuse osteopathy with occult practice. Of course, they are different things entirely. One is not a science at all, and the other—"

"I'd love to hear more," Helen said. "Perhaps we could find somewhere with a little less hubbub, and you can tell me more about your profession?"

Stevens looked at Grace, who nodded. "I'd like that very much, Miss Bell."

"Then let me give you a little tour of our home. We can begin upstairs."

DR. STEVENS WAS AS boring in bed as he was in conversation. Helen had at least hoped for something closer to occult than osteopath, but he hadn't taken long, and he had been considerate, too, pulling out expertly and spilling his seed neatly on her belly. She'd thanked him sincerely, and even complimented him on the size of his load. Osteopaths must be even cheaper than real doctors, she thought, because he left her only with a smile and no tip.

She tidied up and made ready for another staircase appearance. The drugs had settled down and she was thinking about bumping up again, but it was going to be a long night, and she thought it would be better to wait to get high again until after the third or fourth. With the fading of her high came a welling sense of disappointment that Dr. Grand had failed to show.

Helen was only halfway down the staircase, though, when she spotted Grand. Part of her wanted to retreat, turn around and run back up the stairs to the safety of her room. But she thought of Raven and mustered her resolve. She continued down the staircase.

Grand spied her a heartbeat after she'd located him. Their eyes met, and again Helen wanted to turn, but she made herself meet his gaze with a heavy-lidded nonchalance—bedroom eyes, he had called it. He knew the look and smiled hungrily back at her. At the bottom of the staircase, she lost him in the crowd, momentarily. She was making her way over to Grace's side again when Grand intercepted her.

"Helen," he said. "You're looking very well."

"As are you, George," she said, with as much self-control as she could manage. "It's good to see you."

"That's very gracious. I expected you would ignore me entirely."

Helen waved her hand dismissively. "Water under the bridge," she said, swallowing hard. "Forget about it." She put her hand on Dr. Grand's chest. "There *are* some things I can't forget. Things that no one else has ever made me feel."

"You were always my favorite, you know. No one else comes close."

She glanced down at his watch chain. From it was dangling a golden fob in the shape of a Scottish thistle. It seemed half-familiar, but all she could picture was his carnelian and bloodstone spinner.

"Where's your watch fob?" she asked.

He looked down. "Whatever do you mean?"

"You used to wear a different one," she said.

Grand looked somewhat surprised, but also perhaps a little pained. "Ach, girl, how soon you forget. This one is my Scottish thistle. It's for good luck. I wore it every day when we were together."

"Yes, of course," she said. "George, if you'll excuse me, I have to find Grace—for my next performance."

He bowed. "It's good to see you, Helen."

"Would you—ever care to have a drink sometime? Away from all this."

"My, yes," he replied. "I'd like that very much."

"Then we shall. Bye for now, George," she said, trying to hide her disappointment. She walked over to Grace, who immediately took her by the hand and led her toward the piano, where a man was leaning and watching the music roll make the keys move all by themselves.

Grace touched the man gently on the elbow, and he turned.

"Miss Bell," she said, "allow me to introduce Mr. Leland Kennecott."

"Miss Bell," Lee said with a bow. "It's a pleasure."

"The pleasure is all mine, Mr. Kennecott."

"I'll let you two get acquainted," Grace said, and walked back to her desk.

"It's been quite a while," Helen said quietly.

"It has."

"Perhaps we can continue our conversation upstairs," Helen said, eager to be done with him and wishing she could shoot up. She was puzzled and disappointed by Grand's thistle fob, and seeing him and now Lee had brought back the humiliation she had felt on that day.

She had tried, and most of the time succeeded, in suppressing whatever and whoever Helen Crosby had been. Whenever Eva came to mind, she shoved her away. Grand she had treated like some malady from which she had miraculously recovered, if not fully. It had taken a great deal of willpower, and a stupefying quantity of drugs, but she had done it. Until now.

They ascended the stairs without a word, and in her bedroom Helen hadn't even the heart to put on her usual Miss Bell act. She merely started to undress herself, and when she was naked, she stood there quietly, looking at Lee.

"Is something wrong, Helen? Have I offended you somehow?"

"No," she said. "But we both know why we're here, so why don't we dispense with the preliminaries?"

"If that's the way you're going to be then," he said. She watched him as he slid off his jacket and began working the buttons of his vest.

"We have plenty of time," she said abruptly. "Would you mind if I injected myself first?"

"Injected yourself with what?"

"Morphine," she said.

"How long have you been using that?"

"The day Grand brought you over was my first time. Well, maybe the second—I can't quite recall now. But since then, I've had to have it two or three times a day. More and more all the time."

"It's ruinous, Helen. The life of an addict does not end well."

She laughed. "At least I know how mine will end then. Most people don't. I have—a friend who'd like me to take a cure, but that's not in the cards."

Lee stepped over to her and took her gently by the shoulders. "You know, Helen, I never intended things to happen—the way they have."

"We have that in common," she replied.

He stepped back, and she expected him to resume undressing, but then a thought seemed to cross his mind.

"I might know someone who can help you. A chum of mine from medical school opened a clinic in Rochester. He offers a cure for men and women who become enslaved to alcohol or drugs. He's doing amazing work, Helen. I think he could free you from morphine forever."

"That would be wonderful, but as I said, I can't very well leave here to take a cure."

"What day do you have off?"

"Wednesday. Why?"

"I go to Rochester on Wednesdays for a class related to my internship. Listen—come with me this week. We'll get there before midday.

You can relax in the hotel or go shopping while I'm in my class. Then we'll have a perfect evening together, and on Thursday I'll get you checked in to my friend's clinic before I return to Buffalo."

"You're suggesting I run away?" She thought of Raven. "Grace will come after me."

"She'd never know where you'd gone. Who would run away to *Rochester?*"

Helen looked at Lee, towering over her in stocking feet and vest.

"Why would you do something like this for me?"

"That day in your flat," he said. "That was all Grand's doing. I will admit that I was so taken with you that—I went along with it and behaved shamefully. I've regretted it every day since. There are days I hate myself for it. And now I suppose—if I knew I'd done you a good turn, I could forgive myself."

"I don't know what to say," Helen murmured.

"Then say yes. We'll leave it as it is tonight, and Wednesday morning I'll meet you at the Exchange Street Station for the 8:10 to Rochester."

She thought about it a moment. "There's one small problem, Lee. I don't have street clothes. And Grace keeps all my money until I pay off my debt."

He reached into his coat, took out his billfold, and counted out a hundred dollars. "That'll be more than enough to buy you some clothes and a bag. Say you'll do it, Helen. Give me a chance to make things right."

Helen felt a flash of something she hadn't felt for quite some time. Hope.

"All right, Lee. I'll go with you on Wednesday."

Lee gave her a big smile. "Wonderful. I'll just go back downstairs now. Everyone will think I'm just efficient."

Helen laughed, the first time she'd laughed a real laugh since being on the Midway with the other girls.

~

AT LUNCHEON THE FOLLOWING day, Grace's girls were unusually quiet.

"Young Mr. Kennecott was most complimentary about you, Miss Bell," Grace said, trying to be nice.

"That was kind of him," Helen replied.

"The magic pussy never fails," May said.

"He was such a—an imposing fellow," said Alice. "I can't help but wonder . . . was everything, er, in proportion?"

"Oh yes," Helen said, raising her eyebrows. "He's—"

"Can you spare us the gory details?" Raven said.

"Sorry," Helen replied. "Star asked."

"I take it that Doctor Grand's watch fob was in order?" Grace asked.

Helen stirred her food with her fork. "I could have sworn that was his fob. I would have bet my life on it."

"Doctor Grand has many faults," Grace said, "but he's hardly a murderer. Anyway, I don't want any of you girls doing any more amateur detective work. The police will find that man in due course."

"After we're all dead," Raven said.

After lunch, Helen walked slowly back upstairs, suddenly missing Olive. Poor, twenty-one-going-on-thirty Olive. How they'd laughed together.

She got out her syringe and shot herself up. But though she had measured the dose precisely—she was up to two-and-a-half-grains—it didn't have the desired effect. She crushed her last two tablets—another grain—and injected herself again. That put her over the top, and she peeled off the rest of her clothes and lay down on the bed, cruising.

Olive's face came back to her again. She'd been terrified of razors, yet she'd trusted Helen. But how frightened she must have been before the end came. She wondered what Olive had thought in her final moments of life and hoped that some memory of their friendship, or of that wonderful day at the Pan, had eased her way.

Her reverie was interrupted by a gentle rap on her door. "Come in," she said.

It was Raven, looking especially beautiful, her cheekbones accentuated by just a touch of rouge.

"Hello, you," she said to Raven.

"Hello, yourself." Raven closed the door behind her and lay down next to Helen. She buried her face in Helen's shoulder.

"What's wrong, dear?" Helen asked.

"I didn't like hearing about that man's big dick."

"Honey, it wasn't anything. You know, just making conversation."

"I know you and I do—what we *do*, and with lots of people," Raven said quietly into Helen's hair, "but I don't like to think about you *doing* it. Or certainly not *enjoying* it. Which you must, I expect."

Helen leaned up on an elbow and smoothed back Raven's black hair. "Almost all of the time, I'm thinking of something else. I let Helen go somewhere else, and Miss Bell takes over."

Raven nodded. "I understand. I do the same thing. But what is it you think about—where does your mind go—when you're getting it?"

"Do you really want to know?"

"I do. I want to know everything about you, Helen."

"I think of you."

"You do *not*," Raven said with a little scoffing laugh.

"Oh, but I do," Helen said, kissing Raven on the lips.

"And I thought I was the only one," Raven said softly. "Helen— there's been something on my personal dance card, you know, for a very long time."

"What is it?"

Raven wriggled out of her dress and gently crawled between Helen's legs. "*This*," she said, putting her face into the apex.

"My," Helen whispered.

Raven looked up with a sly expression. "May I continue, Miss Bell?"

"On one condition only."

"What is it?"

"That I may have the pleasure of the next dance."

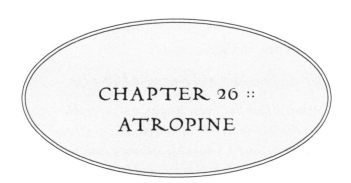

CHAPTER 26 ::
ATROPINE

"Grace," Helen said after luncheon on Tuesday, "can I get some more coke from you?"

"Have you already gone through the last batch?"

Helen laughed. "I'm afraid so."

"You need to slow down, girl," Grace said.

"It's been difficult . . . after Olive. It's the only thing that cheers me up."

"All right, then. I'll send some more up tonight. But take it easy, will you?"

"I will. And also—can you get me some belladonna? Atropine?"

Grace looked at her quizzically. "Why in the world would you want *that*?"

"Not to take," she said. "A few tablets that I can make into eye drops." While Helen wasn't about to ingest the stuff again, she liked using atropine made into a weak solution and dropped into the eyes to make her pupils dilate, giving them a sultry, seductive look.

"Oh," Grace said. "That does look rather good on you. But be careful—too much of that stuff, even in the eyes, will give you very bad dreams. And a lot of other things, too."

"I know. I'll be careful."

"I'll have the stuff brought up tonight," Grace said. "After your shift, though."

EARLY THE NEXT MORNING, Helen took two sheets of notepaper and two envelopes from her writing desk. She removed the cap from her inkwell, dipped her pen, and began to write.

Dear Grace, Alice, May, and Raven (and Charley):

I know it'll look like I've run away, but my problem has now become a deadly threat. If I can find a cure, rest assured I'll come back. If I can't . . . well, what's life without a little risk?

All of you have been good to me, and I am grateful. I hope we'll see one another again soon, and in the meantime, I hope you think of me fondly, as I think of you.

Affectionately,

Helen

She folded the paper, sealed it inside the envelope, and set it aside. Then she dipped her pen again and began a second letter.

Dearest Goh-láh-nah—

I wish I could have told you this in person, but I wanted to remember your eyes the way I saw them last evening, after we made love.
If I can beat this evil thing, I will come back to you, and we will run away for good, together. But if I cannot, then you must, for both of us. Enclosed is all of my tip money, just in case.
After everything, I'd do it all over again—because it all led me to you.

Love forever,

Helen

Helen folded the banknotes inside the notepaper and eased the packet into the envelope. She let the tip of her tongue glide lightly over the gum of the seal flap and smoothed the envelope closed. Then wrote "Raven" on the outside, kissed it, and set it with the other one.

CHAPTER 27 ::

FLIGHT

After Helen finished her letters, she tiptoed down the stairs. It was hours before anyone else in Grace's place—or any of the other joints along Ellicott Street—would stir. She closed the front door softly behind her and, on the sidewalk, looked up at the house that had been her home since—everything.

She had with her only a small carpetbag she'd bought at Hengerer's and was wearing a modest but pretty shirtwaist and pleated skirt, topped with a trim Eton jacket and a smart boater hat with a wide, bright blue ribbon. She had smiled as she examined the ensemble in the cheval mirror back in her room—the first street clothes she'd worn since that wonderful day on the Midway. Even better, she had spent only half of Lee's hundred dollars. The rest had gone into the envelope for Raven.

When she walked up, Lee was standing on the platform at Exchange Street Station, smoking a cigarette, looking not quite handsome but certainly imposing. He was at least a head taller than most any other man in a crowd of men waiting to take the 8:10 to Rochester. When he saw her, he flicked the cigarette onto the tracks, blew smoke out of the side of his mouth, and removed his skimmer hat.

"Good morning, Helen," he said, with a bow.

"Good morning to you, Lee. How are you this morning?"

"It's a little too warm for my taste," he said, "but I'm well enough. Frankly, I was curious whether you really would show up."

"I said I would, didn't I?"

"You did, but—our limited history hasn't been so pleasant as I might like. I was afraid you might change your mind."

"On the contrary. I've been looking forward to our little trip. I've never been to Rochester."

"That sounds like the beginning of a bad joke," he said. "In any event, may I say you look lovely?"

She gave a half-twirl on the platform. "Why, thank you, sir."

"You look like the angel on top of a wedding cake," Lee said.

Helen had to laugh at that. "Now I know you're blowing smoke, and not just from your cigarette. Angel? I rather think not."

"All right, perhaps that was a slight exaggeration. But only a slight one."

Their train chuffed into the shed and, squealing and hissing, drew to a slow stop opposite them.

Lee helped her up into the first-class carriage, and they sat facing each other in the plush, velvet seats.

"You're pulling out all the stops today, aren't you?" Helen said, looking around.

"I have amends to make."

They sat quietly as the train rocked and rumbled through the New York Central freight yards, and then into open country.

"Would you mind if I made a visit to the smoking car?" he asked as the small farmsteads of eastern Erie County began to whisk by.

"Not at all. But you know, they say that nicotine is more addictive than morphine," she replied with a laugh.

"Then if you'll excuse a fellow addict," he said, unfolding his long legs, "he'll go and get his fix."

Helen was happy for the time to herself. She was accustomed to quiet mornings at Grace's, not the rush and babble of crowds and railway stations and smoking cars. Outside, the tidy little farmsteads gave way to larger tracts of open land, all as flat as the top of her hat. It seemed all to be planted in endless rows of corn, now head-high and sprouting jaunty tassels and little plumes of silk.

"Batavia's next!" the conductor called, walking down the center aisle.

Lee returned to her side after the train left Batavia's station, reeking of cigarette smoke. Helen waved her hand in front of her face.

"You stink!" she said. "How many cigarettes did you smoke?"

"Miss Crosby, you don't pull any punches, do you? I had two. You have to remember that there are twenty men in the smoking car, all puffing away at the same time."

"I hope you air out before we get to Rochester," she said.

"We'll be there in a half-hour or so. I've engaged a room at the Whitman House Hotel, which is new to me, but said to be very nice. It's right downtown, and there are plenty of restaurants and department stores nearby. You'll find Rochester a little dull compared to Buffalo, but it's lively enough for a day."

"I'll have a look around while you are in your class," she said.

"Since you've told me one of your secrets, maybe I'll tell you one of mine." He leaned close to her, and the smell of stale smoke was so strong she nearly gagged.

"What's the secret?"

"I don't have a class in Rochester. I go there once a week to make a little extra money. Being an intern at Riverdale doesn't pay terribly well. I have a wife and son to provide for, and just now we have to live with my parents."

"You're married? And already have a child?"

"Yes and yes. I've been married for almost three years, and my son was born in March."

"And you're how old?"

"I'll be twenty-four on September first."

"So young," she said.

"*Too* young. It just happened that way. But I certainly wouldn't advise it."

"What's your wife like, if you don't mind my asking?"

He smiled and looked off in the other direction. "She's a bore, if you want the honest truth. Dull as dishwater. But of course, she wants me to make much of her all the time."

"I'm sorry," Helen said.

"My own fault," Lee replied. "But let's look on the bright side. My wife doesn't care about my outside activities. She's relieved, if anything, that I'm not insisting on humping her every other night. The pregnancy was hard on her, and she dreads the thought of having another child."

"Is that difficult for you?"

"Difficult? How so?"

"It just seems to me that if I had a husband, I'd want to be with him intimately."

He smirked. "Then you're different from every other woman I've ever met. They all play the slut before they marry, and once they do they turn into nuns. You might be surprised that I respect a woman like *you* far more than I do one like my wife. My wife is as much a whore as you are, but she doesn't know it. The difference is that she gets her bed and board provided in exchange. And nowadays she's getting those for free."

"A woman like me," Helen said quietly. "That stung."

He put his hand on hers and patted it. "I didn't mean it the way it sounded. I meant to say that there's more integrity in your world than there is in—whatever you call the home front."

"I have a friend at Grace's who agrees with you, almost word for word," she said. "Now since you lied to me about your class, and we're being so honest with each other, just what is it that takes you to Rochester every week?"

He lowered his voice. "There is a considerable call for, shall we say, a certain type of operation."

"That sounds mysterious."

"Girls in trouble," he whispered into her ear. "Fifty dollars cash every time."

"I see," she said slowly. "But why Rochester? There are lots of girls in trouble in Buffalo."

"That's simple. Doctor Grand."

"What about him?"

"He's got a lock on all that in the Tenderloin. That's why he knows Grace and Popcorn Charley so well. He's been taking care of things for them for years. It's only recently that he's started doing the recruiting."

"Now that makes sense."

"Yes. And he doesn't want me attracting any more attention by doing more in the Tenderloin. It's six months in the penitentiary for illegal operations, and two of us from Riverdale doing it in the same city could get noticed. So he introduced me to a few people he knows in Rochester, and in one day of travel I can make two hundred dollars or more. Per week."

"Are they all—girls like me?"

"No. Some are like you, but quite a few are poor girls. The better sort have family doctors, you know, who'll take care of things at home. I cater to those who can't afford better."

"You're a kind of public servant," she said, looking out of the window.

"I know scorn when I hear it, Helen," he said.

She turned back to him. "No, it's not scorn. Or at least it's not directed at you. I think I'm simply disgusted with life in general."

The train had picked up speed after leaving Batavia and was now stretching its legs across the flatness of Genesee County.

"On a happier note," she said, "when will your duties be done for the day?"

"I'll be back at the hotel by five o'clock or thereabouts. We can have some cocktails and then go out for a nice dinner."

"Perfect. I'm looking forward to it. I feel almost like Helen Crosby again."

LEE AND HELEN CHECKED in at the Whitman House Hotel, under the names of Mr. and Mrs. Leland D. Crosby. The desk clerk glanced at Lee's wedding ring and didn't ask any further questions.

"Room 546," he said, handing a key over. "Checkout is eleven tomorrow, and we have someone on duty all night. Do note that our grill closes at midnight, so if you want anything to eat or drink after that, the Eagleton next door has quite a nice restaurant. They're open until two or three."

"Thank you," Lee said.

"May I call the bellman for your bags?"

"No need," Lee replied. "Since we're stopping only overnight, we have only hand-luggage."

"Very well. The lift is just behind you."

At the fifth floor, the operator opened the elevator door onto a carpeted corridor, and they followed the direction suggested by a small brass plaque. When they stepped inside Room 546, Lee set his and Helen's carpetbags on a low table by the windows overlooking East Main Street. The room was spacious, furnished with a large iron bed, a washstand, writing desk, armoire, and a clothes horse. A bathroom was attached just to the left of the bed.

"Whew, it's hot in here," Lee said. "Let's see if we can get a little fresh air for you."

"That would be most welcome," Helen said, fanning herself with her hand.

Lee opened the windows over Main Street, letting in the outside air and distant sound of the street below. Then he worked the crank that controlled the transom over their door, and soon they were getting a decent cross breeze.

"*Much* better," Helen said. "Now then, when do you have to leave?"

Lee pulled his watch out of his trouser pocket and flipped open the case. "It's almost ten fifteen," he said. "I'd better go. My first appointment is at eleven."

"I'd say good luck, but I don't expect you'll need it," she said.

He smiled and dropped his watch back into his trousers. "I'll see you at five, and then the fun will begin."

She smiled back and looked out of the window as the curtains sucked and slapped in the current of air.

CHAPTER 28 ::
A PERFECT EVENING

Lee didn't return until almost six fifteen, and dusk was starting to come down. Helen was sitting in the dim bedroom when he entered.

He threw his medical bag on the table. "Honey, I'm home," he said with a chuckle.

"Long day," she said.

"Longer than expected. One girl had a lot of bleeding afterward, and I had to fix that up."

"How unpleasant."

"It's fine. At least I had something to look forward to tonight. Normally I just come back to the room and—"

"Jack off?" she said with a laugh.

"You're a naughty one, aren't you?"

"I can be. Cocktail?" She gestured to a pitcher on the bedstand.

"I'd love one," he said.

They clinked glasses and drank.

"Whew, you like them strong," Lee said.

"Just the way it came. But I did pick up a bottle of martini cocktails for later, if we run out."

"I think we'll be face down by that time. So tell me, Helen—how was *your* day? Enjoyable, I hope?"

"I had a very nice day. I took a nap after you left, and then went out for a stroll. And I took in a moving picture show."

"How wonderful. What was the picture about?"

"It was a Western," she said. "Cowboys and Indians out in the Arizona Territory. Shooting at each other, mostly."

"Did you enjoy it?"

"I felt badly for the Indians," she said.

"Why is that? So far as I can tell, they're savages."

"I think that's because you don't know any. And I felt bad because they put up a good fight, but in the end they were still slaughtered."

"That's the way it was in the West, I think," Lee said, taking a drink. "Still is."

"I don't take your meaning."

She took a deep breath. "I mean, one can put up a good fight and still be slaughtered. Like those girls in the Tenderloin recently."

He looked at her strangely. "Yes. That's been very unfortunate."

Helen looked out the window at the gathering dusk. "I suppose some of them fought pretty hard."

"I expect they did. People do when it's a matter of life or death."

"Not that you ought to worry," Helen said, looking at him. "I won't give you any trouble."

"Excuse me?"

"We'll close the windows and the transom beforehand. No one will hear a thing."

"I haven't the faintest—"

"Lee," she said, cocking her head and giving him a pretty smile, "why do you keep your watch in your trouser pocket?"

"Because it's a pocket watch, of course."

"They call them that because they go into the *vest* pocket," she said. "Most men are terribly proud of their watch chain and fob."

"I have a nice one," he said, "but I'm having it repaired just now."

"A gold spinner," she said, "with a carnelian on one side and a bloodstone on the other. The carnelian for your birth month, September, and the bloodstone for your son's. In March."

His eyes narrowed in the darkened room. "Clever girl," he said quietly.

She shrugged. "It took me longer to figure it out than it ought to have. But it does feel good, all the same."

"I do hope you won't try anything foolish," Lee said.

She shook her head. "No. You said it best. The life of the addict doesn't end well. I'm dead one way or the other."

"What tipped you off, if I may ask?"

"I could have sworn Grand was wearing that fob the day you raped me. That's where I went wrong—I remembered the fob well enough, but I mistook the person wearing it. But when you pulled out your watch, I knew for sure."

He listened carefully and then stuck a cigarette between his lips. "Mind if I smoke?"

"Would it matter if I did?"

"No, but I prefer to be polite." He flamed off his smoke and sat back, inhaling deeply. They sat in the dark for a little while, Helen watching his cigarette ember flare and dim, flare and dim.

"I would like to know something," she said into the silence. "I think it would give me some peace to know that Olive didn't suffer. If she didn't, that is. I do want the truth, either way."

Lee took a deep, final drag on his cigarette. "None of them suffered. Well, except that nurse. She was going to rat out Grand—he'd gotten a little handsy with her—and so I taught her a lesson."

"That you did," Helen said.

"But to your question. Surprise is all any of them feel. Once the carotid is severed, they're unconscious within a minute, at most. Now, I have observed that—in every case—the sight of so much of one's own blood is profoundly distressing. But again, that doesn't last long. They pass out and die shortly afterward."

"But how did she get the fob, if she didn't struggle?"

"You'll have to remember I fucked her beforehand. I guess I didn't realize she'd grabbed ahold of it. Whores are thieves, you know. I suspect she thought she could pawn it for ten dollars."

"Olive wasn't a thief," Helen said testily.

"I meant no disrespect to your friend."

Lee lit another cigarette and looked at it appreciatively. "If you knew—or had a strong suspicion—that it was me, I don't understand why you'd come here. It seems suicidal."

"Not in the least. I believe my life is worth a great deal. So I thought we could strike a bargain in exchange for it."

"How intriguing," he said, blowing out smoke. "Now that's a new one. What do you have in mind?"

"You get your prize—me—without the slightest protest. If you will grant me three wishes."

His eyes glowed. "Just like the *Arabian Nights*!"

"Just like," she said.

"And what are your three wishes, my dear?"

"Number one. I don't want it to hurt."

Lee put his finger to his lips. "Easily granted. I keep in my medical bag a bottle of chloroform. Now—contrary to what you see with your vaudeville villains—chloroform takes several minutes to anaesthetize a patient properly."

"I'm listening," Helen said.

"In a surgical setting, I'd apply the chloroform to a fabric cone, which is placed over the patient's mouth and nose. And you would simply breathe in the vapor. You breathe easily and naturally, and in about three minutes drift off comfortably. Now, of course, the surgeon can perform a very complex operation without the patient feeling a thing."

"And in my case?"

"I don't have a proper cone with me, so we will have to improvise just a little. I'll saturate a handkerchief with the chloroform and lay it over your face. The rest is the same, except that the odor will be more intense. But it's not an unpleasant smell, merely very strong. In two or three minutes you'll be in a deep sleep. Once you are, I'll make the incision. It'll be like any other surgery, except of course that you'll never wake up."

"Understood," she said. "And agreed. Now, out of curiosity—do you fuck me beforehand, or after I'm dead?"

He looked at her quizzically. "What kind of monster do you think I am, Helen?" he said, wounded. "I wouldn't have sexual relations with a dead person."

"No offense intended, Lee. It's just been rattling around my head, that's all."

"No offense taken, then. Now then—your second wish?"

"You promised me a pleasant evening. A *perfect* evening, just like normal people have. I'd like to feel that once more."

"You wouldn't try to escape? Or make some kind of scene?"

"If you give me your word that we will do our best to have a pleasant evening, I will give you mine that there'll be no funny business."

"Then you have my word on it as a gentleman. Your second wish is granted. We'll get away from this hotel, lest there be any unpleasant overtones. The Eagleton's restaurant is very good. Would that be acceptable?"

"It sounds lovely," she said.

"And your third and final wish?"

"I know what the symbols mean, Lee."

He looked at her with open admiration. "You truly are remarkable. I oughtn't to be surprised, but I am. I never thought anyone would figure that out."

"Don't give yourself *too* much credit," she said. "It wasn't *that* difficult to work out. But in any case, my third wish is this: that you will promise me that you won't harm any more girls. Including, particularly, any of Grace's."

"You saved the biggest wish for last I see."

"Frankly, it's the only one that matters. If I have to give up the first two to have the third, I will."

"My dear Helen, you were doing so well. Don't start negotiating against yourself before you know what I'll say."

"That's good advice," Helen said. "Though it's probably coming too late in life to be of much use."

He laughed. "Your third wish is granted. And as I am a man of my word, and I had already granted the others, I will not renege on them."

"You pledge to me that you will not hurt any other girls? Including any of my friends?"

He put his hand over his heart. "I won't tell you it will be easy, but I do so pledge."

"Thank you, Lee," she said, extending her hand. He shook it. "Now we can have that dinner you promised. And I'm finding I have a little appetite.

IN THE EAGLETON'S FANCY dining room, they ordered a cold lobster with mayonnaise and a bottle of claret.

"How about a couple highballs while we're waiting?" Lee said to the waiter, who nodded and hurried away.

"You told me a little about yourself on the train," Helen said after the cocktails arrived, "but I'd love to know more. Where you're from, why you went into medicine, that sort of thing."

"There's not much to tell," he said, sipping his drink. "Born and raised in Buffalo. I met Doctor Grand in the parlor of a brothel, and he got me interested in medical school. He took me under his wing, really. As an intern and then with these operations that he and I do. I'd have to say he's been my biggest influence."

"He does have that effect," Helen said. "And I'm curious. Did you know what he had in mind when he invited you to come to my flat that day?"

Lee smiled. "Of course. Grand always has me do the final lesson before a girl's graduation."

"Good to know I could graduate from *something*, after all. But what I don't understand—and if you'll pardon this one bit of shoptalk—it would seem you hate women, given, you know, the things you've been doing."

He looked somewhat surprised. "I wouldn't say I hate women. I do rather *dislike* most of them. But *hate*? That's a strong word, Helen. If I feel anything, and I'm not entirely certain I do, it's that I'm saving them years of suffering, winding up in The Hooks, or—in your case—dying from drugs."

"I see. Ever the public servant."

"There's that scorn again."

"I'm sorry. I couldn't resist that time."

"You want to know who really did hate women?" he asked.

"Who?"

"Jack the Ripper."

"Quite a few people think that the Buffalo Butcher and he are one and the same."

"And I've enjoyed that, because he's a hero of mine. But after a little experience, I have come to accept that I'll always be a footnote in history compared to him."

"Why do you say that?"

"Oh, I dreamed of being the new Ripper, I did. For *years*. Really, it's why I went to medical school in the first place—to learn where all the pieces are. And I thought, the *Pan-American*? What a backdrop!—even better than London. I had it all planned out, Helen. But it wasn't to be."

She raised her eyebrows. "It would seem you've come pretty close."

He shook his head. "Nowhere near. What I've done is pedestrian by comparison. You see, it's not *murder* that makes Jack the greatest of this little fraternity. Almost anyone can manage that, under the right circumstances. It's the *mutilation* that sets him apart from the crowd. To disassemble someone, piece by piece, is a species of revenge, not rage. Cold, malignant hatred, controlled and sustained over a long period of time. I just don't have that ability."

"But you took that nurse's uterus," she said.

"In retrospect, I ought to have mutilated her after she was dead," he said sadly. "She bore the cutting well enough, but Helen—you cannot *imagine* the sound she made when I shoved her own womb into her mouth. I don't care to hear *that* again I can assure you. I knew then I'd never measure up to Jack."

"Well, enough of that," Helen said. "I said no unpleasant talk, and then look at me—I went and dredged all that up. The lobster's quite delicious, isn't it?"

"I love lobster," he said. "More wine, my dear?"

EVERYONE KNEW THAT HELEN must have gone out early that Wednesday morning, which was itself unusual. But when she didn't return by midnight—and Grace was waiting up, ready to give her a piece of her mind—the girls started to worry. Naturally the unspoken fear was that Helen had fallen under the knife of the Buffalo Butcher, but they all reassured themselves that there must be a more pedestrian explanation for her absence. Perhaps she'd buried the hatchet with her sister and stayed overnight on Oak Street.

Raven sat up in her bed the whole evening, unable to sleep, hoping to hear the front door rattle and the sound of her friend's familiar footsteps going down the corridor to her room. Nothing.

Two hours after midnight, Raven walked softly down to Helen's door and knocked. She had hoped against hope that the door would open and there would be Helen, smiling and looking at her in that special way she had. But again, she was disappointed, and she went downstairs in her dressing-gown to find Grace.

Raven went into the back of the house, where the girls rarely ventured, and found Grace in her parlor, smoking a cigarette and reading the newspaper. Grace looked up and stabbed out her smoke in annoyance.

"What's the meaning of this intrusion?" she snapped. "I don't invade your privacy, do I?"

"I'm worried about Hel—Bell. I just knocked on her door and—nothing. It's locked up and there's no sound at all."

"I don't know what's gotten into her lately," Grace said.

"I think we ought to look in her room. She may not be there, and then we're no closer to an answer, but on the other hand—with as much dope as she uses sometimes . . ." She broke off and looked away.

"She would have had to be a ghost to come in without my noticing," Grace said, getting up and grabbing her ring of keys, "but I'm willing to try anything."

The pair walked upstairs and to the rear of the house. Grace unlocked Helen's door and peeked in.

"She's not here," she said with a distinct air of relief.

Raven barged past her into the room. She looked under the bed, in the bathroom, even in the armoire. Grace stood in the doorway, arms folded and tapping her foot, and just as Raven was going to leave in frustration, she spied the two envelopes propped up against the gallery of Helen's writing desk. She turned to block Grace's view, bending over as if to look under the desk for a clue, and slipped the envelope addressed to her into her pocket. The other one she seized up triumphantly and handed out to Grace.

"Look what I found! A note."

Grace tore open the envelope with her forefinger and shook the paper out. Raven crowded next to her, reading over her shoulder.

"She's run away," Grace said. "That little vixen. What in the world will I tell the girls?"

"It's just not like her," Raven said, thinking how Helen could have left without saying even so much as goodbye.

"I've got to go talk with Charley. This is bad." Grace looked at the clock on Helen's wall, the one Helen had watched on so many nights. She stuck a finger under Raven's nose. "Don't you *dare* say a word about this to the others. Go back to your room and stay there until breakfast. I'll figure out what to say by then."

Raven hurried away and Grace locked up Helen's vacant room again, and then went as quietly as a raindrop down the stairs, out the front door, and into the darkness.

In her room, Raven sat down on the edge of her bed and slit open her envelope from Helen.

"Please, please, *please*," she said under her breath.

She unfolded the paper, found the money, and read. Then she turned face down onto the bedspread and began to sob into the pillow. Come back to me, Helen, she thought.

CLOSING TIME AT THE Eagleton arrived at 2:00 a.m., after two more highballs and a bottle of champagne. They pleaded for just one more drink, but the manager said no.

"He doesn't know I have a bottle of martinis back at the room," Helen giggled.

"Then we have the laugh on him." Lee stood and extended his hand. "Shall we?"

Outside, the deserted streets were much cooler. They walked around the hotel's long block, Main to Clinton, Broad to Stone, and back again.

They entered the quiet hotel, nodded to the desk clerk, and found that the lift was out of service. They found the staircase and began their ascent.

"How many more flights are there?" she asked, leaning on Lee's arm and giggling. "I feel like you're making me *climb* all the way to heaven."

"We should have gotten a first-floor room," he said.

"No matter. I'm not going to let a little stair-climbing spoil my good time. The restaurant was excellent."

"I thought you'd like it."

Just then Helen stepped on the hem of her skirt and almost went face-first onto the stairs. "Oops!" she said, laughing.

He took her arm and righted her. "A little tipsy, are we?"

"Maybe a touch."

They opened the door to Room 546 and stepped inside. "Such a pretty room," Helen said.

"It is. They did us right."

He closed the door behind them and angled the back of a chair under the knob. "Privacy, you know."

"Good idea." She took a corkscrew from the washstand and struggled with the cork on the bottle of martinis. Her hands were trembling.

Lee took the bottle and corkscrew from her. "Allow me. Are you doing well, dear?"

"I'm a little nervous, to be honest," she said, and laughed. "I always have been before going on a journey."

"This one will be to a much better place," he said kindly.

She smiled. "I'm not so sure. But it'll be someplace else."

"Try not to be sad. You're a very brave woman, Helen."

"I'm trying to be."

Lee poured them each a tumblerful of martini cocktail, and Helen gulped hers down.

"Now, as I'm sure you'll understand, it will be best if this looks like a suicide," Lee said. "I'll be leaving the hotel directly after we conclude our business, so a letter is the only way to explain things."

"Is that why you registered us as Mr. and Mrs. Crosby?"

"Indeed. Even though no one here knows me, and certainly not as Mr. Crosby, people *have* seen us together on the train and at the restaurant. So it would be well if you could sit down at the desk and write out a note. You know, explaining why you're ending your life. That way, even if I'm questioned, I'll have a cover story."

"Oh yes," she said. "That's very sensible. Let's have a drink while I'm writing."

Helen took her glass and sat down at the little postcard desk, opening drawers in search for some hotel stationery. She found one, jabbed the desk pen into the inkwell, and thought a moment.

"I wonder what tone one takes with a suicide note?" she said.

He sat down on the edge of the bed and began to unfasten his collar and cuffs. "I think most people ask for forgiveness."

"Now, *that* seems a bit hypocritical," Helen said. "I really think I'm the one who should be doing the forgiving. But I'd have to forgive myself first, and that I cannot do."

"Ha. You have a quick wit, Helen."

"It's been good to laugh a little." She straightened the paper and wrote:

Whitman House Hotel
Rochester, New York
August 28, 1901

To all:

To Dr. George Grand—you destroyed my faith in men, but not in God. And I know you'll have to face him one day.

To Eva—I wish you much happiness.

To Grace, Charley, May, and Alice—You've all been good to me, really you have. I hope to see you again.

To Goh-láh-nah—this time, the dove must go before the raven. Trust that I will be with you always.

Helen

"There," she said, waving the paper in the air to dry the ink and then handing it to Lee. He read it over.

"Very well done," he said, handing it back. "A nice balance of pointed and poignant."

"Why, thank you. It's certainly from the heart."

Helen folded the paper neatly and slid it into one of the Whitman's lavender envelopes, then leaned it neatly against the gallery on the top of the desk. She took a deep breath.

"Well?" she said. "You've been as good as your word, Lee, so now it's time I was, too."

"Finally," he said, and quickly stripped off his layers of clothing.

"Good Lord, what a sendoff," she said, nodding at his pecker. "It's a wonder you don't trip over that thing. I guess I was too high to notice on the other occasion."

He rolled his eyes. "You have no idea how tiring it is to hear that all the time, from every woman. How frightening it is. Will they be able to handle it. I can't help it I was born this way. It's a *curse*."

"I meant it only as a little joke. I didn't mean to hurt your feelings."

"It's fine." He looked down at it. "I suppose at least you know you have an effect on me."

"I haven't lost my touch," she said. "Now you make yourself comfortable while I undress in the washroom."

She went into the bathroom, cocktail in hand.

I don't have much time, she thought, closing the door behind her. She sat on the toilet and reached into her skirt pocket for the tiny vial that Grace had given her, the one containing the atropine she'd cautioned her about. It was there, just where it was when she'd left her room that morning.

Helen dumped out the three little white pills into her palm, and crushed them with her thumb. She dumped the powder into her cocktail and stirred it with a finger. Then she undressed and urinated, to keep Lee from wondering what was taking her so long.

She dried herself off and stood in front of the mirror, running her hands over her naked body, thinking of Raven, who after tonight would be safe. As would all her other friends, as well as girls she would never know. But it was Raven's hands that she would miss most.

Bear up, Miss Bell, she thought. One last shift. She grabbed up the glass again and went into their bedroom.

LEE WAS LYING ON his back, his cock gone soft in her absence. When he saw her, though, it came to life again, and fast. She lay down next to him. He was going to mount her when she reached for the cocktail glass, which she'd placed on the nightstand.

"Let's finish this first," she said.

"I've had plenty, thank you."

"Lee, please. Put yourself in my place. I'm frightened. Just finish this one with me, will you?" She took a sip and handed him the glass.

"Very well," he said tartly. Impatiently he drained the rest of the glass. "There," he said, setting the empty tumbler down, licking his lips with a curious expression. "Satisfied? May I now enjoy *my* part of the evening?"

"Of course, Lee. I didn't mean to be difficult."

"Then don't be," he said, gritting his teeth.

She had barely begun to open her legs when he climbed on her and jammed it in with a long groan. Now she remembered that day more clearly, how much it hurt and how his face had shown no pleasure, only delight in causing pain with nothing else but a part of his body.

He began humping her furiously, and she felt a shiver of fear. The atropine would take a good five minutes to work its magic, and experience told her that at this frenzied pace he'd come in a minute or less. Then a few minutes for the chloroform . . .

Bell, she thought, manage the clock.

She pushed her hips against him, hard, and slowed his motion. He was so strong that she had to wrap her thighs around him so that he couldn't thrust, only grapple with her. He tried to push her legs apart again, but in this area her work had made her strong, too, and he failed.

"What are you doing?" he said angrily. "I want to finish."

She looked him in the eye, and she thought that perhaps his pupils were beginning to dilate. Three pills—even in a big body that should be a near-fatal dose.

"It's better if it lasts a bit longer," she said. "I know what I'm doing. Let me bring you off." He nodded.

Helen slowed their rhythm and felt his breathing settle again. In her mind, she felt a minute pass, then another, gracefully undulating together.

"*Now*," she said. "Give it to me. Hard as you want."

He put his palms on the insides of her thighs and shoved them apart. Between that and his big tool, Helen felt that she was being torn in two, but she thought again of Raven. In less than another minute, he collapsed next to her, panting.

She stretched out primly on her back, propping her head up on the pillow. He looked over at her, his eyes very dark, and with some unplaceable emotion on his face. It would have frightened her under normal circumstances, but she could tell that the atropine was taking effect.

"I hope you enjoyed that," she said.

"Do you ever shut up?"

"I don't mean to be irritating. Are we ready for the final act?"

He didn't reply. He slid out of bed and retrieved his medical bag, walking with a strangely stiff gait. He came back with the vial of chloroform, a handkerchief, and a razor, presumably from his shaving kit. He straddled her and put the razor under the pillow. His dick was hard again, but he didn't attempt to penetrate her.

She took a deep breath. "Here we go," she said quietly, looking past him at the ceiling. "May I pray?"

"If you make it fast," he said.

She nodded and closed her eyes. "Lord, into thy hands I commend my spirit," she said softly, and then looked at Lee again.

"Is there—anything else?" His eyes were now all pupil and glassy.

"Make sure you go deep enough," she said.

"You have nothing to worry about. The artery is about an inch under here." He touched the left side of her neck. "I'll begin my incision just to the left of it. I'll sever the artery, and you'll be gone. All you have to do now is to relax while I administer the chloroform."

He saturated the handkerchief with the contents of the vial. "As I said, the smell's not unpleasant, but it's natural to want to hold your breath. Try to resist the urge to do so. Breathe as deeply as you can. The deeper you breathe, the sooner this will be all over."

She nodded. He spread the handkerchief over her face, and she took a breath. "It smells sweet."

"Slightly, I suppose," he said, slurring his words.

She inhaled deeply. "It reminds me of clover—in the summers, when

I was a little girl," she whispered through the cloth. "But deeper, some-how. More dangerous."

"I've put enough on the cloth that your heart is going to slow appre-ciably. That way, when I make the incision, there won't be as much pressure."

"Oh good. I've been worried about making a mess."

"It can't be helped completely," he said, stretching his fingers, which suddenly felt oddly stiff.

She took several more deep gulps of the chloroform. "I feel warm. Like I'm sitting in front of a fire."

"It's beginning to work. Keep breathing, just like you are. Only another minute or two."

"Imagine, I'll be dead in only two minutes," she said softly. "Such a strange notion."

"You'll be *asleep* in two minutes," he said. "It'll take several more after that for you to bleed to death. But you won't be aware of that part."

He felt for her pulse, trying to flex his fingers. "Your heart's slowing down."

"I feel really good now," she murmured. "What a delightful sensation."

"It won't be much longer now. You'll be dead very soon, Helen."

Her whole body felt warm and cozy now, and she imagined that she was in Raven's arms, skin against skin. How I love you, Goh-láh-nah, she thought.

"The girls will live," she murmured.

"I do feel a little bad about that," he replied.

Her eyes fluttered open, and she made a small, urgent sound.

"What is it, Helen?" he said, taking away the cloth and putting his ear to her lips.

"You'll find out soon," she whispered. "I knew you would lie." Her eyes closed again.

"Too late now," he said, replacing the handkerchief.

He let her breathe through the cloth for another full minute, watch-ing her respiration slow. She began to snore softly. When he removed the cloth—fingers still strangely stiff—he saw that she had fallen fast asleep with a beatific smile on her face. There was something about her smile that angered him.

Lee reached under the pillow and found his razor. It took both hands to open it, because his fingers wouldn't respond to his brain's command. He fumbled for a while before he thought to hook the end of the blade with his knuckle and swing it open. Then the damn thing closed on the backs of his fingers, and he began bleeding profusely.

His eyes, too, were refusing to cooperate, and the outline of her exposed throat was blurry, looking like—what was it looking like? he thought. Unable to see clearly, he felt for the pulse in her neck, and after some effort found it, faint but regular deep beneath her soft skin. He placed the very tip of his blade against the throb. He would begin his incision here, cutting deep enough to find the carotid, and then draw across the windpipe, as usual. But this time, mainly for show—what a suicide ought to look like. Ear to ear.

As he was about to push the blade in, he thought of the cocktail she had given him. *You'll find out soon*, he thought. He felt a jolt of anger. She had slipped him something; there could be no doubting that now. The outlines of the room were melting, and he could feel his hand beginning to shake. He felt sure something else had entered the room, majestic and terrifying. He turned dizzily right and left but saw nothing except his own image reflected in the cheval mirror, crouched like a gargoyle over Helen's naked body. Wearing that Mona Lisa smile.

He thought to get up and crawl away, let her live in her hell and he in his. But that would feel like cowardice, and so he dug the razor in, pushing deep into the muscle of her throat. Feeling the wet warmth flooding over his fingers, and the penetrating smell of rust, he knew he'd found her life. He managed to cut almost to her right clavicle before the room went black.

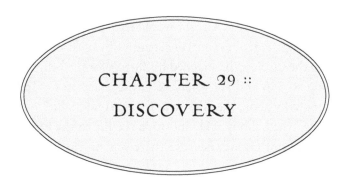

CHAPTER 29 ::

DISCOVERY

A t breakfast, Grace sat down at the head of the table. Only May
and Alice were in their places.

"Where are Bell and Raven?" May asked after a pro-
longed silence.

"Raven's in her room," Grace said. "She's not hungry this morning."

"I'll eat hers," Alice said. "What about Bell?"

Grace took a deep breath. "Girls, I'm sorry to tell you that Miss Bell
has left us."

"Left us?" said Alice. "She only just got here, and she's as pretty as
the day she did. Don't tell me she went to The Alzora."

"No, she didn't go to The Alzora. She's run away."

Alice and May goggled at her, flabbergasted. "Run away?" May
said. "Where?"

"For heaven's sake, Miss Flower. The very nature of running away
means that no one is supposed to know where one has gone."

"Yes, that's true," May said.

"Will you bring her back?" asked Alice.

"Miss Star, the likeliest thing is that Miss Bell will return on her
own. I'm sure we'll have word of her very soon."

AT 11:01 THAT MORNING, the day desk clerk at the Whitman was
officially annoyed. It was a minute past checkout time, there had been no

answer to several calls to Room 546, and the hotel was fully booked for that evening. Mr. and Mrs. Crosby would have to go.

He rang the room one more time, fruitlessly, at eleven fifteen. When he hung up the earpiece, he snapped his fingers for the bellboy.

"Go up to 546 and see what the Crosbys are up to. Tell them if they're not out by noon, they'll owe us for a second night."

"Yes, sir," the bellboy said, and rode the lift to the fifth floor. He hated this kind of errand, because there was no tip in telling someone to scram.

He rapped gently on the door of Room 546, but there was no answer. He rapped again, harder—but again no answer. Then he heard what sounded like the drone of something mechanical, and he put his ear against the door. The drone was clearly audible through the wood, but now it sounded more like a rhythmic series of low moans.

The bellboy put his eye to the keyhole to see if he might get lucky and see a couple going at it. Still no tip, but that would be worth watching.

At that moment, a well-dressed gentleman stepped out of Room 547, directly across the hall, on his way to a luncheon downtown. He saw the boy kneeling in front of 546, peering through the keyhole.

"What in the world do you think you're doing?" he asked indignantly. The bellboy hopped up, red-faced. "I've half a mind to report you to the management, and see you turned out."

"It's not what you think," the bellboy stammered. "The people in here"—he jerked a thumb toward the door—"were supposed to be out by eleven. But they're not. And it sounded like someone's hurt in there."

"You'd better not be putting me on," the gentleman said.

"Go ahead, listen. There's a key in the lock, so I couldn't see anything through the keyhole."

The gentleman pressed his ear against the door. "Why, that is peculiar," he said after a minute.

"I told you so!"

"Do you have a passkey?" the gentleman asked.

"No," the bellboy replied.

"Wait here a minute." The man went back into his room and

emerged with a chair. "Climb up on this. Maybe you can see what's going on through the transom."

"All right," the bellhop said, and climbed onto the seat of the chair, placing his hands on the doorframe to steady himself. He went up on his tiptoes to peer through the transom window.

"God," the bellboy said, pushing away from the transom and almost toppling off the chair. He climbed down, shaking.

"What is it?" the man said.

"It's—it's something horrible," the boy said.

"But what?"

The bellboy tried to stammer something out.

"For heaven's sake, boy, what is wrong?"

"We have to call the police," the bellboy said feebly. "Now."

SOMEONE HAD PROPPED A chair under the doorknob of Room 546, so it took three burly cops to break open the door.

"Jesus Christ," said the first on entering.

The room was sweltering, and the air was thick with the metallic tang of blood, the stench of a slaughterhouse.

Helen was lying naked on the left side of the bed, on her back, legs still slightly apart. Her head was slightly thrown back, eyes fixed on the ceiling above the bedstead. There was a gaping wound across her throat, tracing a graceful arc from under the left ear to where it disappeared under her chemise. The front of the chemise was soaked with an astonishing quantity of blood, which had run down her neck and onto the bed. Some had run down her left arm, which was extended over the edge of the bed. Lightly clutched in Helen's left hand was a straight razor, partially open.

Lee was stumbling around the room, clad only in an undershirt, which was also soaked in blood. His entire upper body was arched backwards, taut as a bowstring. He walked stiffly around to the right side of the bed and collapsed next to Helen's body, the side of his face in what looked to be a pool of congealed blood, dark purple and resembling a large, flat piece of beef liver. Lee was moaning rhythmically, his eyes and mouth opening and closing.

The first cop nerved himself and walked over to the bed. The girl was plainly dead, her dark brown eyes half-open and glassy.

"This fellow's on fire," he said, feeling Lee's forehead.

"Looks like tetanus," the other cop said.

The first policeman picked up the water pitcher from the washstand, and with his fingers splashed some on Lee's face. Lee babbled something and stiffly raised a hand in front of his face. It, too, was covered with blood.

By now there was a little crowd of curious hotel guests gathered in the hallway, peering in.

"Scat," one of the cops said to the group, who hustled away down the corridor, buzzing about what they had seen. "Not you," he said to the bellboy and the gentleman from across the hall. "You'll have to give a statement to the detectives. You don't go anywhere."

"But, officer, I have sales calls to make," the gentleman said.

"Not today you don't."

"Water," Lee croaked, roused again from his stupor by all the commotion. "I need water."

The cop went over to the washstand again and filled a glass. He noticed that the water in the pitcher was a light pink, tinged with blood. He shrugged inwardly and rolled Lee up to a sitting position. He handed him the glass and Lee gulped it down greedily.

"Don't you see them?" he murmured, trying to point something out.

"See what?" the cop said.

Lee didn't answer, but kept snapping his gaze here and there, as if trying to follow a pesky fly.

"What in holy hell went on here?" the cop asked, but Lee didn't answer. "You," the cop said to the bellboy, "have your boss call the main station and send the detectives. Also the coroner. And don't go anywhere until we get your statement."

The boy disappeared down the hallway.

"And you," he said to the gentleman, "go wait in your room until we call you."

When the two cops were alone with Lee, they took turns splashing him with pink water. At last Lee seemed to recover a semblance of lucidity.

"What happened here, mister?" the cop asked.

"What's the matter?" Lee slurred. "Haven't you ever seen blood before?"

"Have you taken anything?"

"The girl gave me a cocktail with something in it," he said. "She tried to poison me."

"Looks like the other way around, buddy. What's your name?"

Lee looked through them, uncomprehending, and got another splash of pink water for his trouble.

"I said, what's your name?"

"Leland Kennecott," he said. "Doctor Leland Kennecott."

"The desk clerk told me that this room is registered to a Mr. and Mrs. Crosby. How is it your name's Kennecott?"

"She was talking about making away with herself all night, and after a certain point I thought it best if I just go with her."

"Excuse me?"

"I need to get back to Buffalo," Lee said.

"You from Buffalo?"

"I agreed to take her away from everything," Lee mumbled.

"Seems like you did a pretty good job of it," the second cop said.

"You two married?" his partner asked, tapping Lee's wedding ring.

"Not really," Lee said.

"There's no point asking him anything," the cop said to his partner. "He's high as a kite."

By the time the coroner and his two assistants arrived, Lee had made some improvement, but had turned surly.

"My name's Phillip," the coroner said to Lee. "Monroe County Coroner. I'd like to take your statement."

"Phillip what?"

"Coroner Phillip."

"I'm thirsty," Lee said.

One of the cops poured another tumblerful of pink water. The coroner took it and squinted, then looked into the porcelain pitcher. "There's blood in this water," he said, dumping the glass back into the container. "Get him some fresh from the bathroom."

"Look at my eyes." Coroner Phillip felt Lee's forehead. "You said he was seeing things earlier?" he asked when the cop brought the fresh water.

"Yeah, swatting at stuff that wasn't there."

"Atropine or hyoscine poisoning, I'd say. He's feverish, thirsty, seeing things, and all this stiffness."

"I told them already—the girl gave me something in my drink," Lee muttered. "She tried to poison me."

"Why would she do that?" the coroner asked.

"For fuck's sake," Lee said, "how obvious do I have to make it?"

"Mind your manners, young man. Why would this girl give you atropine?"

"All night all she would talk about is how she wanted to kill herself. She wrote out a note. On the desk. I tried to stop her, but she wouldn't listen. Then when we came to bed, she gave me a drink and told me to drink it. I did, and when I looked around at her again, she was pulling a razor across her throat."

"Whose razor?"

"I suppose mine. She must have got it from my kit."

"Which hand was it in?"

"Her left." Lee looked over at the razor in Helen's hand. "Just like now."

"And you fell unconscious when she cut herself? You haven't moved since?"

"I couldn't move," Lee said. "Everything was stiff."

"What was the girl's name?"

"Helen Crosby."

"Did you have intimate relations with her?"

"What does that have to do with anything?"

"Why don't you answer the question?" Coroner Phillip said.

"Yes, we had relations. So what?"

"Because you said your name is Kennecott and hers is Crosby. And you're wearing a wedding ring, and she's not. I just wonder what you two were up to."

"Look, she had all kinds of troubles in life," Lee replied. "A man back in Buffalo had taken advantage of her and ruined her, and she had turned to making her living from immorality. Her family turned away from her. I wanted to help her get away from all that."

"So, if I understand, you thought that you'd help her by having sexual intercourse."

"Doing it was all her idea," Lee said.

"You seem a little young to be a doctor," the coroner said.

"I'm an intern, to be precise. At Riverdale Hospital in Buffalo. But very soon I'll be a doctor."

The cop looked over Lee to Helen's body, lying still on the bed. "So you're telling us that she cut her own throat like that?"

"Didn't you hear me? Yes, she cut her own throat. I certainly didn't do it!"

The cop shook his head. "I've seen lots of suicides. But I ain't never seen a woman cut her own throat. Women usually take poison, or gas themselves."

"Well, this one didn't," Lee said.

The coroner turned to his assistants. "Boys, get her into a box and take her to the morgue for the medical examiner to autopsy. Collect up all these bags and so forth so I can give it all to the detectives."

"Detectives?" Lee said. "That's my personal property. And I just explained to the officer here what happened. I expect you to let me go right away."

The coroner stared him down. "It doesn't work like that, Doctor—Mister—Kennecott," he said. "That'll be up to the detectives and the district attorney. "But you ought to expect to be our guest for a while. You've been found with a dead girl in bed with you, and at least from where I sit, your explanation doesn't make a goddamn bit of sense."

WORD CAME AROUND FIVE o'clock, in the evening *Courier*. The headline read:

"BELL GIRL" A SUICIDE!!

Rochester Hotel Room a Charnel House

Medical Student in Custody

Raven came down when she heard the paper hit the front door. Grace had already retrieved it and was waiting for her at the bottom of the staircase.

"Raven," she said, blocking the girl from entering the parlor, "I need to speak with you."

"What is it?" Raven said. "Is there news about Helen?"

"I'm afraid . . . I know how you felt about—"

Raven's eyes flew open. "*Felt?* What has happened, Grace?" She saw the *Courier* lying on the parlor table and knocked Grace out of her way. She picked it up and stared silently at the front page. Then she set the paper down carefully again.

"Raven, dear," Grace said. "Why don't we sit down in my parlor—"

"Grace, *dear*," Raven replied, "there's nothing in your parlor I want. Just leave me alone."

As nine o'clock approached, Anne and May came down the staircase, scrubbed, perfumed, and ready. They sat in the parlor, idly watching the pendulum of the grandfather clock. Something seemed strange, but that was probably just that the place was very subdued indeed without Bell or Raven.

On the stroke of nine, things got stranger. There was no Grace, either, smiling and opening the door to welcome the first gentlemen of the evening. Only the *tick-tock* of the pendulum marking the time.

At last Grace came out of her rear parlor, dressed in black. Her face was drawn and there were large, dark circles around her eyes.

"We're not going to open tonight, girls," she said to Alice and May. "I hadn't the heart to tell you individually—Miss Bell has died."

Alice and May looked back at her, stunned. Grace didn't joke about anything, and even if she did, it wouldn't be about one of them dying.

"She's dead?" May said. "How? Was it the drugs?"

"It seems that when she left here, she went to Rochester with young Mr. Kennecott."

"I didn't like his look," said Alice.

"Oh, there's more to dislike about him than his look," May said. "He's Doctor Grand's final lesson."

"Let's not go into all that now, May," Grace said.

"What a horrible man," said Alice. "Why in the world would Bell run off with someone like that?"

"Enough of all that, girls. The paper said suicide."

"*Suicide*?" May said. "Bell wasn't suicidal. If anything, lately she's seemed especially happy for some reason."

"She took Olive's death hard," said Alice.

"Yes, but she wouldn't kill herself over it."

"I agree with both of you," Grace said.

"Raven will know," May murmured.

"But she'll never say," said Alice.

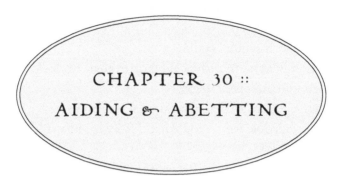

CHAPTER 30 ::
AIDING & ABETTING

After reading the coroner's report and the transcripts of the detectives' interviews, Monroe County District Attorney John Whalen wasn't buying Lee's story, not a bit of it, not for a second. He had Lee transferred to a hospital for observation, under the pretext that he'd said that his companion had given him a potentially deadly drug. There he could keep him on ice for a couple of days, until he decided what to do with him.

Whalen was a youngish man for the job, a vigorous forty-two and showing promise for future political offices. So far as an indictment was concerned, it wouldn't be hard to bring charges against Leland Kennecott, but which ones? Murder, possibly, but the suicide note in the dead girl's own hand presented a serious problem with that charge. Fortunately, the New York Penal Code offered a solution: aiding and abetting a suicide, even that of someone determined to take his or her own life, was chargeable as manslaughter in the first degree. A conviction carried with it the possibility of twenty years hard time in Auburn Prison. That was a serious sentence, and would be a feather in the new district attorney's cap. But murder would be even better—that one could send Kennecott to the chair, which was also conveniently located in the basement of Auburn Prison.

Whalen was on the horns of a dilemma. If, as Lee Kennecott had stated, the girl had drugged him, and then had lain down and finished the job on herself, it would be very hard to prove that he had done any aiding and abetting at all. That was nothing more than being in the wrong place at the wrong time—locked in a room with a crazy woman bent on self-destruction—and no jury of twelve sober and upright men would convict on *that*.

But something didn't settle with him about Lee's version of events. He did, after all, have superficial but very crisp cuts on his right hand—the kind of clean slices that a razor might cause. If he had been holding the razor, and it had closed on him, those cuts would be neatly explained. And Lee had admitted—and he'd signed enough forms now while in temporary custody—that he was right-handed.

Helen Crosby's wound, too, gave the DA pause. The wound started on the left neck; there had been no uncertainty here, and it was a decisive—one might even say surgical—cut at that. The razor had first gone deep, an inch and a half into the flesh, found and neatly severed the carotid artery, and continued across the front of the neck for four-and-a-half full inches, riding over the hump of the windpipe and gradually growing shallower until the blade came to rest against the inside protrusion of the right clavicle. Such a wound would have spurted blood with considerable force; at the very least the young woman's hand—her left, according to Lee's statement—would have been covered with it. There were no two ways about it.

Yet not a drop of blood was found on either of Helen Crosby's hands, neither left nor right, and yet both of Lee Kennecott's, as well as his undershirt, chest, and neck, were covered with the stuff. The razor itself was also free of blood, save for what looked like a thumbprint low on the handle, as though it had been washed off—possibly in the pitcher of pink water on the washstand. When Helen's body was removed, what looked like a huge clot of blood under her neck—always more blood!—turned out to be a wadded-up handkerchief, which had been so saturated that it had coagulated into an almost spherical mass.

No one yet could say whether Helen Crosby had been left- or right-handed. Very little was known about her at all; that would take some digging, and the DA hadn't enough time for that before empaneling a grand jury. Lee had claimed that, after her brief stint as a Bell Girl, she had become a prostitute, and information about prostitutes was notoriously difficult to track down. Most of them didn't use their real names, so even her name may be falsified.

District Attorney Whalen reviewed as much of the information as he could in the space of a few days, during which Lee Kennecott regained his lucidity, and lawyered up. His father came in from Buffalo to stand by him. No one, yet, had turned up for Helen Crosby.

After much thought, the district attorney settled on bringing the one charge before the grand jury that, he thought, could get him a conviction. The apparent suicide note would make a murder charge impossible. Aiding and abetting in the plainest sense—simply encouraging or assisting someone in a quest for suicide—would be impossible to prove, because only Lee remained alive. But Whalen reckoned that aiding and abetting could be expanded to include a more horrifying element—that Leland Davis Kennecott had aided and abetted in the suicide of Helen Crosby by making the lethal cut himself. Even if Helen had cooperated and gone willingly under Kennecott's razor—begged him to do it, even—if the DA could prove beyond a reasonable doubt that it was Lee's hand that ended her life, he would secure a guilty verdict.

District Attorney Whalen laid out his case to the grand jury, which duly returned an indictment against Lee Davis Kennecott for the single charge of manslaughter in the first degree.

A JURY WAS EMPANELED in less than a week, twelve sober and upright men who would have to determine whatever truth had happened in Room 546 of the Whitman House Hotel.

Even before the trial began, each day the gallery was half-full of Lee's loyal fraternity brothers, family, and friends. His dutiful wife, though looking decidedly drawn, came to Rochester and stood by him. As she told the eager reporters, her husband's brief dalliance with Helen Crosby had begun, after all, with the best of intentions.

Lee, for his part, took no pains to disguise his contempt for the proceedings. He gave interviews to anyone with a pencil, calling it an outrage that an educated man such as himself, soon to be a doctor, could possibly be on trial for the admitted suicide of a *whore*. It was a thing too strange to comprehend. And many agreed, their sympathy stirred up by the Buffalo papers, who honored their bargain with the mayor by sending reporters to Rochester and turning the whole thing into a twisted morality play. A *prostitute* was dead, and by her own hand, and yet a respectable up-and-comer was in the dock for it? Probably, the papers suggested, because this thing had happened in Monroe County, and Lee was from Buffalo. Rochester had always felt the sting of inferiority compared to her larger cousin to the west.

There was one more slight *frisson* of scandal when it emerged that the dead girl's photographs had appeared in the recent edition of the phone book. However, few of the books remained unvandalized after the first wave of prurient interest in Helen lost their pages four and five now, and in a hurry. While maintaining a perfectly straight face, the Bell Telephone Company issued a lugubrious statement to the effect that they would not, purely out of respect for the dead, reprint Helen's image in next year's edition. They had, fortunately, already made a handsome profit from three reprints of the current book.

The Buffalo medical community, or a good deal of it, closed ranks around soon-to-be-Doctor Kennecott and helped Lee's wife locate and retain a rather famous defense attorney, George Haynes. Haynes was getting on in years, and had retired from active practice, but he was remembered in Erie and Monroe Counties for his full-throated and stirring oratory, an art still prized and practiced, if decidedly on the wane.

Haynes had even done a stint as Monroe County District Attorney, many years before, and so he knew the game from both sides of the field. He was keen to show the upstart Whalen a thing or two—that an old dog could not only do, but also teach, new tricks.

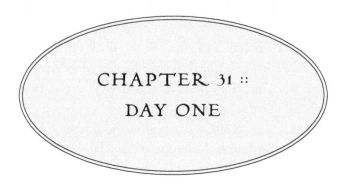

CHAPTER 31 ::

DAY ONE

September 11, 1901
Wednesday

The trial began on Wednesday, with Judge Northland presiding, in the ornate criminal courtroom of Monroe County. District Attorney Whalen's opening statement was concise and went right to the heart of the sole charge on which he hoped to convict Leland Davis Kennecott.

"Your Honor, gentlemen of the jury, we are here to judge the guilt or innocence of the defendant, Leland Davis Kennecott. *Mister* Kennecott—he does occasionally refer to himself as 'Doctor,' but as you'll hear that is an exaggeration—has much to commend him, on paper. Let me tell you some of what I am sure his defense will repeat, again and again—that their client is a medical school graduate, a husband, and a father. I could understand why they would do so, because these masculine attributes are intended to tug at your heartstrings and divert you from the facts of the crime that we will show he has committed.

"But even if you do grant these bright elements of Leland Davis Kennecott's character your sympathy, you must apply equal judgment to the deep darkness present in the man. Yes, he is a husband, and a father. Yet he is a husband and a father who thoughtlessly leaves his wife and infant son at home alone, while he comes to Rochester to cavort with a prostitute overnight in a hotel, under a false name and safely away from prying eyes. And while it is true that the defendant has trained in medicine—specifically in the surgical arts—I will bring out how the victim's wounds could have only been inflicted by a trained and steady hand—the skilled hand of a surgeon corrupted by evil—and not by that of a frightened girl. When you have heard all the evidence presented, you will be alone with your conscience. And in searching your conscience, I am confident that you will find within a verdict of guilty, manslaughter in the first degree."

Haynes sprang up as soon as the DA had taken his seat.

"Imagine, gentlemen," he said, "imagine that—against your own better judgment and, very likely, the opinion of others whose assessments of your character you value—you are moved to pity by the plight of a fallen woman. A woman so distracted and misguided, in fact, that she becomes bent on taking her own life. Imagine, too, that you are a physician—or soon to be one—and you are mindful of your holy oath to use your hands to heal, and not to harm. Indeed, you are a medical intern under a noted surgeon, Doctor George Grand, employed by a respected institution.

"Now because you know that some may misinterpret your good intentions, you take this troubled young woman to a neighboring city. There, you intend to deliver her into capable hands, having already delivered her from the wicked and vicious haunts to which she has become habituated. Now imagine that—despite all your well-intended efforts—this distracted, hysterical, fallen woman goes ahead with her plot to end her suffering by suicide.

"Finally, imagine that despite all this—are you praised for a gallant if futile attempt? No, gentlemen, you are not! Instead, you find yourself charged with a very serious crime which—if you are convicted—may send you to prison for the greatest portion of your productive life. Is this how any Good Samaritan ought to be handled? I think you will agree that it is not.

"I believe that at the end of this proceeding, you will find my client, Lee Kennecott, not guilty of this most unusual and unjust charge."

The prosecution opened its case with Dr. McDermott, Monroe County Medical Examiner.

District Attorney Whalen began, "Doctor McDermott, you examined the body of Miss Helen Crosby?"

"I did," the doctor said. "I performed an autopsy on the deceased."

"Can you take us through your report?"

The medical examiner referred to a few sheets of paper. "Yes, of course. Deceased is one Helen Crosby, five-feet-five inches tall, weight one hundred and twenty-five pounds."

"Any physical abnormalities?"

"Internal organs were all within normal ranges. Small marks behind each knee, typical of regular hypodermic needle use. Stomach contained remains of a recent meal and a quantity of alcoholic liquid. There was a generalized skin eruption around the mouth and over the bridge of the nose."

"What kind of skin eruption?"

"I could not determine its cause. It may have been acne, however."

"Was Miss Crosby with child?"

"No. Her uterus bore no signs of having been pregnant."

"Did you find evidence of any immorality?"

"Contained within her vagina was a quantity of seminal emission."

"Order," Judge Northland said to quiet a tide of murmurs.

"What caused her death?"

"Exsanguination—massive blood loss—from a severed left carotid artery. The decedent had a single wound on the neck."

"Tell us about that wound in detail."

"It was a fine and deep incision—"

"Objection," Haynes said. "'Incision' suggests a medical procedure."

"Sustained," Judge Northland said. "Find another word, Doctor."

"It was a deep slice or wound, a fine cut, made with a very fine blade."

"Such as a razor?" the DA asked.

"Yes, I would presume so. The wound began at the left neck, an inch-and-a-half deep, and progressed in a smooth, arcing line across the wind-pipe to stop at the right clavicle. The jugular vein was intact."

"A cut from left to right, deepest on the left. Does this suggest whether the killer was right- or left-handed?"

"I would say most certainly right-handed," the ME said.

"Very good. Would a cut of this kind require a steady hand?"

"Yes, very steady. It was smooth and didn't wander in any way."

"And a strong hand?"

"Reasonably so, given the depth of the cut, its length, and the resistance offered by the various structures of the neck."

"And in your opinion, could such a wound be self-administered?"

"I find it very hard to believe."

"Why is that?"

"In my experience with suicides who cut their wrists, usually several small, tentative cuts are made before inflicting a more lethal wound," he said. "There is a natural human resistance to cutting one's own flesh. To do so deeply and decisively, and then continue the incis—cut—after severing one's own carotid artery—well, that seems highly unlikely."

"Are you saying, then, that such a wound is more likely to have been made by another person than the victim?"

"I am."

"No further questions of this witness," the DA said.

Haynes sauntered up to the ME. "You said 'in your experience,' Doctor, that suicides make tentative cuts, is that right?"

"Yes, that's right."

"And you said your experience regards those who cut their own wrists, correct?"

"Also correct."

"You have not, then, examined prior to the current case, any victim who cut his or her own throat?"

"No, I have not."

"So you have no experience with self-inflicted neck wounds."

"No, but—"

"'No' will suffice, doctor. You testified that the wound in the deceased girl's neck was not likely to have been inflicted by a left-handed person."

"That's correct."

"Can you be certain? It is *impossible* that the wound could have been made by a left-handed person? Impossible?"

"I can't say anything is impossible, no."

"So it's possible?"

"Yes, but very unlikely."

"Final question, Doctor. You testified that this wound was unlikely to have been self-inflicted."

"That is my assessment, yes."

"But again—not *impossible*? And I would remind you that you have admitted that you've never personally examined a suicide by the cutting of the throat."

The doctor squirmed in his seat.

"Yes or no, Doctor? Is it impossible that this wound was self-inflicted?"

"No," the doctor said wearily. "It is not impossible."

"That's all, Your Honor," Haynes said.

THINGS DIDN'T IMPROVE FOR the prosecution after that. Witness after witness—from the bellboy to the waiter who served Lee and Helen at the Eagleton—either developed sudden memory loss, or had their testimony shot full of holes by the wily old Haynes. As the shellacking went on, Lee's permanent smirk widened into a triumphant smile. Several times he clapped his attorney on the shoulder when Haynes sat down next to him after dispensing with another prosecution witness.

Unless something changed, and quickly, it was clear that George Haynes would succeed in planting the seed of reasonable doubt into the minds of the twelve men sitting in judgment over his client. And the district attorney knew it.

AS THE GALLERY EMPTIED, Grace and Charley sat in the corridor outside the courtroom, talking urgently on a bench against the wall.

"You do understand that once we open our mouths, our businesses are through," Charley said. "Christ, Grace, we'll have to go straight."

"You think I don't know that? But we're going to have to one way or the other. You heard what Chief Ball told us—the mayor's made a deal to clean out the Tenderloin after the Pan. So why not go out with a bang?"

"All right, then. I go where you go."

"Mr. Whalen?" Grace said as the DA hustled by, making for the stairs.

"Yes?" he said, turning and skidding to a stop. "And who might you be?"

"I'm Mrs. Grace Harrington. And this is my friend and associate, Charley Willard. Miss Crosby worked for us."

"She did?"

"She did," Grace said. "And we both loved her, even though I suppose we tried not to."

"I'm terribly sorry for your loss," Whalen said. "It won't bring Miss Crosby back, but I hope we can see justice done, at least."

"This morning didn't seem too encouraging on that front," Charley said.

Whalen scowled at him. "I assure you that I'm doing my best, sir. Now, if there's nothing else I can do for you, I really must return to my office to prepare for the afternoon session."

"Please pardon my idiot friend here," Grace said. "He means well. We don't want you to do anything for us, sir. We want to do something for *you*."

"Grace and I know things," said Charley, "that will put Kennecott behind bars for a very long time."

Whalen scrutinized the two of them. "You wouldn't be putting me on, would you?"

Grace crossed herself. "No, sir, we're not. We've got the goods on him, so long as you give us and our employees immunity."

"You're from Buffalo?"

"Yes," they said.

"Well, I don't have jurisdiction there. I can't grant immunity in another county."

"If you'll tell the Erie County DA that you want a favor for Popcorn Charley and Grace Harrington," Charley said, "he'll do it. And he'll still owe you one. I promise."

"Then come with me to my office. And hurry."

CHAPTER 32 ::

DAY TWO

September 12, 1901
Thursday

"The prosecution calls Grace Harrington," Whalen said. Grace, wearing deep mourning, took her oath and her seat in the witness box.

"Mrs. Harrington," Whalen began. "How did you know the deceased?"

"She worked for me."

"For how long?"

"About three months."

"In what capacity?"

"She was a hostess."

"A hostess? Do you own a restaurant, Mrs. Harrington?"

"I own a Raines Law hotel," she said. "I provide refreshments and light meals."

"Very well," the DA said. "Do you provide anything else for your guests?"

"I provide the society of women," she said to a rush of gasps.

"Women? Prostitutes?"

"I prefer *belles de nuit*, but yes. And you may ask anyone in Buffalo—my establishment is the finest of all. And caters to the most discerning gentlemen."

"It is well that you're admitting to all this in Monroe County, Mrs. Harrington," Judge Northland said.

"Thank you for saying so, Your Honor."

"Now then, Mrs. Harrington, Miss Crosby was a prostitute?"

"She was. And the best of them all."

"And how was it she came to be employed at your—house?"

"Doctor George Grand served as my cadet."

"And what is a cadet?"

"A procurer," Grace said. "A panderer. Think of him as a kind of talent scout."

"Is this the same Doctor George Grand that defense counsel mentioned in his opening statement? The same Doctor George Grand who is in the courtroom today?"

Heads started snapping around, looking for Grand.

"One and the same."

"So Grand brought Miss Crosby to you."

"He did—through Charley Willard, but on my instruction. I needed a new girl, and Doctor Grand is very good at finding them. And training them."

"Training them?"

"Yes. You might say Doctor Grand teaches them the art of love. Then they come to me."

"Does Doctor Grand do anything else for you?"

"He performs abortions when needed."

"He performs *abortions*, you say?"

"That's right."

"And do you know the defendant, Leland Kennecott?"

"I do."

"What is your acquaintance with him?"

"He's an occasional client at my house, and he also is involved with Doctor Grand's training exercises."

"In what capacity? The arts of love?"

Grace chuckled. "Hardly. Kennecott there has a special skill. At the very end of the training, Grand brings him in—"

"Objection!" Haynes said. "Hearsay. The witness has testified that Grand worked for her, not my client."

"Sustained," the judge said, "unless you can establish the witness's direct knowledge of Mr. Kennecott's alleged role."

"Withdrawn," Whalen said reluctantly. "Have you had any direct business dealings with Mr. Kennecott?"

"I have."

"Describe them. As I said, he's an occasional client at my establishment, and he was Helen's final client before she left to come to Rochester."

"When you say 'client,' you mean that he paid you for her favors?"

"That's right. He was at my house the night before she came here with him. He paid me thirty dollars, and they spent time privately in her boudoir."

"Do you find that interesting, Mrs. Harrington? That the defendant was her last client?"

"Of course I do."

"As do most of us, I feel sure. Now let me turn for a moment to the deceased, Miss Crosby. Let's talk about her mental state just before she left you to accompany the defendant to Rochester. Was she suicidal?"

"Objection," Haynes said. "Witness is not an alienist."

"I will restate the question," Whalen said. "Did she express to you any suicidal intention?"

"She did not."

"What about just before she left?"

"Only what she left in a letter to me," Grace said.

"And this is the letter?" the DA said, holding up a sheet of paper with Helen's handwriting. He read aloud:

> *I know it'll look like I've run away ... If I can find a cure ...*
> *rest assured I'll come back ... All of you have been good to me*
> *... We'll see one another again soon ...*

"Does that sound to you like a woman bent on suicide, Mrs. Harrington?"

"It does not, sir. She states quite clearly that she's coming back."

"If she can find a cure. Do you know what kind of cure she meant?"

"She was addicted to morphine."

"Hearsay," Haynes said.

Whalen ignored him. "How do you know this, Mrs. Harrington?"

"Because I provided the drugs to her for her use."

"So Miss Crosby, in your opinion, intended to come to Rochester not to kill herself, but to save herself from addiction? To take a cure?"

"That's right."

"You saw Miss Crosby the night before she left with Mr. Kennecott, correct?"

"Yes, correct."

"Did she at that time have a rash around her mouth and across her nose?"

"No."

"Do you know whether Miss Crosby was right- or left-handed?"

"Most definitely right-handed," Grace said. "I've seen her writing letters."

"No further questions of this witness," the district attorney said.

Haynes jumped up.

"Mrs. Harrington," he said, "what remarkable testimony! In the space of only a few minutes, you've admitted to selling narcotics without a license, to participating in a white slavery ring, and to operating a disorderly house. Isn't that right?"

"My house is very orderly, sir," Grace said to laughter.

"Let me use a less polite term, then," he said. "A brothel. Whorehouse."

"Yes, then, that is certainly so. A very good one, though."

"And have you entered into any immunity agreement in exchange for your testimony?"

"No. Nor am I currently charged with any crime."

"That may change soon enough, Mrs. Harrington. But for the present, perhaps you can tell us why we ought to believe the testimony—any testimony—made by a self-confessed brothelkeeper and drug peddler?"

Grace smiled. "Because this testimony, sir, will cost me one-hundred-fifty thousand dollars a year, for life."

"How so?"

"My business earns five hundred dollars a night, six nights a week. Christmas and Easter weeks off. And my testimony just now has destroyed that business. One doesn't name names in my line of work. Name one, name them all. Not a soul will come to my place now. It's over."

"I'm finished with this witness," Haynes said.

"You are excused," Judge Northland said to Grace. "Court is hereby adjourned for a one-hour recess." The gavel fell with a sharp crack.

"The people call Miss—er, Raven," Whalen said.

Tall and erect, her black hair shining behind her, Raven took her place in the witness box.

"State your name, please, Miss Raven," Whalen said.

"My name is Goh-láh-nah," she said. "Which means *raven* in English. You may, of course, call me Raven."

"Thank you. And your surname?"

"I only have the one name," she said.

"Very well. Now Miss Raven, you knew the deceased, Miss Helen Crosby?"

"Yes, I did."

"You worked with her at Mrs. Harrington's establishment?"

"Yes, and we were friends. More than friends."

"And did Miss Crosby ever tell you that she wanted to kill herself?"

"Never."

"Was she ever morose?"

"Mr. Whalen, there is no prostitute on earth who doesn't get morose at times. It's a discouraging job. But other than the occasional blues, Helen wasn't morose. Quite the opposite. The brightest ray of light we'd had in that house in the years since I arrived there."

"Were you surprised, then, when Miss Crosby departed so suddenly?"

"Surprised, yes, and wounded."

"Did she tell you why she was leaving?"

"She left a letter addressed to me."

"Is this the letter?"

"It looks like it," Raven said.

"Permit me to quote from it," Whalen said, and Raven nodded gravely.

   . . . if I can beat this evil thing, I will come back to you . . .

"What does that mean to you, Miss Raven?"

"I'm sure Helen came to believe that Lee Kennecott—"

"Oh, please, Your Honor," Haynes said. "'I'm sure?' 'Came to believe?' This isn't testimony. It's opinion."

"Sustained," the judge said. "Mr. Whalen, please direct your witness to answer only to what she experienced directly."

"Miss Raven," Whalen said, "did Miss Crosby use narcotics?"

"Yes, she did," Raven said quietly. "Much to my dismay."

"And to your knowledge, was she addicted to them?"

"She was."

"We've heard that she may have come to Rochester to seek a cure. Did she ever say anything to you about a cure?"

"We talked about it a great deal. I urged her on several occasions to seek a cure. She resisted, at first, but then told me she wanted to stop using them. We wanted to run away together, Mr. Whalen. She knew that she had to take a cure for that to happen."

"Thank you, Miss Raven. One last thing. Am I correct that you saw the deceased the day before she died?"

"That is correct."

"And did she have any generalized rash around her mouth and nose at that time?"

"Absolutely not."

"No further questions, Your Honor."

"Miss Raven," Haynes began, "you said that you and the deceased were intimate."

"Yes, that's true," Raven said.

"What does that mean, *intimate*?"

"Um, it means that we shared our private thoughts and also had—other kinds of intimacy."

"If I may read another selection from her letter to you—selections that Mr. Whalen carefully avoided, perhaps you can explain them to the court." He read:

> . . . *I wanted to remember your eyes the way I saw them last evening, after we made love.*

There were murmurs throughout the courtroom, and Judge

Northland raised the gavel threateningly. The courtroom fell silent again.

"Now, Miss Raven," Haynes resumed, "what does 'after we made love' mean?"

"It means exactly what it says. After we made love."

"And just how is it possible for two *women* to make love, Miss Raven?"

"My, you're even older than you look," Raven said with a smirk.

"Your Honor, please instruct the witness to answer the question. Specifically and without sarcasm."

"Answer his question, Miss Raven. Specifically, and without sarcasm, or I'll hold you in contempt."

"Yes, sir," she said. "What it means, specifically, is that Helen and I voluntarily engaged in sexual relations that caused us both to achieve climax."

"Your Honor, the witness is behaving with contempt for this court by openly using obscene and disgraceful language," Haynes said.

"Be careful what you wish for, Mr. Haynes," Judge Northland said. "The witness used explicit but common, clinical terminology not out of keeping with the description of physical fact and not, in my judgment, for any prurient purpose."

"Miss Raven, please try to answer with decorum befitting the court," Haynes said. "Is it not highly unusual for women to engage in such relations?"

Raven shook her head. "Not in a brothel, it isn't. We've all had it up to here with men."

Now there was general laughter in the courtroom, and Northland brought down his gavel.

"Mr. Haynes, I suggest you bring this to a conclusion. You are turning my courtroom into a vaudeville house."

"I'm finished with this witness," Haynes said in disgust.

THE REST OF THE second day was a good one for the prosecution. Grace's and Raven's testimony had impeached Lee's character, one of the pillars on which Haynes was building a defense sympathetic to the young medical student. And likely no juror continued to believe that Helen had been suicidal.

After Raven was excused, Whalen brought up two more doctors, an expert in bladed weapons, and even a barber—who should know how to use a straight razor. All testified that Helen's fatal wound could only have been inflicted by a razor held in the right hand—a strong hand, and a hand experienced in the use of a blade. Lee fit the profile perfectly: right-handed, most certainly of great physical strength, and having had thorough surgical training.

Haynes was looking weary when Judge Northland gaveled the session closed. But the next day—the third and penultimate day—he resolved to make his own.

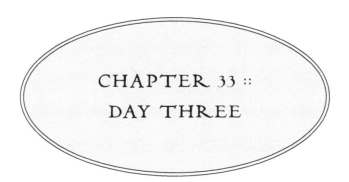

CHAPTER 33 ::

DAY THREE

September 13, 1901
Friday

W hen court began session on the third day, Attorney
Haynes took up the battle for Lee.

"The defense calls Doctor George H. Grand," he said.

Grand slowly took his seat, looking older, somehow, than he had
even two weeks before.

Haynes walked up to Grand, holding a sheaf of notes. "Doctor
Grand, you practice at Riverdale Hospital in Buffalo?"

"That is correct."

"And you knew Miss Crosby?"

"I did."

"When and how did you meet her?"

"March of this year," he said. "We met when she was working at the
Pan-American, at the Bell Telephone Exchange."

"And you know the defendant, Leland Kennecott?"

"I do."

"How do you know him?"

"He is one of my medical interns at Riverdale."

"I see. Now tell us, what was the nature of your relations with
Miss Crosby?"

"We saw each other socially for a while."

"How old are you, Doctor Grand?"

"Forty years of age."

"Are you in the habit of seeing—socially, of course—women half your age?"

"No, I am not."

"Do you know a Miss Anne McClellan?"

"I do. She was a nurse at Riverdale."

"And didn't you see her 'socially' for more than a year?"

"I did."

"How old was she?"

"I don't recall."

"Then let me refresh your memory. When you met her, she was nineteen. When she lodged a complaint against you for your unwanted attentions, she was twenty-one."

"That was a misunderstanding."

"Doctor Grand, did you provide lodging for Miss Crosby at the Delamore Apartments?"

"I did. To help her get on her feet."

"And did you provide lodging for Nurse McClellan at the same place?"

"I did."

"And did you not, in both cases, promise that you would marry these women, and then renege?"

"In neither case was I engaged to be married. There was nothing to renege upon."

"My point is this, Doctor. Did you know that Nurse McClellan became so frightened and discouraged after your long exploitation of her that she has left Buffalo entirely?"

"No, I did not know that."

"You do know that Miss Crosby, in her suicide note, said that—and I quote—you 'destroyed her faith in men'?"

"Women are temperamental creatures, sir," Grand said, red in the face.

"Don't you think perhaps that both became despondent because you were grooming them to be sold into prostitution?"

"Absolutely not."

"We heard testimony here that you are a cadet, Doctor Grand. A procurer."

"Lies," Grand said.

"Perhaps. But by your own admission, you met Miss Crosby when she was working in a respectable position with the Bell Telephone Company. So respectable, in fact, that the company chose to feature her photographs in their directory.

"Yet after some period of time in which you were seeing her socially, suddenly and inexplicably she becomes a prostitute. Might it not seem, then, that you took an active hand in crushing this girl's spirit? Sending her into such depths of despair that death by her own hand would be preferable to a life of shame?"

"I couldn't possibly say," Grand said.

"No further questions, Your Honor."

The DA rose and took his place in front of Grand.

"Doctor Grand, did you love Miss Crosby?"

Grand closed his eyes slowly. "Yes, I did. Very much."

"Were you and she engaged to be married?"

"We were going to be," Grand said.

"But that didn't happen, did it?"

"No, it did not."

"And why was that?"

"The reason," Grand said, "was the defendant, Lee Kennecott."

Haynes stood. "Your Honor—"

"Sit down, Mr. Haynes. The man is giving direct testimony."

The DA smiled. "And why do you say that Lee Kennecott, the defendant, was the reason you and Miss Crosby were not engaged?"

"Because I overheard that she had become intimate with him."

"Objection," Haynes said wearily. "Hearsay."

"Mr. Whalen, please establish whether Doctor Grand has firsthand knowledge to back up his assertion, or move on."

"Of course, Your Honor. Doctor Grand, how do you know—firsthand—that Miss Crosby and Mr. Kennecott had become intimate?"

"As I said, I *heard* it," Grand said, putting his face in his hands.

Haynes leapt up again.

"Sit down, Mr. Haynes. Mr. Whalen, I will not allow hearsay in this court. You are risking a mistrial, sir."

"Your Honor, if the witness can only enlarge upon his statement, I assure you that—"

"One last swing, then," Judge Northland said. "Doctor Grand, continue."

"When I say I *heard* them," Grand resumed, "I mean that on one occasion in June, I believe it was, I brought Mr. Kennecott with me to Helen's lodgings. To introduce them."

"Introduce them why? Because he was your intern?"

"Yes. And I thought Helen might benefit from getting to know other young people in the medical profession."

"I see. Then what happened?"

"We had a cocktail and were having quite a convivial time," Grand said. "I was tired, though, and I suppose that the whiskey had a greater effect than I thought it would. I fell asleep in my chair, but then I was awakened by—"

"By what, Doctor?"

"By the sounds of intimacy from Helen's bedroom."

"You heard the two of them making love?"

"I did."

"So when you said you overheard, you meant that literally."

"I did, yes."

"And what did you do?"

"Neither Lee nor Helen was in the room with me, so I glanced into Helen's bedroom and saw that she and the defendant were engaged in carnal connection."

At this there was a general uproar in the courtroom. Northland banged his gavel three times. "Silence!" he roared. "Or I will clear the court."

"Is that, then, why you broke it off with Miss Crosby?"

"It is," Grand said. "It was horrible. Monstrous."

"You loved her very much."

"I did, sir," Grand said.

"And to your knowledge did Mr. Kennecott also love Miss Crosby?"

"He hated her."

"Objection," Haynes said.

"Overruled. Continue, Mr. Whalen."

"How do you know that the defendant hated Miss Crosby?"

"He told me so directly. He told me that she had told him—after they'd been intimate—that he had raped her. That he was a brute. That made him very angry, and he said he was going to teach her a lesson."

"No further questions, Your Honor."

"Mr. Haynes?" Judge Northland said. "Do you wish to redirect?"

"Most definitely, Judge," Haynes said, standing. He leaned on the witness box. "You mean to say that an *intern* of yours accompanies you to your soon-to-be-fiancée's lodgings, immediately seduces her, and engages with her in carnal connection, all while you avail yourself of a quick nap in the next room?"

"Yes, that's it exactly."

"I must say, if that's all true, you comported yourself with unusual restraint," Haynes said. "Most men might have killed another for such a breach. What did you do instead?"

"I left. Went out."

"You left. That's all?"

"That is all."

"And did you reprimand Mr. Kennecott? After all, he was in your employ."

"He was in the hospital's employ."

"Very well, the hospital's. Did you upbraid him? Chastise him?"

"I did not."

"Do you find that strange?"

"It was a strange situation. I didn't know what to do. My heart had been broken."

"Even after Mr. Kennecott supposedly told you that he hated her? You still let it go by?"

"I did."

"Then you are one among millions, Doctor Grand. Now let me ask you—did you speak with Miss Crosby about this strange event in her flat?"

"I did not. Before I had an opportunity, I received a letter from her in which she stated she had fallen for Mr. Kennecott and did not wish to see me again."

"Can you produce the letter?"

"I burned it, sir."

"How convenient."

"Objection," Whalen said. "Argumentative."

"Sustained."

"Interesting that Miss Crosby should want to see neither you nor, as you allege, my client."

"I believe she blamed me for not intervening when he forced himself on her."

"'*Forced*,'" Haynes said. "An interesting choice of words from a man who has been identified in this court as a procurer and a panderer."

"By a *brothelkeeper*," Grand said, sneering.

"Do you perform illegal operations, Doctor Grand?"

"I do not."

"Yet we've heard direct testimony to that effect. You're saying that's not true? None of it?"

"It's all a damn pack of lies," he snarled.

"I'll counsel you to mind your language, Doctor Grand," the judge said.

"I wonder which George Grand to believe," Haynes said. "The George Grand who claims that another man waltzes into his girl-friend's flat and commences to make love to her, while he sits by idly? The George Grand who denies being a procurer and an abortionist, even when those who pay him for those services testify to that effect? Or the George Grand who says he loved Miss Crosby, yet after a short association drives her into drug addiction and prostitution, and tells him she never wants to see him again?"

"I told you already," Grand thundered, "it's a pack of goddamn lies!!"

"I warned you once, Doctor Grand," Judge Northland said. "You are hereby fined two hundred dollars for contempt. If you cannot pay, you will be held in county jail for seven days."

"No further questions, Your Honor," Haynes said. "This witness has proven himself to be a hot-tempered, unreliable man."

"The witness is excused," said the judge.

IT WAS A RISK, and even the Buffalo papers—who had started to sense some weakness in Kennecott's defense—knew it. So on the final day of the trial, Attorney Haynes called his client to the stand to testify in his own defense.

"My name is Leland Davis Kennecott," Lee said.

"How old are you?"

"I turned twenty-four on September first."

"And you are currently an intern at Riverdale Hospital?"

"Yes."

"Having graduated from the University of Buffalo's medical school?"

"That is correct."

"How did you know the deceased?"

"I was introduced to her by Doctor George Grand," he said.

"When was that?"

"June of this year, I believe."

"In her lodgings, as Doctor Grand testified?"

"Yes, in her lodgings."

"You may also recall that Doctor Grand testified that, on that occasion, you and Miss Crosby engaged in carnal connection, while he slept in the next room. Is that true?"

"It's a fantasy. I would take no such liberties."

"I thought as much. What is your domestic situation?"

"I have been married for three years, and I have a baby son." Lee scanned the jurors, some of whom were smiling back at him. "Born in March."

"Congratulations," Haynes said.

"Thank you, sir."

"With respect for your obvious devotion to your family, I must ask a delicate question. How did you come to be in the Whitman House Hotel with Miss Crosby?"

"I bumped into her on the street, not having seen her since Doctor Grand introduced us. She recognized me, and she immediately began telling me her troubles."

"And what was the nature of those troubles?"

Lee took a deep breath. "She said that Doctor Grand had ruined her—"

"Objection."

"Overruled."

"How did she say he ruined her?"

"She said Doctor Grand had promised to marry her, and then had taken liberties with her. She said that when he tired of her, he cast her aside and left her with debts for lodging and so on. Without resources and with her reputation in tatters, her family turned her away. Subsequently, she'd had no other way to support herself than through immorality."

"Immorality?"

"She was—living in a bawdy house. Grace Harrington's place."

"As we have heard, yes. Very unfortunate. Any other troubles?"

"She said she was using a lot of dope."

"How did such an apparently fine young woman become habituated to drugs?"

"She told me that Doctor Grand introduced her to them."

"Tell me, Lee, what was your reaction to the distressing tale told to you by Miss Crosby?"

"I felt pity for her. She seemed like a nice girl who had come to a very bad spot. I offered to take her to Rochester to seek a cure."

"What happened then?"

"She agreed to try."

"And you resolved to help her?"

"Yes. We came to Rochester together."

"And you purchased her clothing and her train fare?"

"I did. I was moved by her plight."

"But then something went awry, didn't it?"

"Yes. On the train she said no, it was all up with her, and that she had made up her mind to do away with herself. That alarmed me considerably. As a Christian."

"Of course. Now then, when you arrived at the Whitman, what was her mood?"

"She seemed to regain a measure of good cheer. We had a late supper at the Eagleton, and she had quite a bit to drink. That seemed to depress her mood. When we returned to the hotel, she said it was no use. She said she wanted dope, that she didn't care to live without it. I told her not to take it and took it away from her. But she had purchased a bottle of cocktails earlier, and she had some of that, and gave me some, too. She said one way or another she was going to kill herself, and she sat down and began writing a letter."

"Her suicide note."

"Yes."

"And then what happened?"

"Something in the cocktail made me feel very queer, and I must have passed out on the bed."

"When did you awake?"

"Miss Crosby shook me awake. I started up, and I saw her next to me, holding a razor."

"Whose razor?"

"Mine. I had brought it with me for the overnight journey."

"And?"

"She had a terrible expression on her face. I said, 'Helen, what in the world?' or words to that effect. She then slashed at me with the razor. I threw up my hand to defend myself and was injured in doing so."

"And then?"

"Then she immediately lay down on the bed and drew the razor across her throat."

"Did you try to stop her?"

"Whatever she had put in my drink deprived me of the ability to move."

"I see. The coroner has testified that he believes you had been poisoned with atropine. And then?"

"I passed out again and did not wake until two gentlemen burst into the room the following morning."

"Lee, do you swear that Miss Crosby inflicted the fatal wound herself, and that you did not?"

"I so swear. On my soul."

"Thank you, Mr. Kennecott." Haynes resumed his seat.

The DA stood. "Mr. Kennecott, would you say you are a compassionate man?"

"I like to think that I am."

"And a responsible one, too?"

"Yes."

"Already married and with a child. Having graduated medical school and now an intern."

"That's correct."

"That's a great weight on a young man's shoulders."

Lee smiled. "I have broad shoulders." There was some tittering from a few young women who had come to court each day to make eyes at Lee.

"Yes, you do. You have an athlete's build. A strong build."

"I played football in high school."

"And as I recall, you are only twenty-four, Mr. Kennecott?"

"Yes, as of September first."

"Only twenty-four," mused the DA. "All that pressure at such a young age. Do you ever feel like you might like to run away from it all? You wouldn't be the first."

"No," Lee said. "I do not. I would consider such a thing to be unworthy of a man."

"You're not the complaining type, I can tell."

"I most certainly am not. I deplore self-indulgence."

Whalen stroked his chin. "It's a form of weakness, don't you think?"

"I do. Blaming others for one's own failures."

"It's hard to have much sympathy for that sort of thing, isn't it?"

"It is."

"And yet, Mr. Kennecott, you said that Miss Crosby blamed all of her troubles on Doctor Grand. That must have been irritating for a man like you to hear."

Lee looked startled. "Not all of them. Some of them were from the dope."

"No doubt. But you have testified that Miss Crosby told you that Doctor Grand had introduced her to narcotics. So really, she made everything Doctor Grand's fault."

"She said he'd ruined her."

"What was the real reason you came to Rochester with Miss Crosby, sir?"

"As I said, to seek a cure."

"Where were you going to take her for this cure?"

Lee looked over Whalen's shoulder at Haynes, but Whalen moved and blocked his view.

"Mr. Kennecott?"

"So much has happened . . . I have forgotten entirely," Lee said. "A local place."

"I see. And you wanted to help her seek this cure after having intimate relations with her at Mrs. Harrington's house."

"That's a lie," Lee said.

"We seem to hear that a lot from the defense. That everyone else is a liar, and that they alone are telling the God's truth. Why would Mrs. Harrington lose a hundred fifty thousand dollars a year—in order to lie?"

"I have no idea what Mrs. Harrington thinks."

"Do you yet recall where the cure was to be provided?"

Lee hesitated again. "It's so murky, sir. It must be the aftereffects of the atropine I was poisoned with."

"How interesting. Under the effect of this deadly drug, you can remember in minute detail Miss Crosby's troubles, your evening in the hotel, and that she drew the deadly razor across her own throat with her left hand. Yet you can't remember where you were taking her to seek a cure for her narcotics addiction? The thing that started the whole chain of events?"

"I can't account for it, but that's right."

"Moving on, then," the DA said. "I neglected to ask. Did you inform your wife that Miss Crosby would accompany you to Rochester?"

"I did not."

"Did you tell her that you bought clothing for Miss Crosby?"

"No."

"Why didn't you tell your wife these things, Mr. Kennecott?"

"I didn't want to worry her. You'll understand that a mother with a baby already has a full portion of concerns."

"Of course. Who would want to trouble one's wife with an overnight stay with a prostitute?"

Haynes stood. "Is that a question, Your Honor?"

"Get to your point, Mr. Whalen," the judge said.

"Mr. Kennecott, did you have criminal relations with Miss Crosby?"

"I most certainly did not."

"Not in her lodgings, with Doctor Grand nearby?"

"Of course not."

"Nor in the Whitman House Hotel, prior to Miss Crosby's death?"

"Nor there."

"That's interesting," Whalen said, "because you told the coroner, soon after he arrived on the scene, that you had indeed had intimate relations with Miss Crosby."

"I was out of my mind on atropine," Lee said. "I was raving."

"All right, then. Yet the Monroe County Medical Examiner testified that he found evidence of a recent seminal emission in Miss Crosby's vagina."

Northland had to bring the gavel down again.

"So what?" Lee said with a snarl. "What would you expect? The girl was a *whore*."

"You don't like prostitutes, do you, Mr. Kennecott."

Lee's face was quite red. "I don't have any particular sentiment about them."

"I see. Now if I may bring this to a head," Whalen said, "I'd like to ask a few questions about the attack you say that Miss Crosby made on you. You are right-handed?"

"Yes, I am."

"As was Miss Crosby?"

"I do not know whether she was."

"But didn't you see her writing her so-called suicide note?"

"I knew she was writing, but I didn't watch her closely."

"It wasn't much of a *suicide* note, was it, Mr. Kennecott? Full of references to returning to Buffalo and of her love for Miss Raven?"

"It sounded like a farewell note to me."

"Ah. A *farewell* note. Not a *suicide* note."

"I mean to say that she was saying farewell in preparation for suicide."

"All right, then. Miss Crosby finishes writing out a suicide note that, strangely, gives no indication of any suicidal intent. When the fatal events transpired, you were on the right side of the bed, and Miss Crosby on your left? The bed you were sharing?"

"Yes."

"And she had the razor in her left hand, where it was found the following morning?"

"Yes, that is so."

"You're sure?"

"I am."

The DA tapped his fingers on the witness box. "If I understand you, then—a right-handed girl decides to attack a man with a razor, but for reasons unknown she decides to use her left hand. Recalling that she's on your left side, she must therefore swing her left arm across her body to slash at you. Correct?"

"Presumably."

"Presumably? It's a matter of simple geometry. She's holding the razor in her left hand, and she's on the left side of the bed. You're on the right. Would she not have to do as I have said? Yes or no?"

"Yes."

"Good. We agree on that. Now the razor, in Miss Crosby's left hand, is coming down at you from your right, since you are facing her. Your left hand is, therefore, against the bed. What hand would one, in such a case, throw up to defend oneself?"

"I don't know."

"You don't? It would be your right hand, Mr. Kennecott. But the cuts you say were defensive in nature were on the backs of the fingers of your left hand. How would you account for that?"

"As I said, I was drugged. I don't remember."

"Isn't it true that it was not Miss Crosby who caused your wounds at all, but rather that they were caused by your own razor closing on your left hand?"

"That's not how it went," Lee said.

"We will leave it at that, then—that the cuts on your hand are mysterious in origin. But this brings us to an even greater mystery. The girl attacks you. You foil her attempt on your life, and she realizes that you can't be fooled twice. So she promptly lies down and does away with herself. That's what you said to the coroner and the detectives, correct? You saw her do just as I describe?"

"That's right."

"But then she accomplishes this single, deep and decisive, fatal stroke—from left to right, across her throat—using her left hand. *Backhand*. Yet every man on this jury has used a straight razor and can attest that it is close to physically impossible to make such a cut as Miss Crosby received while holding the razor in the left hand. And that is why every medical authority has agreed: the cut was made by a right-handed person."

"You said yourself that Helen was right-handed," Lee said.

"Indeed, she was. But you and others have testified—testimony corroborated in your statement given to the police at the scene—that Miss Crosby was holding the razor in her left hand when she attacked you and when she is said to have killed herself. Where it was found, by the way, at the scene. In her left hand.

"So do you expect this jury to think it reasonable that a desperate, even crazed, woman would attack you with a razor in her left hand, fail in her murderous intent, and then lie down, calmly and neatly sever her own carotid artery, backhand, and do all that without getting any blood whatsoever on the weapon or on her hands?"

"I don't know. I only know what I saw. Or think I saw in my drugged condition."

"Oh, Mr. Kennecott. Remember that the jury is made up of reasonable men. Isn't it far more *reasonable* that it was *you* who inflicted the fatal wound, possibly injuring your hand in the process?"

"No," Lee said, rising out of his chair. "It is not."

"A strong, right-handed man like you, with such broad shoulders, and medically trained? You could easily have held her down, made the cut expertly, and then passed out. Then, when the banging at your door roused you the next morning, you realized the desperate condition you were in.

"You knew you were in trouble, and hastened to make it look like a suicide. You dunked the razor in the water pitcher to clean it off, and then placed it in Miss Crosby's left hand, which was dangling off the side of the bed and accessible to you. And as you didn't know her very well, you didn't know whether she was right- or left-handed. Then, just as the men broke open the door, they found you staggering back to your side of the bed. Isn't that just how it happened?"

"No, it's not true," he said, dabbing his forehead with a handkerchief. "None of that is true."

"If it is not, we have yet to hear a more reasonable explanation of the facts," Whalen said. He turned as if to take his seat, but then turned back.

"By the way, did you notice a rash on Miss Crosby's face that evening?"

"No, why?"

"The medical examiner testified that she had a rash."

"I recall. He said it was acne."

"Yes, but does acne appear after death?"

Lee shrugged. "You'd have to ask a skin specialist about that."

"I suppose so," Whalen said. "I'm finished with this witness, Your Honor."

"Do you wish to redirect, Mr. Haynes?"

"I do, Your Honor," Haynes said, rising. "Mr. Kennecott, you bore no ill-will against Miss Crosby, did you?"

"Quite the contrary. As I said, I wanted to help her out of a vicious environment and an addiction to narcotics."

"I see. And yet, you said that despite your best efforts, as the evening went on, she became increasingly morose. Correct?"

"That is correct."

"And as we've seen, she wrote out a suicide note, implicating Doctor Grand."

"Yes."

"In that note, did she implicate you?"

"No, sir."

"Did she blame you in any way?"

"No."

"The district attorney wishes to tie up common sense in a rat's nest of his own creation. Which hand did this or that, who lay on this side or that, when it's painfully clear that you had in that room with you a despondent young woman, bent on her own destruction, and one who bade farewell to her friends and family in writing. Is that correct?"

"That is correct."

"No further questions, Your Honor. The defense rests."

"Court is adjourned for the weekend," Judge Northland said. "Summations on Monday morning."

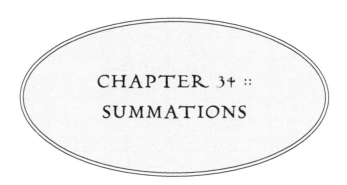

CHAPTER 34 ::
SUMMATIONS

September 16, 1901
Monday

The two opposing attorneys summed up their cases on Monday. Whalen went first.

"Gentlemen of the jury, through this long trial I have waited to hear Mr. Haynes—or Mr. Kennecott himself—explain clearly how a right-handed, hysterical, intoxicated girl—having just allegedly attacked the defendant with a razor—could turn the weapon on herself and, backhanded, cut her own throat, calmly and decisively, ear to ear, and die with a placid smile on her face.

"To go deep—almost an inch and a half!—into one's own neck, to find the carotid, then to draw the killing blade without the slightest tremor all the way across to the right clavicle, in a single, decisive, measured incision . . . that is not the act of self-murder. The suicide would cut shallowly, tentatively, and then perhaps go deep enough to find his life. And once found, stop in horror at the result—the sight of one's own lifeblood, arousing the instinct to self-preservation. Drop the razor, clutch the throat, try to staunch the flow. It would be automatic, instinctual—animal.

"There was, however, no such reaction. Of course there was not—because this was not a cut made by a troubled, frightened woman, pulling a man's unfamiliar razor across her own throat only so far and so deep as her trembling hand will allow. No. This was a single, decisive cut—an incision—made by a strong hand, a steady hand, a hand trained in the use of the scalpel. Indeed, a medical man's hand—the hand of the defendant, Mr. Leland Kennecott. And the incision made by that hand—the hand of that man sitting there—was made on a woman either already insensible or firmly pinioned to the bed.

"Of course the defendant denies it, but why would he not? You've heard him testify that his memory is exceptional in many particulars, and faulty in others—conveniently, those that would convict him. He remembers an attack that he claims happened after being drugged, but can't recall why he brought a prostitute with him to Rochester.

"There is only one reason, gentlemen, that all this can be so. And that is that the defendant is a liar and a perjurer. He has lied in large things and small. He lied to his wife—the mother of his infant son—and went off on a lark to Rochester. Why would a man who lies so fluently to his own wife not lie to you about a matter which may cost him twenty years in prison?

"If you agree with me, gentlemen—then guilty is the only possible verdict. I thank you and this Court for your indulgence."

"Mr. Haynes," Judge Northland said, "your summation."

"Gentlemen of the jury," Haynes said, "you see before you my client, Leland Davis Kennecott, a thoroughly respectable young man. A man whose youthful heartstrings, moved to pity by another's plight, led him to act without a shred of self-interest, perhaps unwisely, yet as a healer ought to do. That is to say: everything within his power to prevent poor Miss Crosby from putting in motion her avowed plan of self-destruction.

"But," Haynes continued, "at last even these Herculean efforts were doomed to fail, and Miss Crosby made up her mind forever. A young woman, brought as low as woman can be by Doctor George Grand, abandoned, cast into the street, had to keep body and soul together by immoral means. What woman would not consider suicide as the more honorable course of action?

"Do not forget that this troubled young woman sat down and calmly wrote out a suicide note. Do not forget that she then calmly poisoned the man who had been her benefactor. Why wouldn't such a one cut her own throat, if only in disgust and self-loathing?

"Simply put: Helen Crosby wanted to die, and she made good on her promise. Herself, and without any assistance from my client. Indeed, she did so against his most strenuous efforts to prevent her from doing so.

"And thus, it is your duty, gentlemen, to find my client not guilty on the one count against him. I know that you will acquit yourselves honorably."

JUDGE NORTHLAND CLEARED HIS throat. "Thank you, gentlemen. I will now issue my charge to the jury.

"Gentlemen of the jury, there is but one count in this indictment. The count states that for the purpose of carrying out Miss Crosby's suicidal intent, the defendant, Mr. Kennecott, himself inflicted the mortal wound. Under this count, you must deliberate only as to whose hand wielded the deadly razor. If you believe, beyond a reasonable doubt, that Mr. Kennecott himself cut Miss Crosby's throat, causing her death, then you must find him guilty of manslaughter in the first degree.

"You must weigh the evidence as you have heard it here presented. You must account for the position of the body, the wound on the neck, the wound on the defendant's hand. And you must render a verdict based on your most sober consideration thereof.

"It is also incumbent on me to observe that while we have heard testimony that Miss Crosby had strayed from the path of the righteous and had fallen far from our ideal of womanhood—that can have no bearing on the defendant's guilt or innocence. In the eyes of the law, all human life is equally sacred. Neither the defendant's personal qualities or shortcomings, nor Miss Crosby's, should enter into your deliberation. Good people can do evil deeds, and evil ones good. Thus, you must assess their actions based on fact and not any prejudice.

"This is a case of profound gravity. Let your action be calm, deliberate, and high-minded. What will remain after we are all dust and ashes, gentlemen, will be your verdict."

The gavel came down, and the jurors were led out of the courtroom.

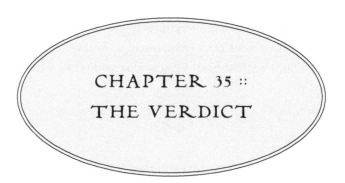

CHAPTER 35 ::
THE VERDICT

September 17, 1901
Tuesday

The jury deliberated into Monday evening before sending notice to Judge Northland that they had reached a verdict. The next day at ten o'clock, Northland gaveled his court back into session.

"Gentlemen of the jury, have you reached a verdict?"

The foreman stood. "We have, Your Honor."

"As to the sole count of the indictment, that the defendant aided and abetted a suicide by willfully and feloniously cutting the throat of Helen Crosby, causing her death, how do you find?"

"We find the defendant, Leland Davis Kennecott, guilty of manslaughter in the first degree."

The room exploded with gasps, exclamations, and a few cheers. Northland waited with uncommon patience for the hubbub to subside. Then he rapped with his gavel again.

"Thank you, members of the jury. You are excused. I will pronounce the sentence later today. Court is adjourned until four o'clock."

❧

IT WAS FOUR-FIFTEEN WHEN Judge Northland reappeared for Lee's sentencing. He walked out of his chambers to find the visitors' gallery full, as expected, and the press gallery . . . empty.

Not a single reporter, local, Buffalo, or New York, remained in the once-full press section. How strange, the judge thought. Sentencing isn't usually considered an anticlimax.

He settled himself behind his bench. "Will the defendant rise?"

Lee and Haynes stood, looking quite calm.

"Mr. Kennecott, you have been found guilty of manslaughter in the first degree. For myself, I will say that I concur entirely with the jury's conclusion. I cannot conceive how it would be possible for Miss Crosby to present the appearance which she did, had she cut her own throat, and I will add that it seems probable from all the evidence in the case that she was not conscious when she received the mortal stroke at your hands. You willfully and knowingly inflicted the mortal wound. Her wish and consent, incidentally, would not absolve you from the graver charge of murder, had you been indicted for that offense.

"And now, sir, the duty is upon me to pronounce an appropriate judgment. I have considered the facts very carefully. Your counsel, Mr. Haynes, has spoken persuasively for you. But I cannot see my duty in any other way than to pronounce upon you the full penalty of law. Therefore, you will be confined in the State Prison at Auburn, at hard labor, for the term of twenty years."

"I move for a new trial!" Haynes thundered, jumping out of his chair.

"Denied," Judge Northland said. He brought down his gavel with a report like a gunshot. "Court is adjourned."

THE BAILIFF LED LEE away, his mother and father in tears. Relieved that it was all over, Judge Northland stepped down from his bench and walked quietly into his chambers. He slipped off his robe and sat down wearily behind his desk, looking at all the paper he'd been reading. All of it would now be filed away, and tomorrow there would be something else. Some other set of facts to pore over. He couldn't know what it would be, but he knew it wouldn't be like *this*.

There was a gentle rap on his door. "Come in." He looked up to see his law clerk, trembling and pale, in the doorway.

"What's wrong, John?" he said, smiling. "Of the two of us, I should be the one looking wan."

"The—the president's been shot," the clerk said. "In Buffalo. At the Pan-American."

"McKinley?"

"The telegraph says some anarchist shot him. That's why all the reporters vanished. Everyone's gone to Buffalo."

"Please tell me he survived."

"I don't know, Your Honor. That's all I know."

"I'm glad you told me, John. Keep an eye on the wire, and tell me what you learn."

"I will, Your Honor," the clerk said, and left Northland alone again.

God help us all, Northland thought, sitting back in his chair.

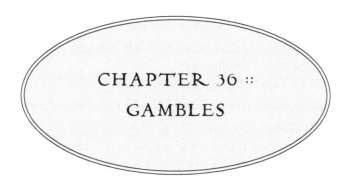

CHAPTER 36 ::
GAMBLES

"Thank you for coming to see me on such short notice, Mr. Haynes," District Attorney Whalen said when George Haynes stepped into his office. "I understand you are preparing a motion for a new trial."

"I am," Haynes said. "And I do hope you won't try to talk me out of it."

"I wouldn't dream of it. I know how determined you are. But I did think it only fair to tell you that if you file for a new trial, I'll be making another filing of my own."

Haynes smiled a little smile of condescension. "May I inquire as to the nature of your filing?"

"I'll be moving to empanel a new grand jury, and to seek an indictment for first-degree murder. And I'll be seeking the chair for Mr. Kennecott."

Haynes shook his head slowly. "You know there isn't a snowball's chance of getting that indictment."

"Oh, I think it's a better chance than that," Whalen said, smiling. "You may be curious why, at trial, I didn't tie up a couple of loose ends that were dangling there."

"Loose ends? You left no stone unturned."

"Not so. But you were too busy with your rhetorical flights of fancy to notice. One was the peculiar position of the girl's body. Peaceful, as if sleeping. Smiling. She gave no evidence of moving a muscle during or after the fatal cut."

"We heard all that. She wanted to die. That was clear."

"Even if you're right, no matter how much someone wants to die, no one could remain so still while her throat is being cut. There would be some reaction, even if involuntary."

"Apparently not," Haynes said.

Whalen ignored him. "The other odd thing was the wadded-up handkerchief found just under the girl's neck. You'll recall that there was so much blood on it that it was originally mistaken for a huge clot."

"So what? A handkerchief? This is your basis for murder in the first degree?"

He held up a hand. "We have the peaceful attitude of the body. We have a wadded-up handkerchief. And we have a final incongruous element—the rash around Miss Crosby's mouth and nose."

"You heard the medical examiner. He believed it to be acne."

"That may be, but Mrs. Harrington, Miss Raven, and your client himself testified that Miss Crosby had no rash prior to her death."

"It came on suddenly, then. Or post-mortem."

"You may recall that your client suggested I consult with a skin specialist about that. And I did—two different doctors. They both looked at the photographs. I didn't use their findings at trial, but I have them right here." He held up two pieces of paper.

"Then we have a mistrial," Haynes said. "If you withheld something."

"I have no responsibility to disclose anything to you unless it is potentially exculpatory," he said. "And these are most definitely not. You see, my doctors—eminent ones, too—determined that the rash wasn't acne at all. It was a light but distinct chemical burn. The blood draining out of the body changed its color somewhat, so it was mischaracterized as acne."

"Chemical burns?" Haynes scoffed. "Next you'll probably assert that my client carried chemicals with him."

"And *that's* where it gets interesting," the DA said. "The answer is so simple—and simultaneously explains the other two curiosities—the blood-soaked handkerchief and the unusually peaceful pose—that I'm angry with myself for not grasping it sooner.

"It was chloroform, Haynes. When doctors anaesthetize patients with chloroform, they first apply grease or petroleum jelly around the mouth and nose, because chloroform burns the skin if it comes in direct contact with it. I will assert before a new grand jury that your client saturated the wadded-up handkerchief with chloroform, anaesthetized Miss Crosby, and then—with her entirely insensible to pain and in a state of surgical sleep—made the fatal incision.

"That explains why she didn't move so much as a muscle while her throat was cut. It explains why there was a bloody handkerchief found next to her face. And it certainly explains the rash around her mouth and nose.

"Now then, let's consider your alternatives. If you file for a new trial, I'll seek—and obtain—a new indictment for first-degree murder. My theory will be that Mr. Kennecott sought to rid himself of this burdensome affinity of his, and use her suicidal tendencies both to put an end to her life, and to his troubles. And that's why he took only his medical kit and his razor with him to that hotel, sir. He had, all along, a certain type of *operation* in mind.

"Or you could stand pat. Your man's been given twenty years, but he'll be out in thirteen—maybe even ten—if he keeps his nose clean.

"Not only will I not oppose your filing a motion for a new trial, Mr. Haynes—I would *welcome* it. So file away at your leisure, but I assure you that you'll be trading his ten years in Auburn for ten minutes in the electric chair. Your choice, but I think it's a pretty big gamble."

Haynes was quiet for a very long moment, looking into his lap.

"Naturally I'll discuss this with my client," he said softly, "but you may expect me to withdraw my petition for a new trial."

"WHAT I STILL DON'T understand," Charley said to Grace, Raven, May, and Alice after their return to Buffalo, "is how Helen determined that Kennecott was the Buffalo Butcher."

"Helen was a smart girl," Raven said. "Before she left, she figured out that the symbols stood for our names. That meant it had to be someone who knew her, and knew everyone she worked with.

"Then there was the fob. Helen could have sworn that she

remembered that Grand was wearing that fob the day he brought Kennecott over to break her in. But you know Helen—she was high at the time, and she must have got it mixed up. I think she figured out that it was Kennecott who was wearing the fob, not Grand."

"But how do we know that it was Kennecott's fob?" Charley asked.

"Because of the stones," Grace said. "The fob had two stones set in it. Carnelian and bloodstone."

"So?"

"On the stand, Kennecott was talking about his baby son, who was born in March. And he said that he was born in September. Remember what Mrs. Dickinson told us? Bloodstone is the birthstone for March, and carnelian is September's. His wife probably gave him that fob when their child was born. I'm sure Helen figured that out."

"But Kennecott wasn't tried for the Butcher crimes," Charley said. "So what good would the fob do Helen?"

"Only to prove that he was the Butcher," Raven said. "But I'm sure she also knew that, even so, she couldn't tie him to the Butcher murders—unless one of those murders was her own. That's why she asked Grace for the atropine. She knew if she gave him atropine, she could immobilize him at the scene of the crime. Then the odds would be that he'd be found guilty of *her* murder and, if he was acquitted, that we'd figure out the rest and find a way to stop him. I think she just took a gamble."

"With her *life*?" Charley asked.

Raven blinked back tears. "I'd like to think that Helen thought she'd win either way. If she was right about Kennecott being the Butcher, she could save us all by dying in our place. And if she was wrong, she'd take the cure he promised, and save herself."

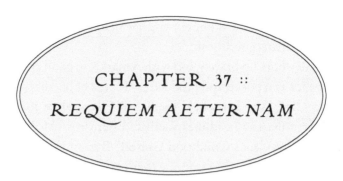

CHAPTER 37 ::
REQUIEM AETERNAM

The shooting of President McKinley in the Exposition's soaring Temple of Music swept Leland Davis Kennecott, Helen Crosby, and the Buffalo Butcher off the front page. Lee's verdict and sentence didn't show up at all in a number of papers; even the *Enquirer* buried it on page eight.

Mayor Lennox and Superintendent Ball now had something even worse to occupy their time. No one had cared about the dead whores, not really—but when they started turning up dead, the success of the Pan-American had hung in the balance. Now that wasn't even a consideration. Whether McKinley lived or died, Buffalo's grand Exposition, this once-in-a-city's-lifetime opportunity for civic glory, would forever be tarnished by anarchy and assassination. After the shooting, the Exposition bravely remained open—pretending to go about its business as usual—but effectively it was over, and more than a few prominent Buffalo men wished that it had stayed on Cayuga Island, after all.

President McKinley had taken two bullets in the gut from a small-time loser from Detroit by the name of Leon Czolgosz. Leon had been born in America to Polish parents, but the promise of the burgeoning nation had bypassed him, or so he thought. He drifted from cause to cause, at last latching on to the teat of Emma Goldman, the mother of American anarchism. Convinced that McKinley and his ilk had to die for the working man to live, Czolgosz resolved to do his part for the cause and drifted to Buffalo. He stalked the president over several days before catching up to him at a public meet-and-greet at the Temple of

Music. Just as he had planned, Czolgosz shot McKinley point-blank with a cheap revolver he'd bought the day before at Walbridge's, a big downtown sporting goods store.

McKinley bore up bravely and with remarkable good cheer, despite being gut-shot and poked and prodded by a corps of doctors still mostly practicing Civil War battlefield medicine. For a while it seemed as if he might rally; the headlines vacillated between "McKinley Will Live!!" and "President's Condition Grave!!" But on the eighth day of McKinley's suffering—the same day that Lee Kennecott was taken by prison train to Auburn—the shooting officially became an assassination. Mr. McKinley, dignified to the very end, said a quiet prayer and gave up the ghost.

As Shakespeare had said of the Thane of Cawdor—a phrase not lost on Buffalo's drama-loving public—nothing in the man's life became him like the leaving it.

Theodore Roosevelt, McKinley's toothy vice president and erstwhile hero of the Spanish-American War—the bully little conflict that had postponed the Exposition, and brought it to Buffalo—was, after some effort, located on one of his frequent hunting junkets, brought to Buffalo, and duly sworn as McKinley's successor.

There had been no murders in the Tenderloin since that day Lee had been arrested in Rochester, soaked with Helen's blood, stiff as a statue. Without any newspaper coverage, though, no one thought anything about it, and that kind of time had passed between murders before. Two weeks after the cortège took McKinley's body away, the grinning new president left on his private train, and Leon Czolgosz went to the electric chair. And still there had been no new murder.

As the weeks and months passed, a consensus grew that Czolgosz, or one of his demonic associates, had been the Buffalo Butcher. It all made sense: He had tried to destabilize the city, and damage the Exposition, by slaughtering a few whores before striking the decisive blow against the president.

And in time—unlike his counterpart in Whitechapel—the Buffalo Butcher faded entirely from memory.

October 1, 1901

HELEN'S BODY WAS LAID to rest in a little cemetery outside of Rochester. Charley, Grace, Raven, Alice, and May took the train to see their friend lowered into the receiving earth.

Grace had ordered a headstone, a nice one, too, but Charley insisted on paying for it. Grace had, of course, told him to go pound sand, but then she saw Popcorn Charley do something she'd never seen before, nor ever would again: He had begun to weep. So Grace relented, and Charley's headstone was duly put in place, while the five of them looked on, lost in their own thoughts. Raven surprised them all by suggesting a Bible verse to follow Helen's name and dates.

The stone read:

Helen Crosby

1879–1901

John 15:13

Then Grace, Charley, May, Alice, and Raven returned to Buffalo, where despite a wet summer, six murders, and an assassination, the Pan still had a month to go.

Of course, the killings stopped as soon as Lee was shipped off to Auburn, though no one ever knew quite why they did. Like Jack the Ripper himself, *someone* was responsible for a terrible spasm of violence, followed by an equally sudden quiescence, but no one knew more than that. Who was the Butcher, and where had he gone? After a while, most concluded that he must have been just some anonymous one of the eight million visitors to the Pan-American, or—more likely—one of Czolgosz's anarchist cabal, trying to destabilize the city before the assassination.

Neither Charley, Grace, nor the girls ever said a word about what they knew. They were the only ones who would ever know for certain why the Butcher's brief reign of terror had ended.

The Pan-American Exposition closed its gates for the last time at the end of the day on November 1, 1901. Buffalo was, if anything, relieved that it was over. The colorful buildings, the glittering lights, all would come to be associated with one thing: an assassination. It stuck to the Pan-American's memory like cheap cologne.

Raven disappeared one month after the Pan-American closed. Grace chose not to look for her, and privately wished her well.

Dr. George Grand was arrested three years later for performing an illegal operation, namely one of the countless abortions he provided in his operating theatre at 45 Erie Street. He did six months in the Erie County Penitentiary, then pulled up stakes and left Buffalo for good. He returned to his native Scotland, living with his brother and family in their little house in the Highlands. After a few years, tired of the quiet of northern Scotland, he resumed his earlier career as a ship's surgeon for a variety of passenger lines. The work—easy duty—took him twice to South Africa, three times to Australia, and four times to New York.

By 1912, he was in such demand as a maritime physician that he was asked to sign on for the maiden voyage of the world's newest, largest, and most luxurious passenger steamer.

After all the shit I've had to take, he thought, signing his new contract. He smiled with satisfaction. Imagine—Dr. George Grand, ship's surgeon, RMS *Titanic*.

THE END

AUTHOR'S POSTSCRIPT

I wrote this book after receiving a number of comments from readers that they would like to read more about the Pan-American Exposition. The first book in the Avenging Angel Detective Agency™ Mysteries, *The Unsealing*, was set in the Pan Year, but only as a matter of stage-setting.

So in this one I had the opportunity to dive deeply into the history of the Exposition and the effect it had on Buffalo, both before and (long) after the event itself. And some of what I found was disturbing and coalesced into this story.

Sex trafficking—enforced sexual slavery—isn't something I made up. It went on in the Gilded Age, and it continues in ours as well. In the United States and around the world, young women (and men) are forced into the life described in this book. How many? No one knows. Statistics are very hard to come by: There is no incentive for victims to come forward. Procurers and pimps are often violent and vengeful. Those victims brave enough to admit being in sex work are often themselves prosecuted as criminals and sent to prison where, all too often, their abuse continues. For most, there is no escape except for the oblivion of drugs or suicide.

People like George Grand still lie in wait for runaways, substance abusers, victims of domestic violence, and those who simply run out of options. Selling one's body for food, shelter, narcotics—or, ironically, to satisfy the human need for love and belonging—is the unfortunate lot of all too many people in our world.

I don't write novels to lecture anyone on this or that, but I do believe that fiction ought to reflect the full range of the human condition and, in so doing, touch our common humanity.

As always, a big thank you to my publisher, Ashwood Press. My boundless gratitude to my wife.

Special thanks are due to my editor, Melissa Stevens, whose surgical skill was invaluable in making this a book I am especially proud of.

Robert Brighton
October 2023

ABOUT THE AUTHOR

ROBERT BRIGHTON IS AN authority on the Gilded Age, an inveterate explorer, and the author of the Avenging Angel Detective Agency™ Mysteries.

He began writing fiction after spending two years researching the liminal period of 1898–1905, in which his novels are set. Prior to that, he has been a bison rancher, mule handler, vintage automobile restorer, and has made several other quixotic career choices. He has traveled to some fifty-six countries and is looking forward to adding the Faroe Islands and Patagonia to his life-list.

When he's not writing, he's either spending time with his wife and their two cats or exploring some new part of the world. He has an enthusiasm for Japanese tin toys, antique weather instruments, and anything mechanical.

Find out more at RobertBrightonAuthor.com.

Milton Keynes UK
Ingram Content Group UK Ltd.
UKHW012008011223
433659UK00011B/154/J